Death
IN THE
REAR VIEW
MIRROR

THE PARLOUS TRILOGY #1

A St Jack Mystery

Kent Weatherby

ISBN: 0615678688
ISBN 13: 9780615678689

Library of Congress Control Number: 2012945970
CreateSpace, North Charleston, SC

"Oh what a tangled web we weave, when first we practice to deceive."

Sir Walter Scott
Marmion, Canto VI, Stanza 17

Chapter One

On the morning of June 23, 2006, fate wrenched the life of Stannard Jackson, dragging his past into the present and forever altering his future. It began shortly after leaving home in rural Wyandotte County for the daily commute to his insurance claims office in Johnson County, the affluent suburb of Kansas City.

At exactly 6:25 a.m., he backed out of his garage on Wolcott Road and drove toward Interstate 435 South and his job in Overland Park. He enjoyed this part of his commute on the narrow blacktop road traversing the rolling oak forest. The car practically drove itself toward the rising sun. He turned the dial on his radio to KMBZ and heard Marla Maye, host of "Early Day with Marla Maye," hyped-up on coffee and trying to awaken the early commuters. *No one is* named *Marla Maye,* he thought. *Why do people have to make up such ridiculous names?* It was a personal judgment he would never have made in his professional life. He turned down the dial, enjoying the calming sight of green pastures interspersed among the trees in the cool dawn. Dairy cows stood in the tall grass. He sighed. All seemed right in his universe. He punched the radio's off button at six-thirty, immediately after the traffic and weather report. *Okay, traffic at Quivira Road is moving, but it will slow down soon.* He told himself to speed up. *You don't want to be late; get through that bottleneck. Road construction, morning traffic, and the inevitable traffic accident will bring it all to a halt.* He glanced at the dashboard clock. At 6:35 a.m., rush-hour traffic should have barely started. But, if today was an indication of a new norm, maybe he would have to alter his departure time. It would require a change, and Stannard Jackson hated change.

At precisely 6:41, one minute behind schedule, he accelerated up the ramp merging K-5 with Interstate 435. His mind wandered. He reflected there were now more people in Johnson County, Kansas, than in Kansas City. Two minutes later, driving in the far-right lane of the interstate, he slammed on the brakes of his 2005 Ford Taurus. He swerved hard to the left to avoid hitting the yellow Corvette flying up the ramp at Leavenworth Road directly into his lane. A dark green Cadillac darted past him in the left lane and closed on the Vette, two cars being driven by madmen. "What the..." The expletive hung, unfinished. Horns blared in the early morning quiet, angry stares shot from driver to driver, and meaty hands slammed hard on steering wheels.

He saw the Cadillac with two men inside catch up to the Corvette before the sports car suddenly sped ahead once more. Hands shaking with uncharacteristic rage, he chased the two cars for the next two minutes. Even at ninety miles per hour, the speeding cars maintained their lead. Only when he reached the repaving work zone did he ease up. Ahead he could see the Corvette in front followed by the dark green Cadillac. He called the Kansas Highway Patrol hotline to report the maniac behind the wheel of the Corvette. As he passed the Kansas Avenue exit, he saw the Cadillac stopped at the top of the ramp. *So he gave up the chase too! Ohio tags; he's come a long way from home to find trouble this early in the morning.*

Three minutes later dispatchers logged two additional calls reporting the wild driver of a vintage yellow Corvette. The dispatchers immediately notified the Shawnee, Lenexa, and Overland Park police departments in an attempt to stop the vehicle. A police cruiser patrolling the busy interstate highway first saw the Corvette at the south end of the bridge over the Kansas River, where it left the pavement.

Just short of Johnson Drive, it narrowly missed the light poles along the roadside before lurching back into the path of frightened commuters. At Johnson Drive, a second patrolman on top the overpass, working the radar unit monitoring the early morning rush hour traffic, radioed his partner, who joined the pursuit. Sirens shrieking and emergency lights flashing, the cops followed the Corvette. They observed the car careen a second time off the road onto the grass median strip and back onto the highway, narrowly missing the 79th Street bridge abutment. After that, following police procedure, the patrol cars dropped back at the direction of their dispatcher.

Additional police cruisers from Lenexa joined the pursuit, at 87th and 95th Streets. A line of police and highway patrol vehicles five cars long now followed the Corvette. The last one joined the procession just as the driver flew past in a blur of speed. The highway patrol trooper saw the man in the Corvette look furtively into his rearview mirror. The trooper would later recall how the man glanced directly at him after looking in the rearview mirror, his eyes wide and wild. The man was seemingly in terror, as if something or someone evil was pursuing him. The trooper later changed his mind, saying the man's eyes gave him the impression he was under some sort of demonic spell.

An instant later the rogue car cut between the cruiser and another vehicle as the driver changed lanes.

The car again left the roadway between 95th Street and the K-10 convergence, careening onto the grass median strip before darting in and out of traffic from lane to lane. The officers lost visual contact for a few moments at K-10, where a second four-lane road funneled traffic from the university town of Lawrence. A police helicopter had now joined in the chase, directing an Overland Park cruiser to drop farther back from the fugitive. At the off-ramp where the interstate highway split, leading drivers to either Wichita or Des Moines, the police watched as the helicopter took up the chase alone. Moments later the officers observed the car appear to drive intentionally into concrete pilings at the Quivira Road construction zone. The yellow Corvette virtually exploded, its fiberglass body breaking into pieces.

The police officer closest in pursuit slowed but said nothing for a few moments. When he did speak, he exclaimed over his radio, "Ugh...What could he be thinking? It was just a traffic violation!" The time was 6:56 a.m. The entire chase—eighteen miles—had lasted thirteen minutes, the average speed eighty-three miles per hour. Moments later all eastbound traffic on I-435 stopped.

Seconds turned to eternity while the officers maneuvered their patrol cars along the shoulder to the wreck. Other drivers looked on in disbelief. Pulling onto the road behind the wreckage with their lights flashing, the officers stopped. They could see all that remained of the driver after the terrible crash. The collision appeared to have launched the man, who had not buckled his seat belt, from a sitting position headlong into the windshield, leaving the impression of his head in the laminated glass. At the same time, the steering wheel had driven back against the body, crushing his chest and keeping him from being thrown from the car. The man was undoubtedly dead. The top of his head and face had caved in upon impact. Blood from the head wounds soaked the cotton sweatpants and T-shirt he wore. The officers approached the car with caution, expecting it to burst into flames at any moment—relieved when it did not.

The trooper at the scene radioed the license tag information to the dispatcher: 2006 Johnson County Kansas personalized tag, HEADOC. Moments later the response came back that the tag was registered to Dr. Loren Parlous and his wife, Lorelei, for a 1958 yellow Corvette. The address on the registration was 5133 Lakeshore Drive East, Lake Quivira Estates, an exclusive gated residential area located on the Wyandotte/Johnson counties line.

"Someone will have to notify the doc and his missus that their Corvette has been in a single-car accident and the driver is dead," one of the officers commented to the other. "I'm glad I don't have to do that. It's bad enough having to investigate these traffic fatalities, but dealing with a grieving family isn't my bag."

"Yeah," the other answered. "Let Public Affairs handle it. They've got chaplains for that."

Then looking around, he continued, "You know, there isn't a lot to be done out here. You and me, we got about all the trouble we need. We were in pursuit, so I suppose there will be some sort of Internal Affairs investigation into our tactics."

His partner in the pursuit looked around then said, "We saw the whole thing. What do you make it, accident or suicide?"

"I don't know. It sure looked to me like he drove into that bridge piling on purpose. I suppose we should put it down as an accident for now."

The other officer thought about it for a second then answered, "Yeah." He then asked, "Do you think it's the doc? The fire department first responders looked for a wallet or some kind of identification. There wasn't anything in his pockets. Maybe it got thrown out in the collision or is somewhere in what's left of the car."

"Yeah, my guess is it's the doc. It makes sense he would be driving his own car. You know how some of those rich guys like to pretend the freeway is a NASCAR track. They pretend to be pros, but they can't drive for shit. We can go through the car when they get it to the salvage yard and look for some sort of identification. Right now we need to get a wrecker in here, get this mess cleared out, and get traffic moving."

The combination of narrowed lanes from the road construction at the point of impact coupled with the far-flung accident debris hindered efforts to remove the wreckage for over an hour. Stannard Jackson sat a mile back in the line of stalled traffic. He had just passed beyond the last exit where he could have changed his route to reach work at even close to his usual time. He sat seething. *What else?* He was too far back in line to know what had happened. All he knew for certain was he would be late getting to his office. An hour and ten minutes after traffic stopped it returned to its normal slow commuter drive through the construction area. Stannard Jackson turned off the interstate at Antioch Road and proceeded south to Corporate Woods. He parked his car in the company parking lot, still quivering from the excitement and rage of the morning commute. Not even the long wait in traffic had completely calmed him.

As he pulled into a parking space, the Morning Sky-to-Drive reporter who monitored traffic from a radio station helicopter reported what happened. The delay had been caused by the crash of a yellow Corvette. *If it is the same yellow Corvette, it could have been me,* Stannard thought as he turned off his radio. But in the days and weeks that followed, he came to realize that it could never have been him. He was a rational person who led an ordinary life, not some idiot behind the wheel. No, the accident had nothing to do with him, though through a strange twist of fate, the event would change his life forever.

Chapter Two

The body of the unidentified man driving the Corvette arrived at the nearby Johnson County Medical Center morgue well before police cleared the accident scene. The man's lack of identity only added to the mystery. At the desk the ambulance driver filled in the admittance forms. At the top of the page he wrote the name "John Doe" as the attendant on duty looked over his shoulder. "What is it, a traffic case?"

"Yeah, but we got no identification. When the police made a search of the vehicle they couldn't find any personal identity papers on the body or in the car—anyway, what is left of the car." He continued filling out the form. *Age,* he thought. *How can I tell?* The man appeared to be in his early- to midfifties, although there was some doubt even as to that due to the severe damage to his head and face. The man's head was so badly damaged it would take someone intimate with him to make the identification. He wrote "fifty, plus or minus." The police, first responders, and ambulance driver all agreed the man appeared to have been in good physical condition prior to the crash; that, coupled with the muscle tone and firm, elastic skin, suggested he would not likely be much over fifty. The attendant moved rapidly through the other questions, most of which he could not answer.

"Where'd it happen?" the attendant asked.

"You won't believe it," the ambulance driver said. "If we weren't in the basement, you could probably see it from here. The guy hit the concrete bridge piling not more than two hundred yards from here… over at the Quivira Road exit off the freeway."

"Well, it's convenient if nothing else. Can I take a look?"

"Why? He's all smashed up."

"So—wrecks like this get my imagination going. What's it to you?"

The ambulance driver thought for a second before answering. "He's yours now. Do whatever you want. I didn't see anything." With that, he turned and walked away, shaking his head in disgust.

The attendant wheeled the gurney toward the refrigerated morgue. About halfway down the hall, he stopped, pulled back the sheet and stared at the smashed face, shrugged, pulled the sheet back over the head, and continued on down the hall. At the end of the hall, he pressed the automatic opener and stood back as the double doors swung open, allowing him to push his cargo inside. "I got a fresh one for you, Doc," he cried out as he entered.

The pathology resident on duty started to answer but stopped. Then he thought about it again and called out to the attendant, "Show some respect." He wanted to call the man a jerk but managed to hold his tongue. Picking up the admittance form, he noted the "John Doe." He continued, "Whoever he is, he was alive an hour ago. How'd you like it if you got treated like that after you died?"

The attendant pushed the gurney off to one side, muttering loudly enough for the resident to hear, "That's just the point, isn't it, Doc? I'd be dead, so why'd I care?"

The doctor turned his back to the attendant, thinking, *I don't know where they find people like him.* "We'll treat him with respect, anyway," he said to the attendant. "Let's get these clothes off him and see what we have."

Chastened, the sulking attendant returned. Working together they began stripping off the blood soaked clothing. What the resident discovered sent a cold shiver down his body. When he removed the dead man's shirt, he discovered evidence of cutting on his upper torso. The man had been tortured and mutilated. His nipples were gone, and his chest and stomach region also bore signs of mutilation. Beyond the mere fact of mutilation, there was something disturbing about the wound. As he peered at the marking, it occurred to the doctor that the image had something of a face about it. He saw, or thought he did, a pointed head with horns and two eyes, slanted and evil, and below that a pointed goatee. What was it? Why did it look familiar?

He grabbed the lab camera and began taking photographs of the body. Having finished that task, he asked the attendant to remove the blood-soaked cotton sweatpants. As the attendant began to slide them down the man's legs, the doctor noted the absence of any underwear just before he registered the greatest shock. The man had been castrated.

Stepping away from the body now totally exposed to his view, he reached for the telephone. Only then did he notice the frayed strips of duct tape adhered to the wrists and ankles of the corpse. Dialing a number from memory, he called the department head. "Dr. Stinson, can you come down here? An ambulance just delivered a body, and I think you should see it for yourself. I'm not certain how to proceed."

Five minutes later, sixty-two-year-old Dr. Jerry Stinson, chief of forensic medicine at the medical center and the Johnson County coroner, walked into the room. "What've you got?" he inquired.

"Over here. This man got here a few minutes ago—DOA. The admittance form indicates he crashed into some of the bridge work being done on the freeway outside the hospital." Motioning to the body, he continued, "But when I started to make my preliminary examination, this is what I found."

Dr. Stinson peered at the body. His black mustache, now touched with gray, twitched ever so slightly. "Well, isn't that something. What do you make of it?"

The resident hesitated before answering. "That's just it—I don't know. When I pulled back the sheet, I saw the head wound and blood consistent with that injury. As we pulled the sheet farther down the amount of blood made no sense. But then when we removed his clothes, I saw this. At first I thought it was some sort of torture, but as I examined the wounds, I couldn't be certain."

"What do you mean?"

"Well, for one thing all the wounds—the excised nipples and the unicursal hexagram—appear to be superficial. None of the cuts is deep. They could've been self-inflicted, though I don't see why anyone would do that, and—" he motioned to the man's groin "—I sure can't see anyone doing that to himself."

15

"I agree," exclaimed Dr. Stinson. "We'll need to get the Overland Park Police in here.

We don't know at this point whether we are dealing with a traffic accident, a suicide, or a torture/murder. We'll need to do a complete autopsy on this one before signing off on the manner of death. Who is the deceased man anyway?"

"We don't know. He's going to stay a John Doe until we make an identification. The first responders, ambulance driver, and police all came away empty-handed. There was no identification anywhere in the clothing or in the car. All they know they learned from the Division of Motor Vehicles. The car belonged to a Dr. Loren Parlous."

Dr. Stinson turned back and, now for the first time, looked at the body with the intent to see if he could identify the deceased man. Dr. Stinson knew Dr. Parlous, but he couldn't be certain the man on the table was him. The badly damaged face and head made it virtually impossible for him to identify the body. "I've met Parlous at social functions a time or two but...I don't know. The body is too badly damaged. We'll need to have someone make a positive identification. To begin with we'll need fingerprints and DNA . One thing is certain—Parlous is, or was, a psychiatrist, not a practicing surgeon. Rumor has it that he was having some psychological problems of his own. It may be possible for him to have made those cuts, but I wouldn't stake my reputation on it based on what we see now."

"So, what do I do?" the resident asked.

"Call the police first and ask them to send over a detective. Then we'll get the body on the list for an autopsy. I'll do the autopsy myself, but I want you to get it scheduled...then assist."

"Consider it done, Chief."

"Check with my people upstairs for a time. There isn't any hurry. He's not going anywhere. I just want to get it done sometime in the next day or so if it can be worked into my schedule." Then, as an after-thought, he added, "If it is Parlous, it will not make our job any easier. He had a reputation for being something of an odd character. Who knows, maybe this was his way of getting attention. If so, then something went desperately wrong."

Two Overland Park detectives arrived at the main gate to the exclusive Lake Quivira housing development at 11:45 a.m., not quite five hours after the crash on the interstate. They were not from Public Affairs, and neither man was a chaplain. They stopped at the guard shack, where they asked for directions to 5133 Lakeshore Drive East. The guard on duty, a retiree of a few years from the Overland Park Police Department, recognized the detectives and offered to lead them. "I'd better show you the way. The house is almost impossible to find. It's in some trees overlooking the lake. If you aren't familiar with Lake Quivira, you could miss the turnoff."

The guard closed and locked the door to the guard shack then hopped in his car and led the way, driving along the east side of the lake. He followed Crescent Boulevard to Hillcrest Road East, around the less developed side of the lake. The security guard made two more turns and then went straight for a quarter mile before making a 120-degree turn off the main road. The narrow lane had pavement barely wide enough to accommodate one car. He stopped on the side of the lane with the back of his vehicle sticking out into the road and waited for the detectives to pull up beside him. "Follow this driveway. You can't miss it." The older of the two cops stared at the overweight guard, who hastily wiped a flake of doughnut sugar off his lip before turning around and speeding back toward the guard shack.

"I see what he meant about missin' this place. They don't even have a mailbox to mark the road," the driver of the unmarked cop car said.

"Yeah, they must have a post office box. I'll bet the FedEx and UPS guys love deliverin' packages to Dr. and Mrs. Parlous."

Small trees bordered the asphalt. Tall grass growing on both sides of the lane brushed against the side of the unmarked police car. The driveway wound downward toward what appeared to be a cliff overlooking the lake. Had it not been for the fact the guard had directed them to follow the path, the detectives would have turned back. After following the lane for a couple of hundred feet, they stopped in a clearing with a grove of stunted oaks. Only a large concrete parking pad fronting on a thirty-foot-wide concrete building with an electrical-powered steel-tracked sliding door was visible from the copse of trees. Had the detectives not known a house stood nearby, they would easily have mistaken what they saw for some sort of warehouse or maintenance building.

"Dr. Parlous must be a weirdo. Look at this place! Where's the house?" the older detective remarked. "It's gotta be here. This is the end of the road." The detectives got out of the car. "You go take that side. I'll go this way." He had not walked more than twenty-five feet when he called out, "Over here. There're steps leadin' down over here."

The younger man walked over and looked down the curving steps. "You couldn't pay me to live in a place like this. Can you imagine comin' home on a dark and stormy night?"

The older man laughed. "Yeah, and you're a cop. They probably park in that building. There've gotta be stairs inside that go down."

Both men followed the outside steps built into the side of the hill. As they did so, they saw that the house had been tucked back so that it could not be seen from the lake. A casual observer would see only a rocky tree line. At the bottom of the steps, they turned the corner and found themselves on a decorative walkway bordered by azaleas and barberry bushes and a profusion of other plants. The neglected landscaping looked as if it had not been trimmed since the year before. It was now more of a jungle than a planned effort at beautification. They stood on a concrete deck twelve feet wide with a native limestone wall that separated and hid the house from the downhill side.

The younger man let out a low whistle. "You ever see anything like this?"

"No. What was it you said about the doctor being some sort of weirdo?

"Yeah, how little I knew."

They paused, looking out at the lake thirty feet below the rock wall. The older man stepped to the edge and looked over. He saw a near vertical rock cliff descending to another copse of wild trees. Beyond that he could see the lake shimmering with ripples in the light breeze. The sun stood high overhead. The temperature was already in the high eighties, and the humidity was nearly as high. The house itself contained more glass than paneling, and the main entrance was recessed into the structure. The main door stood like some great medieval sentry barring entry to an ancient tomb, or so it seemed to the detectives. But for the expanse of glass along the front wall facing the lake, the house appeared to be more of a bunker than a home.

"Where's the doorbell?" the younger man asked.

"Dunno." Seeing none, the older cop reached out and gave the medieval horn-headed knocker several heavy raps. He stood back and waited. Moments later the door opened and a woman who appeared to be in her thirties, dressed in flowing black silk lounging trousers and a white blouse that was unbuttoned to suggest a sensuous body more than reveal it, asked, "Yes, what can I do for you?"

The young cop gaped. The older man spoke, "I am Overland Park Police detective Lieutenant Michael Pezzati, and this is detective Sergeant Pollard. Are you Mrs. Parlous?"

"Yes, what is it you want with me?"

"May we have a few words with you?" Lieutenant Pezzati glanced around. The driveway, the concrete building, the overgrown vegetation, this bunker for a house—and now this woman. His thoughts stopped as he took it all in. None of this fits.

The woman hesitated.

Lieutenant Pezzati opened the leather case containing his identification and badge.

He noticed the woman pretended to look at it before she responded, "Of course, won't you come in?"

"Thank you," Lieutenant Pezzati said. His partner, content to let the older man take the lead, continued to stare. "This is quite a setting. I just commented to Sergeant Pollard it almost seems like a bunker, built as it is into the side of the hill. But then all this glass at the front certainly dispelled that thought."

"Oh, but you were right. That isn't ordinary glass; it's armored, bulletproof. Not even a .300 Weatherby Magnum could penetrate that glass, or so I've been told. My husband had it installed a year ago. It's even supposed to be bombproof. We are quite safe here. My husband didn't believe the security guard at the gate provided much more than nominal protection from intruders." With a wave of her hand she finished, "No one could break into this house."

Pezzati and Pollard glanced at each other. *Too much information that I didn't ask,* Pezzati thought. And, she said "didn't." What's that supposed to mean?

"Why, do you think someone would want to break in or shoot at the house? This is an exclusive address, but…" Pollard started to ask before being interrupted.

"Well, you never know, now, do you? We had our reasons. I've been watching you on our security cameras since that toad of a guard turned onto our driveway." She turned her back and walked into the house, leaving them to trot along behind. "Why not call me Lorelei," she called without looking back.

Pezzati followed, noting the use of past tense for the second time in less than a minute. She said "had," not "have." *She was expecting us!* He filed the slip away for later reference. He followed her into the house, trailed by Pollard. So much for an invitation, he thought. Shifting the conversation back on track, he shot a look at Pollard that said *Don't get suckered; we didn't come here to discuss her home security system.* "Mrs. Parlous, our visit here is official. There's been a traffic accident this morning. The car, your car, a yellow Corvette, registered to your husband, Dr. Loren Parlous, has been in an accident. We are unable to identify the man driving the car. While I hate to state the obvious, it is possible the driver was your husband. No identification was found on the driver."

Lorelei Parlous stiffened slightly. "Why don't you just ask the man driving the car?"

Lieutenant Pezzati saw a look of confusion in her eyes. "We can't. He died in the crash."

Her eyes hardened but no tears came, no catching her breath or quickening of respiration.

She stood silent for several seconds, obviously trying to think what to say before she answered. "That was no accident, the bitch! So she finally got him!"

"Hold on there. What bitch? What's this all about?"

23

The words now tumbled from Mrs. Parlous. "It's his first wife. She's been threatening Loren. She's the reason for all the security around here."

The two detectives looked at each other, wondering at the outburst. The traffic accident, if that was what it was, now began to take on a more sinister aspect.

"Let's take it a little slower if we can," Lieutenant Pezzati said calmly. "First of all we don't know yet that it was Dr. Parlous who was driving the car. Second, even if it was, I don't see how his first wife could have anything to do with it. It's a traffic accident, so far as we know. What we need is for you to come with us to see if you can identify the body."

"Of course. Let me change and get my purse." Lorelei Parlous rose from her seat and left the room.

When she returned fifteen minutes later, she was dressed for a social outing: tight, thin black leather pants showing off her long, slender legs—made all the more attractive by the three-and-a-half-inch heels she wore—replaced the silk lounging trousers. The white silk blouse, with a second button now open, showed more cleavage than necessary under any circumstances, let alone on an errand such as the one she faced.

Pollard looked at Pezzati. The two cops exchanged glances that told what they were both thinking: *What the hell is going on here?*

Lorelei Parlous led the two men through a door that separated the main living quarters from the bedrooms. At the end of the hallway they saw what appeared to be an elevator. Once inside a television monitor showed their police car sitting alone on the concrete pad. She punched in a code, and the elevator rose slowly up to the ground level. At the top she pushed a second button, and the screen on the monitor flickered before showing the inside of a spacious garage. A moment later she pushed another button, and the elevator door opened.

Pezzati marveled at the level of security. The elevator door had to be opened by someone either operating the elevator or who knew the code from outside,. Dr Parlous had not intended to take any chances that they could be surprised by someone lying in wait. She pushed another button, and he heard the steel doors sliding on their track. Outside at last, they walked to the waiting unmarked police car.

Five minutes later, as they passed through the security gate, the guard peered into the car's window and noticed the two cops had Mrs. Parlous with them. Pollard drove by without acknowledging the guard. Pezzati sat in the back with Mrs. Parlous next to him. "Odd," the guard said to no one there. "I wonder what's up? Two cops drivin' off with the cold hottie. I wonder where's the doc?" Taking a bite out of the last of the dozen donuts, he watched as the car sped up and turned left onto Holliday Drive, where it followed the shoddy road along the south bank of the Kansas River toward the interstate.

Pezzati thought people new to Kansas City would have trouble believing the social elite of the city would choose to live in place like this. Secluded, yes; security provided, maybe. But outside the confines of the upscale development, an evil world lurked and you had to drive down an isolated, dark and poorly patrolled road to reach it.

At the ramp leading to the interstate highway, Pezzati sensed a change in Lorelei Parlous. He saw her glance north before they headed south in the same direction the driver of the yellow Corvette had frantically driven just hours before. He turned to Mrs. Parlous. "I don't want to get too far ahead of myself, but just what is it you think the doctor's first wife may've to do with this?"

"Just that she'd been threatening to kill Loren ever since their divorce became final three years ago. It's the money! She got a two-million-dollar policy on his life in the property settlement. The judge ordered Loren to keep paying premiums on the policy even though he no longer owned the policy."

"When was that?"

"Three years ago."

"Well maybe they'd been married for a long time and the judge thought there was a reason for him to provide for her security."

"What?" Lorelei snorted. "Who cares? They'd been married for twenty years—so what? Erin is a medical doctor. She has her own practice. She didn't need anything from Loren. She was just being vindictive."

They drove in silence for several minutes. "How long have you and the doctor been married?"

"I don't see what that has to do with anything, but since you asked, three years next month."

Pezzati noted the coincidence in dates. Dr. Parlous's first marriage ended three years ago, and he had been married to Lorelei for three years. He said nothing about that, but moments later he asked, "Does the first Mrs. Parlous live in Kansas City?"

"No, she lives in either Fort Walton Beach or Destin, Florida...but she was in town last night!" The detectives received the words for what they were, potential evidence, but the way

Lorelei spit them out the accusation was obvious.

"Really." The answer pinged off the old cop's antenna. "And just how do you know that this Erin Parlous was in town?" He took out a notepad and began making a note.

Lorelei looked over his shoulder as he wrote. "She doesn't go by Parlous. She goes by her professional

name, Kasalaitis. It's Dr. Erin Kasalaitis. She's Greek."
She said "Greek" as if the ethnicity had some particular meaning. "I know she was in town last night because Loren and I met her for a drink. We had some business to discuss."

Before Pezzati could answer, the police car turned to go up the ramp off the freeway onto Quiver Road. Bits and pieces of debris from the wreck diverted the car's passengers from their conversation. At the light, Sergeant Pollard turned left and crossed back over the highway. One block later, he turned left again at the entrance to the Johnson County Medical Center. The hospital stood on the hill high above the road, gleaming white in the hot sun.

Pezzati wondered if any of the patients had been looking out their window at the time the Corvette slammed into the concrete and steel bridge piling. For that matter, could anyone in the hospital see the road below? After parking the car, the two detectives escorted Mrs. Parlous to the office of Dr. Jerry Stinson. Minutes later the four took what they believed to be a long walk to the morgue. There, the attendant opened the door to the refrigerated compartment and pulled out the body. Dr. Stinson turned back the sheet, exposing the face but not the upper part of the torso.

Lieutenant Pezzati spoke first. "Can you identify the body?"

Lorelei Parlous hardly flinched as she looked in the direction of the man on the table. "Yes, it's Loren."

She didn't even look, the detective thought. *She looked in the direction of the body but not at it. Was she expecting to see him? Why? What does it have to do with Dr. Erin Kasalaitis?* "Are you certain?" the officer pressed. "The head and face have been badly damaged."

"You don't think I know my own husband?" she snapped. It was not a question but a challenge.

Pezzati noted no grief—just aggression.

Nodding to Dr. Stinson, Lieutenant Pezzati indicated he wanted the sheet pulled farther down. He needed to see what it was the doctor had told him about on the phone.

"Can you provide any explanation of this?"

Lorelei looked at the mutilated chest and the strange carving in the torso. "No, but I suppose it would take some sort of sadistic person to do that—even to Loren."

Pulling the sheet the rest of the way down, Lieutenant Pezzati looked directly at Mrs. Parlous, watching her face intently for some sign of emotion. Before he could speak, Lorelei exclaimed, "The vindictive bitch. It shouldn't have ended this way."

Chapter Three

Three weeks had passed since Stannard narrowly escaped being hit by the yellow Corvette, during which time he had all but forgotten the incident. Only in his disturbed sleep did his subconscious continue to register the near-fatal collision. Otherwise, his life settled back into the normal routine of work during the day as chief claims investigator, conducting investigations, reviewing files, and writing reports. In appearance Stannard Jackson was just another man on the twilight side of middle age, bowed by the years and slightly myopic with thinning blond hair. Routine marked the life of the medium-height investigator. Those who knew him best agreed he had a melancholy nature given to brief periods of euphoria. He was a man who walked the treadmill of life as if afraid of falling off. *Chief claims investigator.*

It sounded glamorous enough when his brain took a flight of fancy, which did not often happen. He saw himself then in the mold of Sam Spade or another of the old detective heroes known only to people his age. On those occasions he knew it might have been true but for the one monstrous mistake he'd made. The mistake had destroyed his career.

This was the man who awakened that morning three weeks later. The recollection that he had lost his temper after nearly being hit on the highway lingered—and that bothered him. There was something else. He dreamed of the man in the Corvette. In the brief glimpse he got of the man's eyes, he had seen terror; the kind of terror that drove men to grasp at straws in the hope those flimsy lifelines could save them. At the time, the only emotion Stannard felt was rage at nearly being killed. Now, in his dreams he recalled how the crazed man had looked and how he'd driven his car. The recollection awakened old thoughts and emotions. The man must have been in fear for his life. That kind of fear reminded him of how his son, Russell, must have felt in the minutes before he had been butchered on that homemade altar, alone, terrified, and helpless in the light of a full moon.

He felt the stirrings of his old self, the successes but mostly the one horrible loss that had defeated him, beginning to rise. It frightened him. The last thing he wanted to remember was the death of his son, Russell, murdered, he believed, at the hands of two boys, both now also dead. He blamed himself for Russell's murder. It had been his clumsiness—no, his arrogance—in investigating a seemingly meaningless crime that had put a target on his son's back. Or so he thought. At the time he had been a Kansas City detective, a rising star in the department assigned to the Metropolitan Major Case Squad, which investigated only the most important crimes. A young man seen as destined for greatness, his colleagues had nicknamed him St Jack, a contraction of his real name. Following the murder of his son, the name became a mockery, and that coupled with the tragedy led to an emotional collapse. Ultimately he had resigned from the force and a couple of years later taken the job as an insurance investigator.

At breakfast he told Caryl he had been thinking about Russell. It was the first time in years that either of them had mentioned their son. When he did so, tears welled in his eyes. He turned away, allowing the pain of the memory to fester as it had years earlier. He did not notice, or care, that his wife also felt anguish at the loss of their only son. For Stannard Jackson the loss was personal and there was room for only his grief. Shaken by the brief mention of Russell, he left the table without giving his wife the good-bye peck that normally preceded the drive to his office. Instead he went straight to the garage. There, he unlocked his car, got in, and began his predrive routine with the precision of a commercial airline pilot readying himself for takeoff. He adjusted the seat. He turned on the automatic cruise control. He adjusted the mirrors. After that, he pulled the tilt wheel down so that it fit his middle-aged girth and arm length. The routine had become compulsive behavior but even more so this morning. The actions were necessary because he always returned the settings to their neutral position whenever he parked the car. He never knew when someone else would want to drive the car and would find his settings annoying. Of course, no one ever drove the car but him. If they did, they would undoubtedly find the settings less objectionable than discovering everything turned off. He reached for the electronic door opener stored in the console for safety and theft reasons. He opened the garage door and backed out.

He arrived at the office a half hour later glad to be away from Caryl and the reminder of his dead son. He sat alone in the empty offices, lit by the rising sun still low in the eastern sky. As he looked out the office window, a soft glow filtered through the dense woods that gave the office park its name. Masquerading as a natural forest, they too reminded him of the place where his son had died. The time passed slowly as he fought off the memories he knew would haunt him if he allowed them. It bothered him that he did not know if he wanted to remember the wooded scene where his son had died. *Why can't I just let it go? Why does my subconscious drag it back to the present?* He covered his face with his hands and tried not to cry.

At a quarter till nine, the claims manager entered his Corporate Woods office, dropped a file on his desk, and plopped his massive body down in the chair opposite. Stannard stared at the pale red file folder. *Claim for life insurance. Okay, what's this all about? Why the dramatic entrance?* He wondered if his eyes were still red. *They can't be. I got over the crying jag over an hour ago.* Something in Ed Johnson's demeanor told him this one was special. Big Ed, as all the investigators called him, assigned routine referrals on a rotation basis so that every eighth one landed on Stannard's desk. His last four had all been matters he completed in less than two working days. The two bungled arson claims had been the most exciting work he had seen since early in the spring, and neither required much of his ability to solve it. Surprise and relief reflected on Stannard's face when he lifted the file and opened the front cover. Routine cases never came with thick files. "What's this? Something out of the ordinary?"

Big Ed Johnson nodded. "We do have something special, something that none of the other guys can handle." He sat in the single chair facing the desk. "I want you to look into it. I think you'll find it to be something that'll get your juices flowing."

Opening the file, Stannard read the cover memo.

"Claim for Life Insurance Benefits.

Allied Life Insurance Company of North America.

Policy Type: Twenty-year term policy with expiration date of September 30, 2006. *Just a couple of months away,* Stannard noted to himself.

"Name of Deceased: Loren Parlous, Lake Quivira, Kansas.

Name of Claimant: Erin Kasalaitis, Fort Walton Beach, Florida.

Amount of Claim: $2,000,000.00 with double indemnity for accidental death.

Nature of Investigation: Cause/Method of Death."

After reading the cover memo, Stannard looked up, "Okay. What is so special about this?

What does the death certificate say about the cause of death?"

"Ah, Stannard, you don't know who the deceased is, do you? It's Dr. Loren Parlous—" he strung out the man's name "—the man driving the yellow Corvette that nearly hit you on the interstate last month. I thought you might have a special interest in looking into this claim."

Stannard picked up the file once more and looked at the man sitting across the desk. "I recall reading the newspaper accounts of the incident and saw the television reports on channels 5 and 9," he said. "I'd forgotten the name." He recalled he had even looked in the obituary section of the paper to see what else they had to say about Dr. Parlous. It hadn't told him much, as he recalled. "What's the point?" He riffled through the documents. "It seems cut and dried to me. That man was an idiot. He was driving as if he was out of his mind and lost control of his car. Little wonder, the way he cut in and out of traffic. If there was ever a man asking for a premature death, it was him."

"Well, Stannard, before you stamp this one for payment, maybe you should take a few minutes and read the file. I think there are some things in there that may, just may, shake your first impression." Big Ed pulled his six-foot-two-inch, three-hundred-pound body from his seat, smiled, and left the office.

Stannard opened the file folder and laid the cover memorandum aside. He read the index of documents.

Accident reports by the Overland Park PD and the Kansas Highway Patrol.

Autopsy summary by Dr. Jerry Stinson.

Death certificate signed by Dr. Jerry Stinson.

When he got to the cause of death, he paused. *Okay, so the doctor died as the result of head trauma and a crushed chest that punctured his lungs, but how did he come to sustain those injuries, accident or suicide? That must be the question.* He flipped back to the accident reports filed by the two law enforcement agencies. There it was—equivocation. No one was going to say with certainty whether this was a case of suicide, accident, or something more sinister. Once again returning to the file, he turned to the autopsy summary and began reading, then stopped in shock. Turning back through the file, he looked for the release forms authorizing the dissemination of information. They were there, executed by Erin Kasalaitis. *Who is that,* he thought, *and why should she be executing these documents for the death of someone named Parlous? A daughter, maybe. No, there it is, she's a former wife. That's unusual—an ex-wife still a beneficiary on an insurance policy. Someone forgot to make a change. I'll bet the new wife, if there is one, isn't happy about that. That's one point for this not being an accident.*

He set the file aside as he thought, *Big Ed might be right. This case could be something to remember. For the first time since Russell died, I'll be looking into a claim where I have some firsthand knowledge.* He gulped hard trying to swallow the emotion. *Russell again. Will that be a help or hindrance?* He had no way of knowing then, but one thing was certain: Big Ed had not done him a favor, regardless of what the man thought. He looked for a place to start. The pathologist who performed the autopsy would be as good as any. Flipping through the report, he found the name of the doctor and the hospital but not the phone number. He opened the greater Johnson County telephone directory and looked up the number for Johnson County Medical Center. The number he dialed connected him with the main hospital switchboard. When the receptionist answered, he asked to speak to Dr. Jerry Stinson.

Three transfers and over a minute later, a man answered the phone. "This is Dr. Stinson."

The voice was warm and cordial. "What can I do for you?"

"Dr. Stinson, my name's Stannard Jackson. I have a file before me making claim for insurance proceeds on the life of a Dr. Loren Parlous. I believe you performed an autopsy on the body."

"That is correct. Who did you say you were with?"

"I work for Consolidated Adjusters. We are an independent investigative service for insurance companies."

"Is there some question about the autopsy findings?"

"Yes…no, well there is…I'm not sure. There are some strange circumstances I just noted in the file… and thought I'd…you know, just take the investigation slow. I'd like to talk to you if you have some time."

The response came back quickly. "Let me just open my appointment calendar." The doctor checked the schedule printed and left on the desk for him by his secretary each morning. "Sure, in fact I have some time at three o'clock today. If you'd like to come over then, I can give you the better part of an hour."

"That's great," he answered, "I'll be there and bring all the documentation with me for your files." The moment he finished, he heard the phone go dead on the other end. Dr. Stinson had not even asked about any releases or authorizations. He looked at his watch: nine fifteen. He had over five hours to do preliminary work on the file. He walked to the copy machine, where he made copies of the release and authorization forms executed by Erin Kasalaitis.

Back in the office, he spun his desk chair around to face the credenza, grabbed the PC mouse, and clicked on Internet Explorer. Instantly the powerful computer sprang to life, and he opened a site saved on his Favorites. The screen filled with the home page of a member-only private medical directory. He clicked the search box and typed "dr loren parlous kansas city bio." Moments later, the screen flickered and the biography of Loren Wills Parlous, MD, PsyD, JD, appeared:

Dr. Loren Parlous is a graduate of Kettering College of Medical Arts (MD 1977) in Dayton, Ohio, and the Columbia University College of Physicians and Surgeons (PsyD 1979) in New York City. Physician and Surgeon licensed since 1979 by the State of Ohio, the State of New York, the State of Missouri since 1980, and the State of Kansas since 1981. Psychoanalyst—graduate of the San Francisco Psychoanalytic Institute. Juris Doctor—graduate of the University of Missouri at Kansas City in 1988. Assistant Clinical Professor, Psychiatry, School of Medicine, University of Kansas, Kansas City, Kansas. Lecturer in the Law and Psychiatry Fellowship program. Former member of the Ballenger Psychoanalytic Institute faculty.

Distinguished Fellow of the American Psychiatric Association and a member of numerous local, national, and international medical organizations, including the American Academy for Psychiatry and the Law. Has authored a well-received professional treatise, *The Manipulative Personality Disorder in the Serial Killer.*

He has written and lectured to medical audiences and is a frequent media expert and commentator on psychiatric, forensic, and mental health issues.

Dr. Parlous has been in the full-time private practice of psychiatry and psychoanalysis since 1985 and currently devotes more than 70 percent of his practice to Forensic Psychiatry and Medical-Legal Consultation.

In January 2003, Dr. Parlous established Forensic Psychiatric Associates Medical Corporation, of which he is the Chairman, Chief Executive Officer, and Medical Director.

All right, that gives me a little background on his professional life, but what about his private life? He opened a window for the *Kansas City Star* obituary pages, clicked on "Archive," and scanned the list until he found what he wanted. Dr. Loren Parlous had been born to a farm family living near Dayton, Ohio. *Humble beginning.* He had graduated from the University of Dayton *(modest start to his education)* before going to medical school *(at prestigious schools, so he must have been smart or good at networking or something else)* and ultimately specializing in psychiatry *(manipulating people).* He was survived by his wife, Lorelei, and an adult son by an earlier marriage *(odd, he's not named),* and there was no mention of where the son now lives. That was all. *Strange! Obituaries of prominent people were generally longer, especially for doctors, lawyers, business leaders, and politicians. Their egos required it, or was it the egos of their survivors? Either way the short obituary raises more questions than it answers. You would not expect there to be a mention of the ex-wife, Erin Kasalaitis, so maybe I should look her up too.* Stannard printed the obituary, made notes in the margin, and placed it on his desk beside the file.

As an afterthought he clicked the mouse on the archives page of the *Kansas City Star* and typed in "Dr. Loren Parlous." He watched with dismay as over a hundred files opened in the queue. One by one he plodded through them until he found one that caught his eye. *Hello, what is this? The doctor was having difficulty with the board of healing arts over some alleged professional improprieties. I wonder if that's public information.* He made a note to check with the board, located in Topeka, Kansas.

He then turned his attention to the claim form and the name Erin Kasalaitis, 4214 Opa-Locka Lane, Destin, Florida. He moved his mouse to his Favorites and clicked on People Search.

He typed in the name and address. Again, within moments the information teaser appeared, telling him he needed to type in his password so that his company would pay for the information the website was about to give him. "Erin Kasalaitis, 4214 Opa-Locka Lane, Destin, Florida. Single. Medical doctor educated at the Kansas University School of Medicine. Licensed in the State of Kansas 1982 and the State of Florida 2004. Prior residences indicated at Leawood, Kansas, and Olathe, Kansas. Additional residences currently owned by Kasalaitis at Key West, Florida. No criminal record." *Not much there,* Stannard thought, *but we have another doctor. Let me see what the medical directory has on her. Funny, the claim file didn't say she was a doc.* He typed in "Erin Kasalaitis, Destin, Florida." He hit the print key and waited for the report to exit the printer. He began to read: "Erin Kasalaitis, MD, Deputy Director at the Emerald Coast Drug Rehabilitation Facility located in Fort Walton Beach since 2004. Formerly engaged in private medical practice in Kansas City, where she specialized in anesthesiology."

The balance of the report consisted of details that didn't interest Stannard. He printed the document and laid it on top of the one relating to Dr. Loren Parlous. With nothing to do before his meeting with Dr. Stinson, he opened the file and began reading the documents, slowly this time, making mental notes of all the important details. When he'd finished that, he searched the insurance companies' computer database for claims filed by or on behalf of Loren Parlous, Erin Parlous, and Erin Kasalaitis. *Okay, no claims filed by any of those individuals in Kansas, Missouri, Nebraska, and Iowa.* He expanded the search to include Ohio, California, New York, and Florida. *Nothing here either.* He expanded the search to include applications and changes to existing policies. *Bingo.* There it was, but what exactly was it? A smoking gun? Only time would tell. Dr. Loren Parlous had on several occasions attempted to cancel the policy under which Erin Kasalaitis made her claim as the owner/beneficiary. He flipped back to the termination date on the term policy. *Now, isn't that fortuitous. If the doctor hadn't died when he did, the policy would've been terminated in ninety days.* Stannard filled the remaining hours before his meeting with Dr. Stinson reading the confidential files relating to Dr. Loren Parlous's efforts to have the policy canceled. He read the letters of denial with particular interest. He noted the increased anxiety as Dr. Parlous made a second and then a third attempt to have the policy canceled.

Having done his background on Dr. Parlous and his former wife, he turned to the autopsy report:

AUTOPSY SUMMARY REPORT
    IDENTIFICATION NO.: 232-06
    AUTOPSY NO: A91-21
    HOSPITAL: KS046
    NAME: Parlous, Loren Wills
    AGE: 58
    SEX: Male
    RACE: Caucasian

HEIGHT: 5 feet 10 inches
WEIGHT: 178 pounds
HAIR: Brown
Date and hour of death: 6-23-2006 — 6:56 am
Autopsy performed: 6-23-2006 — 7:30 pm
Check one: Full autopsy [x] Head only [ ] Trunk
only [ ]

CLINICAL HISTORY

This 58-year-old Caucasian male was transported
DOA by ambulance to the hospital on June 23,
2006. Police records indicate the automobile driven
by Parlous had collided with a bridge structure
on Interstate 435 at the Quivira Road off-ramp in
Overland Park, Kansas. The initial observation indicated massive trauma to the head, a crushed thorax,
and a broken right tibia. Shreds of what appear to
be duct tape fibers and glue residue adhered to both
wrists and ankles.

Closer examination of the body revealed both
areolas had been surgically removed, by superficial
incision 2mm in depth. The thorax showed signs
of additional mutilation by incising a design identified as a unicursal hexagram. These incisions too
were superficial, being 2mm in depth. Although
the design is that of a unicursal hexagram, the lines
had been incised by lifting the lancet. The wounds,
being of uniform depth, appeared to be made by a
person having surgical skill. A second wound scar,

old and superficial, was visible on the left forearm. There were no other discernible scars. The testicles had been removed shortly before the incident resulting in the patient's death in a manner suggesting surgical skill, although the procedure was incomplete and had the appearance of being clumsily performed.

In addition to the accident injury to the right tibia there is indication of a childhood break to the left humerus. That injury had healed without further pathology.

Examination of heart, lungs, and gastrointestinal tract were unremarkable.

Examination of the brain revealed a subdural hematoma resulting from the automobile crash.

Toxicology screen revealed lidocaine administration to the area of the thorax wounds. More significantly, no such pain inhibitor was evident in the area of the inner thigh and scrotum, suggesting the upper body cutting was not used as a means of torture before the surgical castration was performed. Most significant of all was the discovery of the NMDA receptor antagonist ketamine in combination with ephedrine and selegiline. This combination of chemicals constitutes the street drug known as Ecstasy, a drug known for its hallucinogenic and neurotoxin properties. Liver section analysis failed to substantiate rumors of persistent recreational use of cocaine or other controlled substances.

FINAL PATHOLOGICAL DIAGNOSIS

Based on the results of the examination and the limited personal history of the patient available, it is not possible at this time to say with certainty whether the patient died as the result of an accident or suicide. The wounds to the thorax, scrotum, and thighs are consistent with surgical technique. While the patient practiced psychiatric medicine, he had previous experience in the medical profession as a surgeon. The areola were removed by two half-circle incisions being made around each areola, with the wound to the right areola being less precise, consistent with a right-handed person performing the procedure on his or her self. Incisions forming the unicursal hexagram were consistent with the wounds removing the areola.

The compression of the patient's chest cavity and the resultant collapsing of the lungs together with the brain injury are the cause of death.

MANNER OF DEATH

Undetermined.

Jerry E. Stinson, MD
Pathologist

Satisfied he had done all he could to prepare for his meeting with Dr. Stinson, he left his office at a quarter till three knowing the three-mile drive to the medical center would not take more than about ten minutes. Arriving in even less time, he began circling the parking lot looking for an empty space. At five minutes after three he gave up, pulled into a space marked Doctors Only, and got out of his car and locked the door. At ten minutes after three, he walked into Dr. Stinson's office.

"Jackson?" the doctor began. "I thought maybe you had changed your mind about our meeting."

"Sorry, I couldn't find a parking place."

"I know. Only doctors have the luxury of designated spaces."

"I know. That's where I'm parked."

"Well we'll need to get you out of here as soon as possible. The fine for parking in one of those spots is pretty hefty. I hope your company is lenient about those kinds of things."

"They're not. Maybe we'd better just get on with this." He handed over the copies of the authorization he'd made earlier. He then pulled out his copy of the autopsy report. "I suppose this is as good a place to start as any."

Dr. Stinson nodded and pulled out his copy of the summary. The autopsy did nothing to answer the overriding question: Did Dr. Loren Parlous die by his own hand, by accident, or was he somehow murdered? He did not know and would not speculate. Once more, he read the report, recalling the conversation he'd had with the detectives, who struggled with making the decision of whether or not to open a criminal investigation. He had wanted to be certain the findings and conclusions were all there, knowing the police would undoubtedly press him for more. He had told them what he could, even speculated privately with them.

Dr. Stinson set down his JOCO MED mug of decaffeinated Earl Grey tea. He removed the tea bag and twisted the string around the soggy residue, squeezing the last drop of the precious liquid into the mug. "Well?"

Stannard did not speak for over a minute, thinking before he responded, his left hand stroking his chin and the report lying on the table in front of him. "I don't know. What's your take on it? Off the record—are we looking at a suicide?"

Stinson anticipated the conversation would go in this direction and answered quickly, "I've asked around the medical community, and it seems Dr. Parlous had a history of mental problems. I'm certain you realize that that shouldn't come as a surprise. Practitioners frequently go into specialties because they have some predisposition for the same ailments. His psychiatric specialty was in the area of manipulative disorders."

"And what'd you find out?"

"It is all hearsay and speculative, but the word is that Parlous had a recreational drug problem. The autopsy did not substantiate that rumor though. If it had then some flags would have been raised."

"Like what?"

"People with drug problems frequently inflict wounds on themselves. Without evidence of drug abuse, that likelihood goes down. It's possible he inflicted the wounds on himself, although that would, I think, suggest something more disturbing than simple manipulative disorder. Somehow, I just can't see anyone emasculating himself without a powerful topical anesthetic."

Stannard nodded.

The coroner continued, "Of course, there is the possibility he committed suicide. If he did though, it is going down as the strangest case of suicide I've ever seen."

Stannard considered whether he should speak, then remarked, "Well, there may be something to the idea that the doctor inflicted the wounds on himself in order to manipulate someone else. He may have had a reason to believe his ex-wife wanted him dead. She owned a life insurance policy on him worth a face value of two million dollars, four million in case of accidental death or murder. Parlous couldn't persuade her to cash in the policies, and the insurance company refused to cancel since he didn't own them. Maybe he did this to himself in order to lay the blame on her and get the company to do what he wanted. It may have just gone too far."

"Interesting" replied Dr. Stinson, "that would certainly be something worth looking into. Since you don't have much to go on and I'm not ready to certify that the cause of death is the result of a simple accident, or suicide, possibly we should take the next step and do a psychological autopsy."

"Huh, what's that? The man is dead. How do you go about doing an autopsy on the thought processes of a man who's dead?"

"It's a method developed about twenty years ago, although we have rarely had occasion to use it here. It is a screening method to determine whether suicide is likely. The basis is the historical and medically significant events in the light of the patient's personality and relationships, his moods, fears, phobias, and the timeline of events just before his death. I can place a call to the State Mental Health Hospital. They have people qualified to conduct this type of autopsy. It won't be cheap though."

Stannard heard the words and questioned, "What's your idea of going beyond cheap?"

"My initial estimate is somewhere between ten and fifteen thousand dollars. When I mentioned it to the police, they just shook their heads."

Stannard flinched. He had no idea how his bosses would react if he approached them with the idea of performing a psychological autopsy, especially under these questionable circumstances. He answered at last, "Let's try to do it. I'll get it cleared by my boss. You make the necessary contacts, and I'll look for the money." Picking up the autopsy report and preparing to leave, he stopped for one last question. "You know, this is strange, Doc. Here we are nearly a month after the fact, and we still do not know what we're dealing with. What's even stranger is that weird marking carved in his chest."

"It's called a unicursal hexagram. It is a symbol that shows up in so much of history and religion. You know it mostly as a Star of David. Two overlapping equilateral triangles form the design. The normal hexagram is one triangle pointing up and the other pointing down. It signifies the relationship of God to man and man to God. Unfortunately, the unicursal hexagram has another meaning too. For centuries it has also been used as a symbol of evil and demonic power. The hexagram we have here is simply a stylized form of the one we normally see. Think about it. The hexagram consists of six lines, six points, and six triangles. It makes the number 666, the mark of Satan in the Book of Revelation."

Stannard felt the room begin to spin. *Russell, just like Russell.* His brain screamed at him, *Evil.*

Regaining his composure, he asked, "What do you suppose it means?"

"I don't know. It would seem to have a sinister meaning here. This hexagram is a stylized version of the religious hexagram, giving it the appearance of a horned head with eyes and a goatee. The goat is, of course, one of the symbols of the devil."

"Are we looking at some sort of ritualistic killing? Is this satanic worship of some sort?"

He felt his body beginning to perspire. He wondered if the doctor could see his respiration quicken.

"I don't have a clue. There is one more thing. The fact that the lancet was raised in making the design is a point in favor of Parlous doing this to himself. I don't believe a man could make such a design on himself without raising the lancet." Stinson paused before going on, measuring whether to say anything that smacked of religious significance. "Making a hexagram would seem to imply that the numeral one has some importance, though I cannot say what. It may be some sort of satanic play on the ancient Hebrew, you know, 'The Lord our God, the Lord is One.' If so, then the fact that the incision is not a continuing one may also indicate the person making the design intended to make a break with God."

Stannard shuddered. "You are suggesting we're dealing with some satanic ritual here, aren't you?"

"Good heavens, man," the doctor replied, "how can we know that? For all I know, it means nothing. Certainly it means nothing from a medical standpoint. What I can say with certainty is that if Dr. Loren Parlous did this to himself, he was one sick specimen of humanity."

Stannard's head reeled from the interview, but before leaving he had one more question.

"What about the castration? Could a man do that to himself? And if so, could he drive a car afterward?"

"Good questions. The answer is yes, but it's not likely. As I said in the report, the surgical technique lacked the skill of a practiced surgeon. Parlous had surgical experience but had not practiced recently, so far as I know. He would need a surgery setting to do it properly. If he had that, why rely on Ecstasy as an anesthetic instead of something more conventional."

"What about driving?"

"Oh, he could've done it, but it would've been difficult. Did the car have an automatic transmission?"

"Yeah, I believe it did."

"Well that would make it easier. As I said, he was hopped up on Ecstasy at the time of death, so he wouldn't have been feeling too much pain. The vas defers was tied and the scrotum sutured, although the stitches burst in the collision, so...yes, he could have driven."

"Is it likely?"

"That, my friend, is outside my expertise. That is for you to discover."

Stannard started to leave. He reached the office door when the doctor's words stopped him. "One more thing, Mr. Jackson. The man driving the Corvette did not have on shoes when the ambulance driver brought in the body. The soles of his feet were scratched too. It appears he had run across a hard surface shortly before the accident. Do you suppose that means anything?"

Stannard paused before he answered, "Possibly, but I don't know what. Thanks." Stannard left the hospital no more enlightened than when he arrived.

Chapter Four

Back in the office, Stannard flipped through the file, looking for the police report on the accident. *There they are...highway patrol, Lenexa PD, Overland Park PD; nothing about who it was Dr. Stinson talked to though.* A quick call to the doctor's office revealed the names of two OPPD detectives, Lieutenant Pezzati and Sergeant Pollard. He next called the OPPD to find out what they had done. On the third ring of the phone, a receptionist answered and directed his call to Lieutenant Mike Pezzati's extension. A moment later a man answered the phone. "This is Detective Pollard. I am Lieutenant Pezzati's partner. He isn't available now. Is there something I can do for you—or take a message for the lieutenant?"

The detective listened as the caller identified himself. "This is Stannard Jackson. I'm an insurance investigator making inquiries into the death of Dr. Loren Parlous. He died three weeks ago in a single-car automobile incident on I-435. A claim has been made under a life insurance policy, and because of the unusual circumstances we are making an independent inquiry." Pollard did not answer, so Stannard continued. "I got your name out of the file and from Dr. Stinson over at the Johnson County Medical Center. He said he had talked to either you or Lieutenant Pezzati. Would it be possible for me to come by sometime today and talk to both of you?"

"Sure, that'd be fine. Pezzati is in a meeting now, but he should be finished in about a half hour. Come on over. You know where we are located?"

"Yeah, I do. A half hour it is." Stannard took a minute to walk down the hall to Big Ed's office. "I just got started on the Parlous case. It's early but there are some points suggesting this may not be an accident. I just don't know whether to thank you for assigning it or not."

Big Ed smiled. "I thought you'd want to handle it. Frankly, you're the only person in the office quali-fied to investigate something as weird as this."

"I owe you," Stannard answered. "The question is what do I owe you—gratitude or a payback?"

Upon arrival at police headquarters, Stannard was shown into a semiprivate cubicle with five-foot-high walls marked by plastic nameplates outside bearing the names of Detective Lieutenant Pezzati and Sergeant Pollard. When he entered, Stannard stood still. His face slowly broadened into a big grin as Pezzati stood to greet him. "Jackson, it has been a long time."

The name on the door read "Pezzati," but the man standing to greet him was his boyhood friend and former neighbor, Mike Forman. "Forman, what gives here? What's with the name Pezzati?"

Pezzati grabbed Stannard by the shoulders, giving him a great big bear hug, and in true Italian fashion kissed him on both cheeks. "Hey, *paisano,* what's in a name? Forman or Pezzati, I'm still the same guy! What's it been, twenty-five years?"

"More like thirty—maybe longer—but what about the name Pezzati?"

The detective shrugged. "You know, my dad was Irish, but my mother was Italian."

"Right, but that doesn't answer my question. What's with the name Pezzati?"

The detective looked disturbed. "Yeah, well after Dad ran out on us, we moved from the neighborhood."

"I remember. We were what...juniors in high school. You went to Saint Louis."

"That's right. Mom moved us back to be close to her family, and after that she married a guy by the name of Pezzati. He adopted me after my Dad died. I was an adult but he did it because it cemented the relationship we had. He was a cop, from The Hill, and I just followed in his footsteps. About five years ago my wife and I moved here. I feel guilty about not calling you. I heard you had gone into the cops too. Always thought I'd just run into you. What about you? I heard they were calling you by a nickname—St Jack, isn't it? I heard you and Caryl got married and had a kid. How are they?"

Stannard's shoulders slumped. "Caryl is fine but the boy…" His voice cracked. "The boy was murdered years ago. No one calls me St Jack anymore."

Pezzati stood speechless for a moment, stunned at the information, then answered. "I'm sorry, Stannard. I didn't know."

"It's okay," Stannard answered forgiving the blunder. "How could you know? It was years ago and we had lost touch. I try not to think about it. I haven't thought about it much lately—at least not until today. Something brought it to mind the last few weeks. But what about you—you been back for five years? Why didn't you give me a call?"

"I should've called, but you know how it is. I wasn't sure you'd even remember me."

"Not likely, buddy. How could I forget?"

Pezzati laughed out loud. "So then, you do remember how we met?"

"We were only about six years old when you moved into the neighborhood. You decked me when I came over to play with you."

"Yeah, do you remember why?" Pezzati bristled with mock machismo.

"Sure, you said it was because I hadn't asked permission to come into your yard."

"Well, it is a good thing you called ahead today, pal. I'd hate to have to deck you again. Now then, what is it you want to know about Dr. Parlous?"

Everything! It was the Parlous case that brought up the memory of Russell. I've got to know everything. Stannard listened as Pezzati told him what had been done in the way of investigation by the police. Just as Dr. Stinson had said, there had not been any psychological autopsy by either the coroner's office or the Overland Park Police Department. No money. But more important, Pezzati related the strange events surrounding their visit with Dr. Parlous's widow when they had gone to inform her about the accident.

Back in his office Stannard read the report Pezzati gave him of the interview he'd had with Mrs. Parlous. As he did so he tried to visualize the scene as Pezzati had described it.

"Mrs. Parlous, I think under the circumstances we should take a complete statement from you concerning this business with the first Mrs. Parlous. We can either do that now or schedule some other time…"

Lorelei did not hesitate. "No, I'd rather do it now," she said, her voice steady, quiet, and unemotional.

"If you're sure. We know this must be a shock to you. We can always come back in a day or two."

"No, let's do it now."

The car proceeded slowly along the golf course before turning away to follow the narrow road into the wild woods surrounding the Parlous house. At the concrete parking pad, Pollard exited the driver's seat and opened the rear door for Mrs. Parlous. The detectives waited while she punched in the security code to unlock the massive door. The elevator ride to the fortress house below passed in silence. When the door opened, they were greeted by the sound of a woman singing softly to herself in Spanish.

"I didn't realize anyone else was in the house," Detective Pollard said.

"There wasn't when we left. That's Maria. She comes in twice a week to do housework and help out with cooking." Then, in a loud voice she continued, "Maria, I'm home."

The small, attractive Mexican woman a few years younger than Lorelei Parlous appeared from another part of the house. "Oh," she exclaimed, a little startled, "I didn't know there were others with you."

"It's all right, Maria. These men are police detectives." She walked past her maid without further notice then addressed the detectives. "Gentlemen, would you like something to drink, coffee, tea, water?"

Pezzati looked at Pollard and answered for both. "Just some water, thanks."

Lorelei turned back to Maria. "Bring us three glasses of water and then continue with whatever it was you were doing." Addressing the detectives, she continued, "Let's go into the den. We can have privacy there." Minutes later Maria followed the three into the room. She set the tray with drinks on the coffee table and left, closing the door behind her. Lorelei watched Maria as she went to the door. At the moment she heard the quiet click as the latch caught, she took charge of the session. "All right, how do we proceed? Do you ask questions, or do I just talk?"

She's a cold one, Pezzati thought. *Here we are just minutes after she identifies the mutilated body of her dead husband without even looking at it. She shows absolutely no emotion. Shock does strange things to people, but this goes beyond that.* "Let's get started with a few questions so we can get some of the background. Where and when did you and Dr. Parlous meet?"

"We met just about four years ago. I worked in the same complex of buildings as Loren, though we were not in the same building. I worked in the administrative section of a different medical practice."

"Was the doctor married at the time?"

"Yes, I guess you could say that. I suppose there are people who would say I broke up their marriage, but that wouldn't be true. That marriage was finished anyway."

More information than I asked, Pezzati mused.

"There was some talk of a special friend, a lady friend," Lorelei said.

"Who's that? Who had a lady friend?"

"Erin. Everyone rumored that Erin had a girlfriend and it was more than platonic."

Pezzati made a note. *I may want to get back to that later.* "How long had they been married?"

"About twenty years."

"Mrs. Parlous, as we were leaving the house you made a pretty serious accusation against the first Mrs. Parlous. What makes you think she had something to do with your husband's death?"

"Loren told me. He said she tried to hire someone to kill him. He even showed me some letters he'd received from someone in Florida who said Erin had approached him about doing it."

Pezzati caught the glance from Pollard and dropped his eyes as if to say I'll take it. "Who was that man?" Pezzati asked.

"I don't know. The letters were anonymous. I think there are two of them in Loren's desk. I'll look." Lorelei rose from her seat on the sofa and walked across the room to her husband's desk. She searched through the drawers, one at a time, until she found what she was looking for, two single sheets of paper from the bottom right-hand drawer. Each sheet had an envelope stapled to it. The envelopes bore postmarks dated October 12, 2004, and April 29, 2005.

Convenient, Lieutenant Pezzati thought, but he asked, "May I take a look at those?"

"Of course," Lorelei answered, handing them to the detective.

Pezzati read. "October 10, 2004. Dr. Parlous, I think you should know your ex-wife wants you dead. She tried to hire me to do the job. She wants it to look like an accident. I told her I'd think about it but decided to warn you instead." The letter had been written using word processing software. It was unsigned. The envelope bore a postmark from Fort Walton Beach, Florida.

The second letter was to much the same effect. It read, "April 29, 2005. Dr. Parlous, You should be warned. Your ex-wife is not giving up. She called me again. I told her no! She sounded angry and said she'd get someone else, someone who could be trusted to do what she wanted." Like the first letter, this too was generated electronically and unsigned. The envelope for this letter bore a postmark from Destin, Florida.

"Did your husband report these letters to the police?" Lieutenant Pezzati asked.

"Yes, he told me he did. He said they told him that since the letters were not signed and we'd both handled them, there wasn't much they could do with them. He said they dusted them for fingerprints, but all they found were ours."

"How did they know the prints were yours and Dr. Parlous's?"

"We gave them our prints for comparison."

"Who'd he contact concerning these letters?"

"The Kansas Bureau of Investigation. After all, whatever it was, it would require cooperation by both Kansas and Florida police agencies."

"Do you know if he heard anything else from them?"

"He said they wouldn't help."

"How did Dr. Parlous react to the letters and the answer from the KBI?"

"He was scared. He kept saying she would do it. It seemed like he became more and more obsessed with the reality of the threat as time passed. It got to the point where hardly a day passed that he didn't talk about it. Some days he would be so upset he didn't go to his office. He became paranoid about it. He said someone would shoot him on the highway or throw a stone or something from an overpass onto his windshield. I told him that only happened in stories, but he couldn't get it out of his mind."

"You said she was after the proceeds of life insurance. What is that all about?" Pezzati looked at Pollard to make certain he was taking notes.

"Loren had taken out a one million-dollar whole life policy on his life when their son was born. He took out another million-dollar policy about ten years later. Loren told me he converted the policies to a single policy a few years later. I don't know anything about that though. I never saw the policy or policies. What I do know is that Erin convinced the judge that I'd wrecked their marriage. She became owner of the policies in the property settlement instead of just being a named beneficiary. To make matters worse, the judge ordered Loren to keep the policies in force. Loren tried to let them lapse, but she had him back in court under an order to show cause why he wasn't in contempt. The judge threatened Loren with contempt of court and jail if he didn't make the premium payments."

Threatened, the police officer thought. *Judges don't threaten—warn yes, but threaten no.* "So what did Dr. Parlous do?"

"What could he do? He paid the premiums and tried to get the insurance company to cancel the policies. Of course they said no, because he wasn't the owner of the policies."

"When did that happen?"

"You would have to check with them, but I'd say they gave a final and definite answer sometime within the last six months."

"How did he take that news?"

"He became even more depressed, said he didn't know what to do. Sometime before that, he had the windows replaced in the house. After that, he worried that we were in such an isolated location someone would be able to break in. He said that we were too isolated to get help fast. Then he started talking about moving from here."

"What good would it do to move? If Erin Parlous wanted to get at him, she could surely find him easily enough. After all he is...was a noted psychiatrist, and the medical association or insurance company could be counted on to provide his location if all else failed."

"I know, but you didn't know Loren. Once he got something in his head, it had to happen. They say psychiatrists go into specialties based on their own personal predilections, and Loren had done a significant amount of work in immature personality disorders."

Lieutenant Pezzati paused to consider what he heard. The routine traffic accident had become something very much different from ordinary or routine. He wondered where this would take him, so he continued. "Did Dr. Parlous ever talk about committing suicide?"

Lorelei Parlous's eyes narrowed slightly as she answered, "I wouldn't say so in so many words. What did bother me was he started talking about some of his patients. He'd never done that before, and the ones he did talk about were the ones who had attempted suicide. He seemed interested in how they'd tried and why they failed, if in fact they had failed. He kept talking about how anyone who wanted to die could do it easily enough.

"The ones who failed just wanted attention or were trying to control someone else by appealing to a nurturing instinct in the people they wanted to control. At one point he even said it could be a good way to get back at someone who hurt you. He laughed when he said the ultimate joke on

Erin would be to commit suicide and pin a murder rap on her."

Pezzati did not respond.

Lorelei waited. Still no response. Then she asked, "What is it? You don't think Loren committed suicide, do you? I have been telling you it's Erin! She's behind this. I don't know how, but I am certain she has had something to do with it."

"But..."

"But nothing—all that suicide talk being made to look like murder was just Loren blowing off steam, trying to make himself feel better."

Pezzati continued to hesitate, taking in all that Lorelei had said so far. He had initially thought this interview would be pretty much routine, but now he knew it would be anything but. At last, he said, "I'd like to know more about the meeting you and Dr. Parlous had with Erin Parlous last night."

As Lorelei began to answer, Pezzati thought he could see some hesitation on her part, as if she were weighing her words carefully. "Her name is Kasalaitis. I thought I told you that." She stopped to make certain someone made a note. "The meeting was Loren's idea. After the insurance company refused to cancel the policies on his life, he said the only way he would ever get any peace of mind was to buy Erin off. I told him it wouldn't work, that it wasn't just about money. Erin wanted revenge. She resented my relationship with Loren and wanted to punish both of us..." Lorelei paused, waiting for Pezzati to pursue the line.

"You said Erin lives in Fort Walton Beach, Florida. What was she doing up here? I mean, why here?"

"I guess at least some of that is my idea. I told Loren that if he was serious about talking her into dropping the policies, we would need to show her some good faith. Loren sent her a cashier's check for twenty-five thousand dollars and asked her to come to Kansas City to talk about the insurance policies. We'd checked with an economist who ran some figures for us, you know present value of two million dollars against his life expectancy. I know that sounds dumb now, especially since Loren believed she planned to kill him. His life expectancy had nothing to do with actuarial tables. His life expectancy had to do with however long it took Erin to get someone to do what she wanted. Anyway, the economist told us the tables said a healthy man at age fifty-eight could expect to live for twenty-four years at least. We thought maybe we could buy her off now for somewhere around half a million dollars. That's why we sent her the check and asked her to come to Kansas City—to talk about a business proposition. She flew up from Fort Walton Beach yesterday, and we met her a little after five o'clock at Jimmy's Jigger on 39th Street. We planned to have a drink and discuss our proposal. It was a public place, and everyone could feel safe there."

Neither Pezzati nor Pollard showed any sign of disbelief at the time, though later when they discussed the interview both men agreed that the story did not sound plausible. First of all, half a million dollars is a lot of money, even for a psychiatrist. Neither man knew much about the profession, but both believed it could not possibly be as lucrative as, say, neurosurgery. Of course, Dr. Parlous and his wife lived well—but half a million dollars?

Pollard responded to Lorelei's story. "So, how did it go, the meeting with Erin, I mean?"

"Not well. As I said, she had issues that had nothing to do with money. Of course, we didn't offer her the half million up front. We had a drink, and by the time the second round came, we thought it would be a good time to let her know what was on our minds. Loren probably got the conversation off on the wrong foot by accusing Erin of wanting to have him killed. She got in a snit and told him that wasn't true and she resented the accusation. I tried to act as peacemaker and told her that we were glad to hear that from her, because in a way it would make our proposal all the more reasonable. I told her we wanted to talk about how much money it would take now for her to agree to cancel the insurance policies on Loren's life."

Pezzati asked, "How did she react to that?"

"She didn't seem too surprised. In fact, she said, 'I thought maybe that was what you had in mind when you sent the cashier's check.' "

"It concerned me that Loren would offer her too much money. After all, raising half a million dollars would put us into debt. I answered before Loren could speak and told her that we thought a quarter of a million was fair. After all, she'd have to wait for twenty years if the life expectancy table had any validity. By the time she saw any of the insurance money, she would be pushing seventy-five and the money wouldn't do her much good. She looked at me as if I was crazy and said she wasn't interested. She made a rude comment about our being suckers and thanked us for the twenty-five thousand. She said she'd enjoy spending it, knowing it would be the last 'gift' she'd get from either of us."

"What did you or your husband say to that?"

"Nothing—we didn't say anything."

"So what happened then?"

"She got up to leave. She turned back toward our table when she was about ten feet away and said, 'I guess I'll have to get to work for whatever I get next.' With that she walked away and drove off in her rental car."

Pezzati probed for more. "Is that all?"

"No, not quite. Loren got angry with me for making what he thought was a ridiculously low offer. He told me that I knew very well the economic value of the policies was around four hundred and forty thousand dollars. We argued for about a quarter hour, and then Loren left, saying he was going to find Erin and make a legitimate offer. I had to take a cab home. I never saw him again—alive."

"What time was that, when he left, I mean?"

"Just a few minutes after six."

"Are you sure of the time?"

"Yes. The TV had been on in the bar and the network evening news went off just after Erin left. Loren left to follow her at about six fifteen. The local weather was just coming on."

Pezzati considered her comment, a lot of detail, more than he had expected. "He didn't come home?"

"No."

"Weren't you worried about him going to have it out with someone who he thought wanted to kill him?"

"Yes, but I was angry. I felt like he blamed me for everything, wrecking his marriage and now...now he is dead." For the first time, Lorelei Parlous began to cry, big wet tears that rolled down her cheeks and smeared her mascara.

Pezzati and Pollard, realizing they had gotten all the information they could for the moment, excused themselves and retreated to their office to go over the notes they had taken and consider the strange direction the investigation had taken.

Stannard laid aside the report summarizing the interview with Mrs. Parlous. He reread the copies of both threatening letters Pezzati had given him. After that he locked his desk, got up and walked out of his office. Pezzati and Pollard were right—the story Lorelei Parlous told wasn't plausible. Parlous knew the value of the policy wasn't half a million dollars. That twenty-year stuff was just so much bunk. That policy was going to expire in three months. If he was afraid, maybe he had good reason. He walked to his car, where he began his predrive routine, only this time he forgot to complete the entire process before he drove out of the parking lot. The details about satanic symbols and mutilated bodies, about mentally unbalanced people, tore at the core of his being.

There was no doubt that Dr. Loren Parlous died in an automobile accident but there had to be more to it than that. But what—murder or some attempt at manipulation that had gone wrong—he had no way to tell. He also wondered if his boss would authorize a psychological autopsy. He doubted it. What's more, Pezzati had been emphatic. He had pursued the matter as far as his superiors would allow. Officially he and Pollard were off the case. The Overland Park PD was content to call it a traffic accident.

As he drove north toward Wyandotte County, another incongruity popped into his head.

Everyone agreed Dr. Loren Parlous had a recreational drug history, yet the liver sections taken during the autopsy failed to reveal anything other than the cocktail of hallucinogens he had ingested shortly before his death. *I don't get it,* Stannard thought.

Chapter Five

Stannard arrived home late that evening. When he drove into the driveway just off Wolcott Road at 6:35 p.m., Caryl had dinner on the table. She greeted him with her usual affectionate reserve, but her eyes betrayed her concern. "You're late," she commented, noting it was the first time in over six months that her husband had not been home just as she finished setting the table. What was even more disturbing for her was that he had not even bothered to call and let her know he would be late.

"I know," he answered in a distracted tone. "I've been working a new case."

Caryl did not respond. She turned to get the yeast rolls out of the oven. She had not seen him so mentally distant since his days as a police detective. Now he had the same look etched on his face.

"So what's so special about a new case that you would deviate from your schedule?"

Still distracted, Stannard sat down and reached for the meat loaf.

"Stannard," Caryl complained, "I haven't even sat down yet."

"Oh, yeah. Sorry." With that, Stannard stopped and waited for his wife to reach the table, then he dived into the meat loaf and mashed potatoes, helping himself to an unhealthy mouthful while he pondered what to say. He hardly chewed his food before he swallowed, then he said, "Remember a few weeks ago when I almost got sideswiped getting onto the highway?"

"Yes, what about it?"

"Well, that's the case." He continued to eat.

Caryl stopped eating and laid down her fork. "All right, Stannard, what's this all about?

Something has upset you, and I want to know what it is." Her husband did not bring his work home from the office. He left all that behind when he came home. Only now it refused to stay in its place.

"There is something wrong with this case. It is evil, or demonic. I don't know what to make of it, but it bothers me, and you know why." His eyes welled with tears. "I am afraid something will happen...to you...or even worse...to me. What would you do then?"

Caryl understood something had touched Stannard's soul. If anything happened to him, her life, her security would end. Stannard did not fear for his own life—he was afraid for her. She rose from the kitchen table and walked around the table, where she leaned down to kiss him on the cheek.

He drew in a quick breath and sniffled.

"Does this have something to do with Russell? Don't take the case if it does. You can always go to Big Ed and ask for it to be reassigned to someone else. Every time something comes along that brings up—" she choked "—you know, it ends up pulling us both down." Caryl felt a wave of helplessness sweep over her. "You brought up Russell's name this morning. Do you want to talk about it? It might help."

He felt the wave of despair pass over him, believing she worried about his state of mind. He started at the beginning, reminding her about the Vette that nearly hit him weeks before. It was him. The case he had was about the man driving the car. He then told her about his conversations with Dr. Stinson and the detectives. He hoped that in the telling it would bring a measure of acceptance. It had happened to Dr. Loren Parlous, not him. He had only been a witness to a portion of the tragedy, and now he had been called to investigate. As he related the story, his subconscious prompted him to think, *I should just go to Big Ed and ask for the case to be reassigned.* Only when he reached the part about the mutilation did Caryl begin to understand. She listened carefully, her eyes glistening as he continued. "In so many ways this reminds me of what happened to Russell."

Caryl swallowed hard. The last thing she needed to do now was break down in front of her husband. He would not understand—or care. Because he blamed himself for what happened to their son he had never had room for her grief. "That's all in the past. Surely this has nothing to do with that."

"But the cutting, the marks on the body..."

She grasped at a solution, any solution to the agony she knew they would both have to endure if he investigated something as gruesome as this case promised to be. "Why can't your company just leave it to the police? Let them investigate and then piggyback on their results."

"The Overland Park Police Department has closed its file. They're apparently willing to leave it as an accident or some sort of demented suicide."

"And you don't believe that, do you?" she asked.

"No, would you?"

"So then, what are you going to do?"

Each of them posed a question in answer to the question of the other, neither of them wanting to face the obvious.

"Investigate. What else can I do?"

"So then you just begin where the OPPD left off." She knew this would not be an ordinary insurance investigation; it would take her husband back to a life he had abandoned over a decade earlier.

"I suppose so. I'll begin there and do some digging on my own."

"Just don't go digging up the past. Remember, no one calls you St Jack anymore."

"Well, almost no one. I ran into an old friend today over at the OPPD, a detective by the name of Pezzati. You won't believe who he is. Remember Mike Forman?"

"Sure. What has Forman got to do with anything? His family moved away years ago. You didn't hear anything from him after about two years. I lost track of his sister about the same time. We were all teenagers."

"Well, Detective Lieutenant Mike Pezzati is Forman. His mother remarried and his stepfather adopted him. He called me St Jack today. I have a feeling that before this file is closed, St Jack will be called upon."

The dinner still lay on the table, uneaten, but neither of them wanted a cold supper. They washed the dishes and went outside to the patio, where they let the early evening sun warm their bodies and spirits. They sat in silence, watching as it set behind the oak-forested hill to the west.

Lightning bugs swarmed in the night sky, their lights flashing on and off at wildly intermittent places. Twenty minutes later they went inside. Stannard turned on the early nine-thirty news while Caryl picked up her knitting to do a couple of rows on the prayer shawl she had promised the church.

At ten o'clock Stannard turned to a second channel to catch the news there. After that they retired for the night, on schedule, just after the weather report. It promised to be another fine summer day, with overnight lows in the low seventies and a high near ninety with low humidity and clear, clean air quality. The schedule may have returned but not Stannard's normal sense of calm. As they lay in bed, Caryl could sense the tension in Stannard's body. She pretended to be asleep, hoping he would drift off. At 11:45 p.m., his breathing finally slowed, and she knew he had gone to sleep.

At five after one, Caryl heard him rise quietly from their bed and tiptoe out of the room.

Ten minutes later, she too rose and stealthily followed him to the den. She stood in the dark hallway, peering into the dimly lit room. She did not need to see what it was he had before him. She knew he would be looking at the scrapbook of their dead son. He was crying. She said nothing; did nothing. She understood he needed to be alone with his memories, guilt, and fears. Stannard Jackson may be many things, but he was no coward. If he had fears, they were real. He would not run from them, and he needed to face them in his own way and on his own terms. Caryl went back to bed.

Sitting alone in the dimly lit room, Stannard knew the exact page where the feeling of guilt would begin. It always started at the same place. He looked at the faded pages of the scrapbook. The small lamp cast an eerie shadow across the room as his mind raced back in time.

Three bored cops sat at their desks in the corner of the squad room assigned to the Major Case Squad. It had been over two weeks since there had not been a major case for the Kansas City, Kansas, Police Department to investigate. As a result the captain had to listen as other detectives complained about the number of cases they each worked while the three men in the corner sat reading cheap novels and drinking burnt coffee. The men in the corner could not have cared less. They knew they had earned their place in the police hierarchy, and each had the swagger and ego that went with the honor. They were too good to have their time wasted on routine matters. The youngest of the three men, the one they all called St Jack, gave the appearance of having more arrogance than his two older colleagues. The new case assignments irritated all three that Monday morning but especially St Jack, who resented being pulled down to the level of those he believed to be inferior.

"All right, fellas," Captain Simms began, "it is time for you goldbrickers to get back to work." The words at first promised relief from boredom, but when he continued the emotion changed to something else. "I need you to help pick up some of the slack in the workload."

"What's that supposed to mean?" the lead detective on the squad wanted to know.

The captain answered, "For one thing it means there are no new major cases for you three prima donnas to work, but you can help out with some of the case backlog."

That was when the grumbling started. None of the three saw himself working routine cases, certainly not investigating mindless matters just to placate some bureaucrat who thought meaningless statistics would impress his superiors.

"Ah, come on, Captain, that's demeaning," St Jack whined. "You were put up to this by the other guys, weren't you?" He spoke the words they all thought.

"No," the captain lied, "these cases deserve a look just as much as any other, and you three are not doing anything else. Put yourself in the shoes of the victims. How would you like it if your case got ignored just because no one would investigate it? Besides, none of these files should take much time, and if something major comes along you can pull off and take up the important work."

Captain Simms distributed the nine case files as if they were playing cards, dealing the three detectives one file at a time without regard to subject matter. Each detective marked the spot in his novel then picked up his files, each grumbling as he did so. St Jack spilled coffee from the cheap foam cup onto the top manila folder as he looked at the signed complaint. Dead calf—here we go. Intercity drug gang war with two dead bodies left on the street in Quindaro one week, and dead calf in Leavenworth County the next. He read on. A Leavenworth County stockman asserted two or three boys from Wyandotte County had crossed the county line and slaughtered—mutilated, really—a calf that spring. The complaint bore a date four months old. St Jack flipped to the next page. The report and file requesting assistance had been forwarded by the Leavenworth County sheriff. St Jack looked with disgust at a disturbing picture of the animal slit open with its genitalia removed. He flipped to the second page of the report. The same farmer had complained the autumn before of a similar incident. Easter and Halloween, St Jack mused. Whatever is going on has something to do with religion, Easter when Christ defeated the power of evil and All

Hallows' Eve, Halloween, the day before All Saints Day. Even though he had never been a particularly faithful practitioner of religion, St Jack did know that much. His Catholic friends had explained the significance of the autumnal holiday from the perspective of the nuns who ran the parochial school his friends attended. So, what was this file all about? Probably just some kids fooling around with the occult. They'd probably already outgrown the mischief. "Captain, there isn't anything to this," he opined after reading the file. "You know what this is. It's just a couple of kids messing with some old man. The case is already old. What can we do? I doubt anything."

The captain frowned. "Jackson, I gave you the file because I want the boys identified in that file questioned. That's why we have files—in case you forgot. Maybe it leads somewhere, maybe not. I don't care. I want you to look into it, so get on it and stop complaining. There are worse things I could assign, you know."

Resigned to mediocrity, St Jack snatched the file folder and stormed out of the squad room. He'd do it, but the sooner he finished with this foolishness, the better he'd like it. In the parking lot, he walked to his unmarked Crown Victoria, unlocked the door, and sat behind the wheel. These were the days before his compulsive need to have everything orderly. Inside the messy car, cigarette butts cluttered the ashtray and ashes covered the dashboard. Hot embers had burned holes in the seat. Food wrappers from the Hardee's on State Avenue and crumpled paper coffee cups littered the floor. *Okay,* he thought, *who are these kids the old man thinks did it, and where do they live?* The file identified them as John Phillips and Tim Peters, both eighteen. Both boys lived in the Piper area on Donohoo Road and attended Piper High School. *They are just high school kids, for crying out loud. They're just schoolmates of Russell.*

He arrived at the high school building at lunchtime, checked in at the office, and located the two boys eating lunch in the cafeteria. Just as he expected, the boys denied any knowledge of the incidents. Casting glances at one another, they laughed when he told them he did not believe them. It had been sloppy police work. He should have talked to them one at a time. St Jack knew it at the time, but he had been irritated. Stannard Jackson knew it now. What he had not seen was the look on the two boys' faces when he finished talking to them and moved across the cafeteria and sat down with a boy sitting alone without friends. John Phillips and Tim Peters had watched with interest. They both knew Russell Jackson but had no intention of giving the fact away.

Remembering the failure burned in his chest. He wept. Caryl did not hear when he returned to bed. The following morning, her husband appeared his normal self at the breakfast table, though somehow more alive and melancholy at the same time. He left for work promptly at 6:18 a.m. and, after following his usual predrive routine, backed out of the driveway at 6:25 a.m. During the night something had happened to her husband, and Caryl wondered if she'd just seen the first faint glimmer of the man she married, a man everyone had called St Jack.

She watched as he drove away from the house, then turned and walked into the den. The scrapbook still lay on the ottoman, where her husband had put it before he returned to bed. She opened it. He had rearranged the contents of the book during the night. On the first page, she saw the familiar two pictures, the baby picture taken at Saint Margaret's hospital on February 14, 1973. *Valentine's Day,* she mused. *What a wonderful gift.* The second picture was of a smiling five-year-old. Her gaze then fell on the *Kansas City Kansan* newspaper article dated October 31, 1987, which he had moved to the second page. The headline read "Boy Found Dead in Ritualistic Killing." The tears came. How could this bring strength to her husband while it devastated her?

Chapter Six

Caryl may have thought she saw the old St Jack in the way Stannard prepared to leave for work, but for him the process had only begun. His mind raced as it struggled to escape the vortex where it had existed for so many years. When he reached the ramp leading from Kansas Highway 7 onto Interstate 435, his brain began to relive the events three weeks earlier. By the time he reached the point where traffic merged with the Leavenworth Road on-ramp, he felt his nervous system tingling. The police academy training he received so many years ago and his past experience stirred within him. Instead of trying to suppress the bad memories, he let them come and allowed his brain to remember all it could. Even so, it would not be easy. The memory of his son dying at the hands of satanic fiends crowded in on his effort to recall that June day when the Corvette came within inches of ramming him. He fought through the emotional pain to recall those recent events. The man had driven as if possessed. At the time all he had thought was that the crazy fool had nearly sideswiped his car.

His mind then raced back to his son, Russell. He wondered if he would ever be able to forgive himself. What would he have thought if the driver had been his son, fleeing for his life? But it had not been Russell. It was Dr. Loren Parlous. There was no connection between Russell and Dr. Parlous. Then, in an instant the jolt of reality once more gave way to his nightmare of the past. As a junior member of the Major Case Squad, he had been investigating the animal sacrifices that somehow escalated to human sacrifice. If that were not enough, his son had been the sacrifice. It took a concerted effort, but he pulled his mind away from that tragedy and began to focus on the problem now facing him. Big Ed could not have made the company goals in the matter any plainer. "We are on the hook here for some major bucks," he had said. "The way the police agencies left this thing, a legitimate claim may be made for double indemnity. Obviously, our client doesn't want to pay that."

Okay, Big Ed had defined the problem. Insurance companies never wanted to pay on claims, at least not if they had a way to deny them. But the truth of the matter was it might be difficult to avoid paying the claim. After all, the doctor died, and no one could deny the circumstances. Accidental death seemed the most logical solution. But if the company wanted that off the table, he would have to find another answer. So, what did that leave? Suicide would be grounds for denying the double indemnity, but that seemed unlikely under the circumstances. Still he would have to look into it as a possibility.

His brain ran once more to the recollection of his son's death, sending an electric jolt through his body that culminated in an icy shiver that ran down his spine. By force of will, he pulled his thoughts back to the Parlous investigation. *What if the widow was right? What if the doctor's ex-wife had been involved in having him killed? We would not have to pay her, and there had not been an alternate beneficiary named on the policy. Would that change anything? I'll have to ask the company lawyers about that. In that event, maybe the client wouldn't have to pay anyone.*

His mind once more drifted to his son. The boys who killed Russell Jackson had done so without a motive as good as a two million-dollar payout. Aloud, Stannard tried to focus his thoughts. "Stop it,

Stannard. This is not about Russell. This is an insurance investigation, and you need to stay focused. Okay, so I have two possibilities. If I can prove it was a suicide, they will only have to pay the face amount of the policy. Or if I can prove the widow is right, they can just deny the claim outright." He suddenly saw the Antioch Road exit. Lost in thought, he'd driven all the way to Johnson County but could not account for the time. He cut across a lane of traffic and up the ramp and turned south, following the street to Corporate Woods.

Upon entering the office suite, he was greeted by the sound of Big Ed's voice. "Stannard, is that you?"

"Yeah." Stannard walked across the reception room and down the short hallway to the open door.

"I've been thinking about that Parlous claim I gave you yesterday. Any thoughts?"

Stannard sat down opposite his boss. "Questions are more like it. The obvious solutions are there, but I'm having trouble getting a meaningful start. Whatta you think?"

"The client won't like a finding of accidental death. I'm certain of that."

Stannard responded, "I suppose not, but they may end up with that. Suicide is a remote possibility, but the facts are certainly strange for that to be true. About the only thing we have to suggest it are the statistics that show single-car accidents involving bridge abutments are frequently suicide. We don't have a note. Suicides normally leave a note, but that may not mean anything either. Dr. Parlous had a reputation for being something of an odd duck. I think maybe I should do some digging into his background. What little I looked up yesterday didn't tell me much."

"Good idea," Big Ed replied. "There is the suggestion of foul play here, but I don't see a clear path to proving it. Let's focus on the suicide angle. Denial of the double indemnity will be a large enough coup." Then as an afterthought he continued, "Don't give up on the idea of homicide though. I gave this case to you because you are the best investigator the company has ever employed. It had nothing to do with your special knowledge of the incident leading up to Dr. Parlous's death."

"Thanks for the vote of confidence. You know this will be difficult for me...my son...you know."

"Well, yes. I didn't think about that until this morning. Sorry." Big Ed meant it, but putting sentimentality aside, he continued, "So, where'll you start?"

"The widow would be as good a place as any, better than most. The police interview didn't go very far. I think they must've been ready to call it

an accident early on. For sure they weren't calling it a homicide or a suicide. If that's the case though, I can't see any reason to send homicide detectives to do the initial investigation. Public Affairs would normally send a chaplain to do that sort of thing."
I don't get it, Stannard thought to himself. *I didn't get much encouragement from Forman or Pezzati, whatever his name is now. He talked murder but didn't say they were doing anything.*

Stannard left Big Ed's office. An hour later he checked his e-mail and phone messages. The clock gave the time, 8:20, late enough to be calling the Parlous house. He opened the file, found the phone number he wanted, and dialed. No one answered. After the sixth ring, he heard the answering machine click on and a warm female voice come on the line. "If you hear this message, I am either not available or away from home. If you need to talk to me that urgently, you can try my cell phone…" She rattled off the number in a staccato cadence. Stannard did his best to write down the number. He punched in the number he had written on the paper but got a wrong number and a dressing down by the man he had obviously awakened. He dialed the house number again and listened closely. The voice did not sound like that of a grieving widow, but it may be an old recording, Stannard thought. He copied the last three digits of the number and dialed it. No answer. He heard the click of an answering machine. This time it was the automated voice of the telephone service telling him to leave his name and number. He did neither.

Instead he called the office of Forensic Psychiatric Medical Associates, LLC. *If I can't talk to his widow, I'll talk to his professional associates,* he thought. On the third ring, a receptionist answered the phone. He again checked his watch, eight-thirty, early for any medical office to be taking calls. "Hello." He heard his voice sounding like someone in urgent need of help. "My name is Stannard Jackson. I need to talk to someone. I don't know where else to turn right now. Can you help me? It's important." *Why does calling a shrink's office make me sound like a kook?*

There was a pause, and then a calm voice on the other end answered. "If this is a crisis call, you should call one-two-HELPU."

"No, no," Stannard answered. "I'm not about to commit suicide or anything like that. I just need to talk to one of the doctors. It is important. It is about Dr. Loren Parlous."

The voice on the other end replied, "I am sorry, but Dr. Parlous is no longer associated with the clinic."

"I am aware of that. I am an insurance investigator looking into a claim for life insurance proceeds."

Ouch, too much information. St Jack would have handled that more smoothly. Now she'll stonewall me for sure.

"Oh, in that case I will put you through to Dr. Berger."

The phone made a clicking sound then the strains of Dmitri Shostakovich's String Quartet No. 3 filled the void. A moment later, he heard another electronic interruption.

The voice at the other end answered in a guarded voice. "This is Dr. Samuel O. Berger. I am…was…an associate of Dr. Parlous, and you are…?"

"Stannard Jackson."

"What's this all about?"

Not so formal now. "It is a life insurance claim investigation into the death of Dr. Parlous.

I need to talk to someone about him, someone who knew him well." Stannard paused. Would this approach work? There was no sense in taking another tack. *I let the cat out of the bag when I answered the receptionist.*

"No one knew Parlous well. I don't have time for this now. If you want to make an appointment, fine. If not, that's fine too. I'll put the receptionist back on the line."

The phone went dead then Stannard heard the receptionist. "Do you wish to make an appointment?" Her voice now had an icy tone.

"Yes, I would."

"What did you say your name was?"

"Jackson, Stannard Jackson. When can I get in to see Dr. Berger?"

Another pause. "He can give you an hour at two this afternoon, if that is convenient."

"Put me down. I'll be there at two." *Samuel O. Berger, SOB, a sweet old bird. I'll bet the SOB charges me for the hour.* He hung up the telephone and considered Dr. Berger's words, "No one knew Parlous well…" *What's that supposed to mean?* Before his mind could ponder that question further, his phone rang.

The voice on the phone had the warm tone—some would say sultry alto—he had heard on the answering machine that morning. "This is Lorelei Parlous. Did you just call me on my home phone?"

"I did." Stannard did not say anything more. He had not expected a return call, certainly not this soon, and thought he'd wait to see what the widow had to say first.

"I didn't recognize the number," she said. "I wondered who would be calling me this early in the morning."

Interesting. How many people call back numbers they don't recognize? Don't they just assume it was a wrong number when they hear the voice on the answering machine or hear the click when the caller hangs up without leaving a message or identifying himself? "My name is Stannard Jackson. I would like to talk to you about your deceased husband, if I could."

The voice at the other end purred with sensuality. "Well, Mr. Stannard Jackson, I would be happy to talk to you about Loren if I knew you, but since I don't you will have to explain who you are."

"I hope this will lead to a yes. I'm an insurance investigator working a claim made on a life insurance policy. Would it be convenient if I came to your house?"

"Well then, the answer is a qualified yes. I definitely want to talk to you, but not here. I was just leaving for Cedar Creek Estates. Do you know where that is?"

She's dropped the sensuality. There is a detachment in the voice now. "I do. When and where can I meet you?"

"I'm meeting friends at the Cedar Creek club pool before it gets too hot. If you can be there before ten, then we can talk. If you're late—" she paused for effect "—I may be gone."

"Done. I'll see you before ten." He hung up. She was gone before he finished. *Strange call,* he thought. *If all she is doing is meeting someone at the club swimming pool, why is there any question about my having to be there in such a hurry?* Forty minutes later he checked his watch, grabbed his keys from where he had dropped them on the desk, and headed for the exit. The receptionist, Marjorie, looked up from her typing as he walked out of the office. "I'll be back later. You can get me on my cell phone if you need me," he called to her as he opened the door.

He did not hear the reply, "Well, be sure to tell me all about it just in case Big Ed asks."

He began to make a run-through of his predrive routine, realized he had not turned off all the electronics, shrugged, and started the engine. He then backed out of the parking space and exited onto 119th Street, looped around to Antioch, and headed west on the freeway. Slowed by the traffic, he swore at himself for not going down 119th to Renner. He checked his watch as he drove down the ramp onto Kansas Highway 10. He would be on time. He exited on Cedar Creek Parkway with five minutes to spare. Three minutes later he turned at the sign pointing the way to the swim and racquet club.

"Mrs. Parlous?" he inquired of the three women at the pool.

"I'm Lorelei Parlous," a voice answered.

Sweat glistened on his face in the July heat as he came face-to-face with Lorelei Parlous, who was wearing a skimpy black bikini barely covering all the necessities. Its blackness was the only evidence of grieving he could discern. She lounged in one of the comfortable chaise chairs on her stomach, the string of her bra untied so she could get an even tan. Two women of like age similarly dressed sunned themselves nearby.

Lorelei had been watching for his arrival. She rolled over to greet him, her gray-green eyes holding him in their grasp as he approached. He looked away, embarrassed, as she reassembled her attire.

"I'm Stannard Jackson," he stammered, stating the obvious.

"Well, good for you Stannard Jackson. I wasn't expecting Santa Claus." She laughed, eyes twinkling, eyebrows arching.

What's this all about? Stannard thought. *She's flirting.* Nothing so far had gone as Stannard expected. *If this is a grieving widow, she has to be one of a kind.* "Is there somewhere we can talk?"

Casting a glance at her companions, she answered, "Yes, here." Stannard could not tell if she had winked as she answered. Maybe the morning sun caused her to give that impression.

"I had a place with some privacy in mind," he countered.

"This is private enough. These girls are my friends."

Stannard's response was drawn out for effect. "O-kaaay, but some of this may get personal."

"Ask away." She arched her back as she answered.

She is flirting. She is intentionally flirting.

Lorelei clearly intended to control the interview. Stannard did not understand why she was behaving in this manner, but he had a schedule to keep. The appointment with Dr. Samuel O. Berger was not the only thing on his mind. Unless the company denied the claim for valid reason, under the terms of the policy it would be deemed approved for payment. A week had already been lost by the bureaucracy moving the paper one desk-one agent at a time to the head office. After that the head office reviewed the claim and then sent it on to his company for investigation.

Before he could ask his first question, Lorelei once more took charge of the interview. "This is about Loren's first wife, isn't it?"

Stannard evaded her question. "A claim has been made for life insurance, and my company has been asked to look into the merit of the claim." He would not tell her, or let her know, that he had read the police reports and talked to Lieutenant Pezzati. Who made the claim and the face amount of the policy would be his business and his alone for the time being. "Because of the unusual circumstances under which Dr. Parlous died, it's routine for us to be brought into the matter."

Lorelei interjected playfully, "Oh, sure it is. Just listen to yourself—you used the words *unusual* and *routine* in the same sentence. Which is it?" She sat up, posing, and looked directly at him.

Puzzled by the mixed signals he received, first flaunting sexuality, then openness and cooperation, and now soft confrontation, Stannard continued. "In cases like this, it's customary for us to inquire into certain personal matters. What kind of man was Dr. Parlous?"

Shifting position back to cooperation, Lorelei answered, "I don't know how to answer that. He was a man like any other, a man who knew what he wanted and generally got it." She paused.

Now she's being coy. What gives here?

"He was my husband, and we had a good marriage. He was a good doctor who cared about his patients…"

As she paused, Stannard considered her responses, all safe and giving away nothing. *If he was so caring, what was the medical board complaint all about?* He waited; she didn't say anything more. "You are considerably younger than Dr. Parlous. Were you married long before—" he hesitated to get the word right "—his death?"

"Not long. We were married in Acapulco three years ago last December."

"And before that…?"

"Loren was married; I was not."

"And you say your marriage was a happy one?"

"Yes, but where is this going? What does our marriage have to do with his death?"

Stannard didn't want to surrender control of the interview. He answered, "This is all background. I have just begun my review of the case and need to get some feel for the deceased.

You say your marriage was a happy one?"

"We had what I believe was a perfect marriage. Loren went his way, I went mine, and we met in the middle the rest of the time." She smiled to see if he caught her meaning.

The two women friends of Lorelei shifted positions on their lounge chairs and laughed. Stannard sensed their increased interest in the conversation. He blushed.

"Meaning what?"

"Meaning we had what is commonly known as an 'open' marriage. I had my friends, and he had his. Who we slept with and when was our own business."

"And neither of you ever got jealous of the other?"

"No, why should we? How about you, Mr. Stannard Jackson?"

"No reason, I guess—if it worked for you." Stannard ignored the last half of her question, and in any event he did not really believe her, but he wanted to keep her talking. "Did it lead to complications with any of the others—you know, hard feelings, possessiveness, anything like that?"

"Not that I am aware."

"So then, Dr. Parlous didn't have any enemies?" *Now's the time to move the conversation.*

Stannard wondered if she would mention his ex-wife again or go in another direction.

"I didn't say that. Our private lives, within our marriage, did not lead to enemies, at least not as far as I know. Loren did have one enemy, but then I'm sure you know all about her, or else you wouldn't be here."

"So then, you don't believe his death was an accident or a suicide? That's what my file shows." The file indicated no such thing, but how would she react?

"No, it wasn't an accident, and it wasn't a suicide. It was murder, but I can't prove it. That is your job, isn't it?"

"Not really, Mrs. Parlous. I'm just investigating an insurance claim. If his death was suicide it's one thing, if not and it was an accidental death, it's quite a different matter. Questions of murder are for the police. The only thing they have decided so far is to allocate their resources to other cases right now. Based on that, it may be they are leaning toward suicide or accident." The raw nerve Stannard touched had been intentional. The response he got was a surprise.

Lorelei's voice rose slightly in volume as it lowered in pitch. "Erin killed Loren, or she had him killed. At the very least she knows who did kill him.

You should talk to her instead of me. If you really want to know what happened, you should go to Florida. That's where she lives. That's where you will get answers."

He sat in silence, waiting for more.

Resuming her normal tone she added. "Now, if you'll excuse me, I have another appointment and need to change." She rose from her chair and walked away, her two friends trailing along behind. As they approached the gate to the pool area, she stopped and looked back over her shoulder, "One more thing. I gave a lengthy statement to the police. I am certain you have it, but if not, you should get it. I'm sorry about my having to leave. You just got here. Give me a call some other time. I want to help you all I can."

He watched the retreating forms of the three bikini-clad women as they moved around the pool toward the exit. *I wonder...*but his reverie stopped there. He followed her to the parking lot, where she stopped at the BMW sedan and removed a small bag. As he walked to his car at the far end of the lot, she waved to him.

Marjorie looked up from her keyboard as Stannard came through the modest entrance to the office. "You weren't gone long."

"No. Is the boss in?"

"He left right after you did…said he'd be back in an hour or so. What do you need? Can I do anything for you?" Marjorie was not only a good secretary and receptionist, but she would have also made a good investigator. She worked for the company when Stannard had come on board. The rest of the staff saw her as a mother figure, even though she was only a few years Stannard's senior. He never ceased to marvel at her ability to get information from those trained to get it, not give it.

"Yeah, you can work up a tentative itinerary for me to go to Fort Walton Beach."

"In Florida?"

"Well, yeah, unless you know of another one."

"Going to see that Kasalaitis woman, huh?"

Stannard didn't answer. His look said all there was to say.

"When do you want to go?"

"Get it set up for tomorrow, morning—early, if you can. Keep the return open. I don't know how long I will be down there."

He went to his office while Marjorie opened another window on her PC. She Googled Expedia and typed in the relevant information. In seconds, the flight options appeared on the screen. She clicked on the 7 a.m. Northwest flight out of KCI. He would have to change planes in Memphis but had over an hour between flights. He would arrive at the Okaloosa Regional Airport at Fort Walton Beach on the edge of Eglin Air Force Base a little after 11 a.m. The return flight she left open.

Chapter Seven

The temperatures in Kansas City during the month of July and August are high. The combination of heat and humidity that greeted Stannard as he stepped off the curb at the north end of the small commercial terminal at Fort Walton Beach, Florida, introduced him to an entirely new reality. *Fish don't need to stay in the ocean to live down here. The air is so thick they can breathe on land as well.* He looked to his left toward the direction the car leasing agent told him to go. At the end of the long, low building, he found the large rental car parking lot. He looked around for a sign that said Hertz but saw nothing. Alamo, National, and a regional car rental company did not announce their place in the world either. The woman at the Hertz counter had said he would find his car in space one-five-nine, located just beyond the north end of the terminal building. He looked at the lot and saw numbers painted on the ground behind each vehicle. As he walked along, he saw the rental cars jumbled together without regard to company. *One-five-seven is a National car; one-five-eight is Alamo.* Then he saw the Ford Escort with a Hertz sticker in the window. S*pace 159.* He unlocked the door to the vehicle and felt the trickle of sweat run down his back, the car's interior temperature reaching at least 130. Looking around to be certain no one would hear him, he said, "I've got to lose some weight. Either that or stay out of the Deep South."

He got into the car and felt at home. Hertz did things right. All the electronic settings in the Escort were either in the neutral or off position. Stannard began his routine. He adjusted the seat, then he turned on the automatic cruise control. He adjusted the mirrors. After that, he pulled the tilt wheel down so that it fit his short arms. Only then was he prepared to meet the unfamiliar traffic along the Florida Emerald Coast.

He drove along the tree-lined boulevard leading from the rural airport setting toward town. He reflected on the meeting with Dr. Samuel O. Berger, associate director of Forensic Psychiatric Medical Associates, LLC. Associate director...right! The thought hit him with a wave of sarcasm. *There were only two doctors in the practice, Dr. Parlous and Dr. Berger. It's amazing how some egos have to have the affirmation of a title. I'll bet he has the title* Director *stenciled on the door before the week is out. He waited a month; that should be long enough.* His thoughts turned from personal to what the man had said. Berger was a close-mouthed character. *He gave me very little information, and he did bill the company for the time he spent in the interview. Jerk! The practice appeared to be lucrative, but appearances can be deceiving. Berger said Parlous was depressed and he'd asked Berger to prescribe something for him. Of course, he wouldn't confirm whether he had done so. HIPPA, or so he said. Doctors always say they would cooperate but then hide behind HIPPA. We're a country filled with privacy freaks constantly worrying about our precious privacy and all the time telling the world everything we do and think. And another thing, what about that board of healing arts inquiry? Berger refused to even discuss it, claiming professional courtesy. What kind of crap is that? The man is dead; there isn't any professional courtesy. It just makes my job more difficult.* He gave his mind a jerk. *Pay attention to the road.*

Following the Eglin Parkway south, he crossed the two bridges on Choctawhatchee Bay. The scene unfolding as he approached the city appalled him. He had expected to find the place crowded. After all, this was vacation season and the Emerald Coast had a reputation for its white-sand beaches and clear water. Expensive condominiums and resort hotels were what he expected, but that's not what he found on the north side of Fort Walton Beach. It reminded him of Truman Boulevard back in Kansas City—squalid little strip malls with dirty gas stations, poorly dressed young people roaming the streets, junk cars cutting in and out of traffic. Thankful for the GPS system on the Escort, he followed the directions it gave toward his destination. At Hollywood

Boulevard he turned west and started looking for the building. Suddenly it appeared before him, sandwiched between the Waterfront Rescue Mission and the Chester Pruitt Recreation Center. Only a small hand-painted sign on the side of the building beside the door announced Emerald Coast Drug Rehabilitation Facility. *Not a very prosperous-appearing place. From the looks of the building, her salary can't be too good. Quite a come down from what she had to have made in KC. Maybe she does need the money—but even so, would she kill to get it?* He slowed, looking at the mildew-covered white stucco building, then drove on. He had not intended to stop at the facility until he got a feel for the lay of the land. He only wanted to get a look at the place where Dr. Erin Kasalaitis worked as deputy director.

His mind drifted back to Dr. Samuel O. Berger. About the only thing Berger had told him of any consequence was that Dr. Parlous had approached him about buying out the practice or closing it down. Berger thought that proposal was fear driven. After saying Parlous was paranoid, he'd gone on to say he didn't know what to make of the proposal since Parlous was a master at manipulating people, he said. He had to laugh, though, when Berger realized he might have made some diagnosis or violated HIPPA. He retracted that comment in a New York second. "Now, don't think that is a medical opinion. That is my personal opinion," he'd said.

Before doing more, he decided to check in to the motel Marjorie had booked for him. He found the Econo Lodge Fort Walton Beach on Southwest Miracle Strip Parkway. Turning in at the office, he shook his head. That would be just like Marjorie, always looking out for the company's expense account. Well, it would be for only a night or two, and anything that didn't include bedbugs would do. Forty minutes later he had unloaded his gear in room 123 and had called the Emerald Coast Drug Rehabilitation Facility and made an appointment with Dr. Kasalaitis to meet at her home after work. Dr Kasalaitis had initially been coolly cordial on the phone. As soon as he identified himself, and who it was that he worked for, she understood the nature of his visit. After that her tone warmed, as if she had been expecting the call all along. When the call ended, he headed out to scout Dr. Erin Kasalaitis's home. The trip from his motel didn't take as long as he thought it would. He followed the instructions given by his Garmin GPS. The Emerald Coast Parkway took him east to Destin, where he turned onto Emerald Bay Drive. He turned back inland where the GPS told him and slowed. Just before he reached the gated community ahead at the end of the road, he saw Opa-Locka Lane to his right. *Okay, so she doesn't live at the Regatta Bay Golf and Country Club or the Emerald Bay Golf Club. For that matter, it isn't even the near-high-rent housing area between them. She's trying to live the high life but without the cash to pull it off. What was it my dad used to say? Yeah...close only counts in horseshoes, hand grenades, and atom bombs.* Opa-Locka Lane, despite the somewhat exotic name, was just a moderately upscale residential neighborhood making a short loop off the Emerald Coast Parkway. He drove by, looking over the neighborhood. *I expected something larger.* The three-story structure on the small lot on the north side of the Emerald Coast Parkway contained two units on each floor. The condominiums on the south side of Emerald Coast Parkway, those having beach frontage, were what he had expected. Still, the immediate contrast between the workplace and the home was striking. *Erin Kasalaitis,* he made a mental note, *may not live in a million-dollar condominium, but she didn't live in squalor either.*

Satisfied, he drove back to the drug rehab clinic. He parked across the street and watched the building, hoping to get a feel for the clientele Dr. Kasalaitis treated. What he saw came as no surprise. A mix of young men and women were interspersed with a few ancient hippies, holdovers from the 1960s. At 5:25 he saw a woman he felt certain might be Dr. Kasalaitis exit the building. He waited several minutes after she left before retracing his route back to Destin.

He arrived at 4214 Opa-Locka Lane at twenty past six for his six-thirty appointment. He parked his rental car in one of the handful of visitor parking spaces and flipped open his cell phone to call Caryl. Ten minutes later, just as he finished his call, a rough-appearing man wearing khaki pants and a flowered shirt worn loose outside his trousers exited the main entrance. As the man walked past, he noticed that his shirtsleeves were cut off at the shoulders, showing the tattoo of a nude woman on his biceps. *Odd,* Stannard thought, *not the sort of man you would expect to see living in a home like this. He belongs at the drug clinic, not here. He's clearly out of place.* As Stannard started to get out of his car, he saw a woman standing on the third-floor balcony. Dr. Erin Kasalaitis. It had been her he saw leaving the clinic an hour earlier. She seemed to be watching both Stannard's car and the other man at the same time. *Well, that might explain it. She is, after all, a drug rehab doctor, and the man who just left definitely looks like someone who has been, or should be, in drug rehab. Still and all, it seems odd that he would be here instead of at the clinic.* The man glanced over his shoulder to look back up at the balcony, and when he did so Stannard took his picture then snapped the cover on his cell phone shut. *You never know when something or someone like this will turn out to be important.*

The woman on the balcony retreated inside. Stannard sat in his car until the tough guy had gone, then he walked to the entrance. He tried the door. Locked. He glanced to his right and saw the callbox on the wall. There it was, Dr. Erin Kasalaitis, Unit Five. He pushed the button and waited. She had to see him, so why the wait? Then he heard her voice. "Yes, who's there?"

Her voice sounded a little shaky. "Stannard Jackson, Dr. Kasalaitis. I called earlier today at your office. I'm a little early...I hope I'm not too early." His senses had gone on full alert the moment he saw the south Florida tough guy come out of the condo. *The doctor is flustered. A tough-looking man driving an old Ford leaves her building just as I arrive early. She is outside on the balcony watching for what or who.* He waited to see if she would take the bait. She did not.

The voice came back firm and in control. "I'll buzz you up."

The modest lobby to the building held a community mail pod, with each condominium having its own locked box, and an ornate table scratched by parcels placed on it while residents and guests stood waiting for the elevator. A grouping of pictures depicting sailing on the Gulf of Mexico hung on the wall above, and two chairs flanking the ornate table completed the furnishings. *Cheap—worse than it looked like from the outside.* Just past the elevator, two numbered doors obviously led to the ground-floor units. Stannard took this in with amusement. *With only the occupants of the upper-floor units needing to use the elevator, you'd think they could hold their packages until the elevator came.* He poked the elevator call button, and seconds later the door opened. He smiled. Validation. He pushed the button for the third floor, and the elevator rose. When the door again opened, he stood in a small alcove with two doors. The one to his right bore an ornate number 5, the 1,200-square-foot home of Dr. Kasalaitis. The doorbell had hardly sounded when the door opened and an attractive woman about fifty years old greeted him.

"Welcome, Mr. Jackson. Please come on in."

Stannard showed surprise on his face. "This building is a surprise. I would have thought the need for security would have dictated both a locked outside door and a key-operated elevator." *My early arrival didn't get a response, but maybe this will.*

Erin, having recovered, answered with an amused expression, "You are right. The elevator only opens for someone having a key or when someone in the condominium authorizes entry."

Nothing; she isn't shaken a bit. Maybe I had the Florida tough guy all wrong. "That's good. You can never be too careful. I just saw an unsavory sort of guy leaving the building as I drove up." He thought he would try again.

"Yes, I saw you as he left. He was a former patient of mine. He rang me up, but I didn't let him in."

"Odd," Stannard replied. "I would have sworn he came out of the front entrance."

"No, you must be mistaken. He didn't come from my apartment." Changing the subject, she asked, "Can I get you some iced tea? It's Kansas City tea, not the sweet tea they drink down here. I could never abide that syrupy flavor. Of course, if you use sugar in your tea, or artificial sweetener, I have it."

"Tea would be fine," Stannard answered, not really interested in tea but thankful for the moment it would afford for him to take a quick look around.

The former wife of Dr. Parlous was out of the room for only a minute, but Stannard used the time to take stock of what he could see. *Nice place, modern furnishing, she likes glass and steel.* He noted the white plush carpet and the white chairs and divan. The pieces of art hanging on the walls were all reproductions but good ones. Two in particular caught his attention. They were duplicates of pictures hanging in the office of Dr. Samuel O. Berger, the first being a stylized hexagram and the other a candelabra. *Is Erin Kasalaitis Jewish? The connection between the Greeks and Jews is an old one. Maybe that's all. Berger is Jewish. That would explain the ancient Hebrew symbols in his office. But if Erin Kasalaitis is not Jewish, then there could be another connection to those symbols. Dr. Stinson thinks so. What appears to me to be a Star of David and a menorah on Berger's office wall may be something quite different here.*

A moment before Dr. Kasalaitis returned, he noticed the photograph of her on the reading table. *That must be her favorite chair. The likeness is good, but it must be a few years old. She's aged since then, but I doubt anyone could ever mistake those dark, wide-set eyes.*

Dr. Kasalaitis returned with the tea. She motioned to a chair as she handed him his drink. She sat in the chair beside the picture. "What is it you wanted to discuss with me? You were a little vague over the phone." She smiled gently, her voice smooth and soothing.

She has a kind face. They sat and talked. Only once during the conversation did she appear agitated, and that was when Stannard mentioned Lorelei Parlous.

"She told you I wanted Loren dead, didn't she?" Dr. Kasalaitis challenged.

"Yes, she did." *Now there is a leap in understanding. I didn't say anything about Lorelei Parlous wanting to pin a murder rap on her. I wonder where this'll lead.*

"Well, it is a lie. I loved Loren until she insinuated herself between us. You would do well to think about what she tells you. That woman is a manipulative seductress. Remember this, when you point one finger at someone, the other three are pointing back at you."

"Nevertheless, you aren't sorry he's dead are you?"

"No. Why should I be? She got everything she wanted. She's the one living in the big house. She's living in my house with all the security system while I live here. You see how I live."

How does she know about the security system? It was only installed a year ago. She and Dr. Parlous had been divorced for at least two years by then. Stannard did not respond.

Forty minutes later Stannard finished his tea, thanked Dr. Kasalaitis for her time, and prepared to leave the condominium. "I like the artwork. Those are ancient Hebrew symbols, aren't they? I saw some just like them in Dr. Parlous's associate's office."

"You mean Berger. He doesn't have pictures like these in his office, but Loren had some in his office."

"Oh—well, maybe Dr. Berger met me in Dr. Parlous's office when we met the other day." *That's interesting. Berger is moving into Parlous's office. He sure didn't wait for the corpse to get cold before making his move; so much for waiting a month to stencil in the name.*

A minute later back in his car, he realized he had forgotten to set all the controls back in their neutral position. Before starting the engine, he made some notes of things he did not want to forget. When he had finished, he looked up at the third-floor balcony but saw no one. Then, just before he backed away from his parking spot, he noticed movement in a third-floor window curtain. *She's watching me. She's not what I expected. She certainly didn't have the hot-blooded Greek temperament the current Mrs. Parlous alleges.* The thought had barely crossed his mind when his college philosophy class in mythology came back to him. *There's more of Hippocrates about her than the Greek Furies. Her name is Erin. Isn't that name derived from the Greek Furies, the Angry Ones? Their name was Erinÿes. It might fit though. The tough guy who was here ahead of me had an angry look about him. Besides, I'm not sure I buy into her explanation. That was a slip about the security system though. She knows more than she's saying. Greed and hatred are powerful motives. But I just don't see how she could be involved.*

The interview had taken forty-five minutes, and Stannard felt his stomach growl. He backtracked toward the city, looking for a place with a little local color. He found what he wanted, a beachfront seafood joint crowded with tourists. There he stood in line for his seafood gumbo and a parts-is-parts fish sandwich, advertised as Gulf grouper fillet on a kaiser roll with mostly mayo in the tartar sauce and wilted lettuce. *Nothing fast about this place,* he thought as he sat on one of the outdoor tables eating his food while rowdy children ran circles around him. *That's how this case feels to me. They are all running circles around me.* He then moved his car down to the beach, where the sun now low in its westerly descent toward the Gulf of Mexico appeared to grow into a large red ball more than double its size as the mirage it created fell into the water. He parked his car in one of the overpriced public parking lots and put money in the meter. A dollar and a half bought him thirty minutes. Removing his shoes and socks, looking every bit the impromptu tourist he'd now become, he strolled along the white-sand beach, darting toward the dunes covered with cockleburs to avoid the rising tide as it rolled in. He wondered what was worse, getting his trousers wet or pulling the barbed stickers from his tender bare feet.

Having walked half a mile down the beach, watching families enjoy the sun and beach and children playing in the water, he returned to his car just as the red flag came up telling him and the local beach patrol his time was up. He brushed the fine-grained sand from his feet the best he could. He sat in the front seat of the rental car, feet outside, and put on his socks and shoes. It offended his sense of neatness and order to make a mess inside the car. The rule applied to rental cars as well as his.

As he drove away from the parking lot and headed toward the motel, he noticed several old cars, obviously locals. One resembled the old Ford he had noticed at Dr. Kasalaitis's condominium, the one driven by the man she said had not been in her building.

Two hours later, back at his motel, Stannard finished dictating his notes. Marjorie would undoubtedly second-guess him for what she always considered his incomplete "interview." He spent the next two days watching the clinic and the condominium. As Dr. Kasalaitis walked from her office to her car, he took a picture of her for use in his investigation. It wasn't a good picture, but he had caught her face. You could see her eyes. That was important in taking a woman's photograph. People tended to remember the eyes, he told himself. He followed her from a distance to see whom she met and where she went. He did not know what he believed: what she told him in the interview, or what Lorelei Parlous had said about her. Maybe this had nothing to do with either of them. After all, hadn't Dr. Berger been anxious to take the office occupied by Parlous? And, hadn't Berger said Parlous had approached him about buying out the practice? What easier way to get the practice without paying for it than... He stopped. *I'm thinking of this as a murder when I still don't know what it is. Just follow the string And go to Dayton, Ohio. She said Dr. Parlous had an aunt living there.*

The permanent population of the resort town may be only twenty thousand, but it swelled to over a hundred thousand in the summer months. It surprised Stannard that with that many people roaming the streets, he would see the man with the tattoo of a naked woman on his arm driving an old Ford two more times as he followed Dr. Kasalaitis. He couldn't help wondering, *Who's he following—Erin Kasalaitis or me?* The first time he noticed the car he thought his imagination was working overtime. When he arrived at the airport to catch the last flight of the day to Dayton, he got his answer. The man had been following him while he followed Dr. Kasalaitis, and now he was following Stannard—just as he had at the beach.

By the time the plane reached the far end of the runway at Okaloosa Regional Airport, the old Ford had already turned onto the parkway and was headed back toward downtown and the Emerald Coast Drug Rehabilitation Facility. The driver of the car checked his wristwatch and saw that if he hurried, he would just barely make his scheduled appointment with Dr. Kasalaitis.

Chapter Eight

The flight to Dayton went through Atlanta and after a two-hour layover did not arrive until late afternoon. The downtime spent sitting in the terminal and on the cramped airplane gave Stannard time to think about what he had learned in Florida. *The death of Dr. Loren Parlous gets more complicated with each interview. One thing is certain, both doctors, Loren Parlous and Erin Kasalaitis, were strange characters. If Dr. Kasalaitis didn't have something to hide, why'd she associate with the driver of the old Ford and why'd she have him tailing me? If she did. And why did Dr. Kasalaitis and Dr. Parlous have identical pictures hanging on their walls? Was it coincidence or something else? In light of what Stinson said, maybe it foreshadows something sinister.* He'd wanted to ask her more about it but decided the timing couldn't be worse. A good investigator didn't charge through a case like a rampaging elephant. But, being a thorough investigator, he planned to pursue those questions when time and circumstance came together. The most important information he garnered from Dr. Kasalaitis had to do with her ex-husband's life before she'd met and married him. That life had been spent in Dayton, Ohio, where she said he'd been born and lived until after graduating from college. She even gave him names. Before leaving Fort Walton Beach, he had verified the names and addresses of Dr. Loren Parlous's living relatives in the Dayton area on one of the many Internet telephone directories.

After checking in to the Airport Marriot Hotel, no thanks to Marjorie, he followed the directions given by the clerk at the rental car counter to the home of Parlous's sole surviving aunt, widow of his biological uncle. He arrived at what remained of her farm, now surrounded by the city, a half hour later. As the Vandalia suburb expanded, she had sold the farm to developers. A modest farmhouse, and acreage too small to plow but too large to mow, was all that remained. The original farm originally planted in corn now showed an abundant crop of fescue in need of mowing. He parked his rental car in the gravel driveway and approached the front porch of the two-story, two-bedroom house. The eighty-three-year-old widow greeted him.

"Hello, young man. You appear to be either lost or just a long way from home. Do I know you?"

Stannard smiled. "The answer to your question is no, I'm not lost, but yes, I am a long way from home—and no, we've never met."

The old woman laughed. "I thought as much. What with all these new-fangled devices you young people use, you don't get lost very often, do you?"

"You are right there, although I have trouble working them from time to time." He almost laughed out loud at her reference to him as "young."

The old woman set down her lemonade and rose from her swing. "If you are looking for Elvira Parlous, then you have found her."

"I am, and I'm glad to make your acquaintance. My name is Stannard Jackson." He stepped onto the porch and took her hand. He felt the soft coolness of an old lady. Even in the afternoon summer heat, her body did not warm as his did.

"Well, you might as well sit a spell. It gets lonely out here all alone. The city has taken most of the farm, but not many folks have time for an old woman. I doubt many of them even know they are living on land that once belonged to me." She shook her head.

Stannard surveyed the scene. The house and property testified to the business acumen of the old woman. She had obviously made a good bargain when she sold the land. Her house stood on the highest point around, from which she could see three directions from her porch—the nearest house still close to an eighth of a mile away. He sat on the metal retro lawn chair as she began swinging once more, creating a small breeze as she moved the swing back and forward. Stannard imagined he saw Elvira many years earlier, as a girl, doing the same thing to cool herself in the days before air-conditioning. She continued, "Now that you've found me, what is it you want?"

"I'd like to talk to you about your nephew, Loren Parlous." He wondered if his expression gave away the emotion he felt. *The old lady reminds me of my aunt, sweet but tough as nails. It won't be long now before she skins some developer for the rest of this land, but who'll inherit the money?*

"Okay, I can do that, but first you're going to have to tell me who you are. I know your name, Mr. Jackson, but I don't know who you are or why you want to know about Loren."

Stannard took a business card from the black leather case he carried and handed it to her. "I am investigating a life insurance claim filed by his former wife, Erin. She goes by the name of Erin Kasalaitis now."

"So, Loren's dead. I didn't know that, but it doesn't come as a surprise. What happened—did he kill himself, or did someone do it for him?"

Stannard tried not to show his surprise at the directness of her response. "That's why I'm here. The coroner noted the manner of death as undetermined on the official report. As it stands, that would probably be interpreted as accidental death. My company needs to find out the truth before paying out on the claim. The circumstances are so strange that it could be suicide or even a homicide. We just don't know yet."

Aunt Elvira did not wait for Stannard to begin asking questions. "He was sick, you know, sick in the head! Folks around here were afraid of him. Even as a boy he had a way of looking at you that made your skin crawl. For years, everyone kept quiet about him because of that." The initial outburst over, she asked, "How did he die?"

"He was killed in a car crash on the freeway in Kansas City. When did you last see him?"

"Years ago. He came back for his twenty-fifth-year high school class reunion. That was a bad scene too, from what I heard."

"Oh, how's that?"

"About half his class still lives around Dayton. I don't suppose any of them would have gone to the banquet if they'd known he would be there. He stopped by here for a few minutes before he went. He told me he wanted to surprise everyone. He hadn't paid for the dinner. I don't even know if he planned on eating. It was like Loren. He always liked to shock folks."

"So what happened?"

"You would have to ask them. All I know is there was quite a ruckus before they asked him to leave."

Stannard made a mental note to get the names of some of Loren Parlous's classmates. "I guess you knew him from the time he was born."

"No, just from when I married his uncle. I didn't come from around here, so I didn't know him until we were engaged."

"How old was he when you and your husband got married?"

"He was just six. His mother insisted he be the ring bearer. That proved to be a big mistake. I guess it was my mistake too, because I agreed."

"Why was that?"

"He hid the ring right before the ceremony and wouldn't tell anyone where it was until he got what he wanted."

"Really? What was it he wanted?"

"A bicycle with training wheels; the hardware store had a Western Flyer bike. He wanted it and knew how to get it. Thankfully, the wedding was on a Saturday and they were open. He just held us hostage until he got what he wanted. He knew he would. They gave in, as they always did. They got him the bike so the ceremony could start."

Stannard thought about the image of the scrub-clean boy holding an entire congregation hostage in a church with the windows open as the heat of the day rose. He then thought about the pictures of the mutilated body, matted hair obviously in need of a cut, and the dirt under the fingernails taken during the autopsy. He wondered if his death too had something to do with getting his way. "They took the bike back after the ceremony, I suppose."

"No, you're wrong there. He kept it. His mother and father were the weakest parents I ever did see. It almost seemed like they intentionally did things to warp that boy's mind. From what I know about him, they started giving in when he was an infant. He would throw a tantrum until they gave him what he wanted. It just went from there. His father died of a heart attack when he was fourteen. His mother remarried within a year. He didn't get on with his stepfather and just kind of ran loose."

"Did he have any siblings?"

"Not from his mother and real father. She had another son with her new husband, but he died in an accident down at the pond when he was only about two and a half." The old woman stopped to think about what she had said. "I suppose there are some who would say Loren had something to do with that too. He had been really difficult just before the boy died, and afterward his mother doted on him all the more."

"So the pattern of getting his way continued?" Stannard probed. Aunt Elvira was going to prove to be a fountain of information.

"Oh, yes, you can look up some of his old class-mates while you are here. I have no doubt they'll be happy to talk to you now that he is dead."

"You mean to say they wouldn't talk if he were still alive?"

"I doubt it. I know I would be a whole lot more careful what I say if I thought word of any of it would get back to him."

"Have you got any names of his old schoolmates I should try to contact?"

"You bet. Pete Johnson lives nearby. I'll look up his phone number for you before you leave. You definitely need to talk to Pete. Loren got that boy in a passel of trouble when they were in high school. Pete can give you the names and phone numbers of some others." She paused, uncertain whether to tell him more or let him hear the story from Pete.

"Tell me about it." Stannard's curiosity was piqued, and he wanted to keep the old woman talking.

"Well," she began, "Pete wasn't the first or the last boy Loren got into trouble, but that caper sure got a lot of attention at the time. You see, Pete is an impressionable fellow. Some folks would say he's weak or a little slow in the head. Always has been.

Loren picked on people like that. He would get them to do what he wanted then he turned on them. I think he did it just for his own amusement."

Stannard began to despair she would ever get to the story, and reluctant as he was to press her, he said, "So what did he do to Pete?"

"I'm getting to it young man, don't hurry me. This isn't anything I've thought about for a long time, and no one hereabouts has talked about it. I don't know how many folks even know the truth."

Stannard settled back in his seat and waited. Whatever she wanted to tell him would have to come in her own good time. He looked at the old woman, who now appeared to shrink in size as she recalled something repressed in the deep caverns of her mind.

"He was evil," she began. "Loren was evil through and through, and he was a manipulator. That poor, poor boy. He's had to live with this for so many years. No wonder his mind is weak. For years, everyone shunned him. Everyone believed it was him." *She must be talking about the boy she called Pete.* At last her rumination ended and she told the story. "Peter Johnson was always a little slow. That's why Loren picked him." Her mind seemed to wander again as she thought about Loren as a young man. "He started out by just being mean. You know, he would catch grasshoppers and put them in a tin can. Then he would put a larger can over that so they could not get away. He'd build a fire and put the cans in the fire. You should have heard him laugh when they roasted. He said they sounded like corn popping. Well, he just went on from there to bigger things. Eventually he got to torturing small animals, dogs and cats."

Stannard's head began to spin. He knew where the story would go. It was just like Russell. When Russell had been born a year after his marriage to Caryl, he felt a pride he'd never known before. Even as a baby, the boy had looked like him. As he grew, the similarity between father and son became even more noticeable. He hoped the boy would grow taller and more athletic than himself, but when that didn't happen, he reconciled himself with the knowledge the boy had his intelligence. That would surely make a difference. But it didn't. Time and culture had changed the dynamic among youngsters. Kansas City had changed as well. The places Stannard went as a boy, the things he did, were no longer safe in the city, which suffered the inevitable consequences of one-party political rule. Graft was rampant. Political incumbents purchased votes with the cheap currency of patronage or the promise of never-ending social programs. With that came a continuation of political power. The change that came with such programs was bad. Social order disintegrated. Crime increased. Schools declined. The adolescent Russell lived in a cruel world. Boys and girls alike teased him, ridiculed him for his small and frail stature as well as his bookish ways. The boy felt the sting of rejection and wanted to be a part of a larger group. Russell was so very different from Peter Johnson in many ways yet so like him in others. Rejection had led both boys to seek the approval of the wrong people. In Peter Johnson's world, it ended in rejection. In Russell's world, it ended in death.

Elvira continued, "After some time had passed, it got even worse. Of course, no one knew then that Loren had anything to do with any of things that happened. What began as pranks soon became criminal. Someone was killing and mutilating dogs and cats, cutting out their genitalia.

Then it got worse. A farmer found a dead calf. The poor animal had its throat cut, and it too had been mutilated."

Stannard could not help himself—a small cry escaped.

"Are you all right, young man?," Elvira asked. "I know this is a gory tale, but you asked me to tell you about him."

Drawing a deep breath, he slowly exhaled. "It is okay, ma'am. The story just strikes close to home, that is all. Go on."

"You can imagine the outrage in the whole area. Folks started getting together and comparing notes. No one knew who to suspect. Loren had been good about keeping his activities secret. I don't think anyone but my husband and I knew about the cats and dogs. For sure, no one suspected he had anything to do with it, and we didn't tell. Thinking on it now, we should have. Anyway, one thing they soon discovered was that every time something like this happened, Peter Johnson's old pickup truck had been in the area. The poor boy had a speech impediment, and folks had trouble understanding him. When the sheriff questioned him about the coincident of his truck always being seen, he just clammed up. A few weeks later, everyone thought they had the culprit."

"What happened?" Stannard had to know the rest.

"After the calf incident, folks started seeing Loren with Pete. They were always in Pete's old truck. You would see them driving around aimlessly day and night. At first, I suppose everyone thought Loren was just being nice to poor old Pete. Like I said, he was slow and the kids didn't have anything to do with him. For all his odd behavior, he still had a good reputation with a lot of people in town at the time. He went to church regularly, and he was polite to his elders."

Stannard fidgeted in his seat, wondering if she intended to go off down another rabbit trail. She did not.

"Loren was a sophomore in high school, so that would make him what, sixteen I guess. Anyway, he was a year behind Pete. Talk got started about how he needed to be careful because Pete wasn't right in the head. I think they all suspected Pete had something to do with that calf killing. When school let out for the summer, the two boys were together more all the time. That's when someone found the second calf. That was the second time the sheriff tried to talk to Pete. His truck had been seen near the pasture." Elvira stopped.

Stannard knew she had reached an even more disturbing part of her story. *Russell again, two high school-aged boys, dead and mutilated calves.* He wondered if he could stand to hear the story.

She sat silently for a full minute, her head down. Then she began again. "One morning toward the end of summer when the boys had been out fishing, Loren came running up here alone. Blood was running down the inside of his thigh. He said Pete had cut him. He showed us the cut. It didn't seem to be too deep, but it was up near his groin and it'd bled a lot. We took him to see the doc. It took nine stitches to close the cut, and he ended up with quite a scar. After that, we went to see the sheriff, and Loren told him what happened."

"You are going to tell me Loren did it to himself, aren't you?" Stannard volunteered.

"Not so fast," Elvira answered. "Loren told the sheriff that when they got through fishing and got in the truck Pete, all of a sudden, took his fishing knife and cut him. He said he got away from Pete and ran here because it was the closest place. They'd been fishing in a pond in the next quarter section." Stannard wanted to ask if it might not be the same pond where the younger brother drowned but held his tongue. "Well, sir, the sheriff started looking for Pete, but the boy had run off. They finally found him that night. He had gone home after dark. When they confronted Pete, he was incoherent. He just cried, saying he didn't know what to do. They found his fishing knife on the floorboard of the truck. It had a blood stain on the handle."

"So when did you find out the truth?" Stannard asked.

"We found out years later, after Loren moved away. You see, by then everyone was afraid of Loren. No one said so, and I don't even think they were aware of it, but as time passed and he graduated from school, he just had a funny way of looking at folks. He was smarter than they were, and they knew it. Of course by then he'd done some things to kind of set folks off."

"What sort of things?"

Elvira looked tired. She was old and the strain of talking about her dead nephew had taken a toll on her. "I just don't want to talk about it anymore."

Stannard probed one more time. "I understand, but I need to know one more thing. How did you find out the truth?"

"Pete told my husband. Twenty years had passed, and my husband was sick with the cancer. He couldn't keep up with the farm anymore, and he got Pete to help him. One day out of the blue, Pete just up and told him it was Loren. He said when they got back to the truck, Loren was carrying their stuff, putting it in back. He said when Loren got in the truck, he had the knife and cut himself and then he laughed. Pete was scared and Loren told him that everyone thought he was the one who had killed those calves and that if he told the truth Loren would cut him the same way. Pete was slow-witted and scared, so he just ran away."

"So Pete got blamed for everything Loren did."

"Yes, and if Pete hadn't told my husband I never would have found out the truth, although I think deep down I never did believe Pete had done anything wrong."

"Did you tell anyone the truth about what happened?"

"Yes. Some folks felt sorry for Pete, but what could they do? It was all in the past."

"And Loren got away with it."

"Of course. Too much time had passed for the law to do anything."

The interview continued for an additional fifteen minutes, but nothing new came of it. The old woman had told Stannard all she intended to about her nephew. If he wanted to know more, he would have to talk to some of the schoolmates who still lived in the area.

Chapter Nine

Stannard spent the next day looking up former high school classmates of Dr. Loren Parlous. Pete Johnson refused to talk to him at first. Only when he produced a copy of the obituary from the *Kansas City Star* and a certified copy of the death certificate from his file did the man agree to tell his story. At the end of an hour, Stannard had confirmation of what Loren's aunt had told him and much more. Pete provided the names of four more classmates, both boys and girls who had in one way or another been subjected to Loren Parlous's manipulative behavior. By the time he verified each of those stories, he learned that self-inflicted injury, or the threat of it, and blackmail was common behavior for Loren.

The day following that he went to the University of Dayton but found only one of the doctor's former teachers, a man now nearing compulsory retirement age, still in his classroom. Professor Donald Briggs had been his faculty adviser. Sizing the man up, Stannard concluded he couldn't be more than ten years older than Parlous, if that. It came as a surprise when the professor said he remembered a student from forty years earlier.

"Loren Parlous, yes, I remember him. What about him?"

The man's look said a lot. "He's dead, and I'm investigating the circumstances of his demise."

"Okay, what has that got to do with me?" The question sounded almost defensive.

"We don't know whether he died as a result of suicide, accident, or murder. I'm looking into his past to see if there's anything there that might give us a clue."

The man didn't answer right away. As Stannard watched he could see the man considering what to say. *Even now they are all afraid.*

"Let's go back to my office. This may take some time." The walk between the buildings passed in silence. Students enrolled in summer school greeted the teacher, who clearly held a special place in their lives.

"You seem to be popular with the students," Stannard commented.

"I suppose I am. I try to be their friend as well as their teacher, mentor, and adviser. In some cases I've even been confessor."

"And in which of those roles did you know Loren Parlous?"

"All of them at one time or another. He was a complex boy. I'm certain he became an even more complex man. Here we are, Briggs Hall. My office is on the third floor."

The two men climbed the stairs, turned right, and stopped at the second door on the left. "So," Stannard said, "Briggs Hall—is it named for you or one of your relatives?"

"Actually yes, the building is named for my father, Truman Briggs. I come from a line of teachers and feel honored to continue the line, although I fear it will stop with me. I have no children. I suppose that may account for why I've taken such an interest in the students who have passed through here."

Stannard looked around at the office. To him it seemed just a little larger and more commodious than the normal professor's office. He watched as Professor Briggs went to the sink in the corner and filled a carafe with water. Ten minutes later the old-fashioned coffeepot finished perking and Briggs poured two cups. "Do you take cream or sugar?"

"No. As it comes."

Briggs handed him the cup and sat down behind an ornate wooden desk. "The desk belonged to my father. The school did some remodeling after he retired and converted part of an old classroom where he taught into this office so he would have a place to come, sort of a perquisite emeritus for his years of service to the university. Now, what do you want to know about Loren Parlous?"

"Do you remember Parlous well?"

"Oh yes, of all the students I've had in class, I remember him best."

"Really, and why is that?"

"He was a brilliant student but one of the most troubled young men I've ever known or for that matter ever heard about."

"In what way?"

For the next hour Professor Briggs talked without interruption. If Stannard had any doubt about how well the professor remembered the youth, it disappeared in the first few minutes. As the professor talked, Stannard removed a small spiral notebook from his pocket and held it up as if to ask permission to take notes. The professor nodded his approval without stopping. The words flowed from the man as if they had been bottled up for the four decades since Parlous had been a student at Dayton. The attempted suicide, Briggs said, had troubled him most. "He attempted suicide as a sophomore by taking pills and then drinking alcohol." The cause of the attempt, he learned, had been trouble over a girl whom Parlous wanted to date but who'd rejected him. Briggs felt certain the suicide attempt hadn't been genuine, but it had very nearly ended in the boy's death. Parlous had merely wanted to manipulate the girl. It had worked and the girl later became pregnant. He later learned that Parlous had done that sort of thing before to get his way. Only this time it nearly backfired. He'd taken a nearly lethal dose of drugs and alcohol.

The day after that Stannard caught the eleven forty-five Northwest Airline flight from Dayton to Kansas City, his head reeling. He'd left Kansas City at the first of the week under the belief Dr. Parlous had been somehow murdered. Now he wasn't so sure. *Loren Parlous had been one sick human being. On that, everyone who knew him as a boy and young man agreed. Would anyone, even someone who suffered from a serious mental disorder, mutilate himself and then intentionally drive his car into a bridge abutment? It could be an accident following self-mutilation.* If so, wouldn't it be consistent with what Professor Briggs told him about the girl at college?

What about murder? I can't rule that out either. Parlous's ex-wife is a strange case too. It doesn't take an ex-cop to see she had someone follow me all the time I spent in Florida. What's her angle? He didn't have enough facts to know. What he did know with certainty was that she knew more than she'd told him. It may be nothing more than investigative intuition, but he intended to find out.

The Northwest flight to Kansas City International Airport had an estimated time of arrival at 2:35. The short flight had given Stannard time to think. There were many sick people in the world. A few would always fall through the cracks. Dr. Loren Parlous appeared to be one of them. The boys who he believed had been solely responsible for killing his son, Russell, were others. There had been telltale signs all along the way that pointed to the bizarre, sometimes evil, behavior of those people. Somehow a few people like that always managed to go through life undetected until they did something horrible. He understood the anguish Aunt Elvira and Professor Briggs felt. They should have sounded an alarm when they saw what a manipulative personality Loren Parlous had as a child and young man. His fellow high school classmates also had their share of blame for allowing his behavior to go unchecked. The same went for the people in the town outside Dayton. *I'm always running along after the fact,* Stannard mused. *It's not until something bad happens that I get involved.* He caught his breath, stifling a sob. *I should've been ahead of the curve with*

Russell, and I failed. For an instance he felt the black cloud of depression descend on him. Deep in the recess of his mind he knew that this case was probably his last opportunity for redemption. If he did not overcome evil, unmask it, his failure would plunge him back into a hole of depression from which he might never escape.

Composed by the time the flight arrived, Stannard collected his car from the airport parking lot twenty minutes later. He considered driving to the office but only for a moment. He would not arrive there until nearly four and would accomplish nothing before the office closed. He drove the twenty miles from the airport to his turnoff on Wolcott Road and went directly home, where he called the office from his driveway. Marjorie answered. She listened politely while he made his excuse for not coming to the office, then she answered, "I'll tell Big Ed you're back in town and will be in the office tomorrow morning. You do have some phone calls you may want to know about. Lorelei Parlous called a couple of days ago. She wants to meet with you again. She said something about meeting for a drink. What've you got going there, lover boy? I never took you for a player."

He chuckled. "You don't have to worry. Only you and Caryl have a place in my heart. I'll give her a call tomorrow when I get to the office." Nevertheless, he was flattered by the call and would definitely follow up on it.

Stannard told Caryl about his trip after dinner, about how the layover in Memphis had allowed him to try out some of its famous barbecue. It didn't measure up to all the hype. Kansas City's barbecue giants—Gates, Arthur Bryant, Oklahoma Joe's, and Hayward's Pit, where he frequently ate lunch since it was near the office—all beat the food in Memphis. Under questioning by Caryl, he admitted that the barbecue at the Kansas City airport, even those carrying the same name, also failed to measure up to the original restaurants. He told her about the white-sand beach along the Florida Panhandle and the walk he'd taken, barefoot, while the tide rolled in as the sun had set. He omitted the part about first noticing the man who had left Dr. Erin Kasalaitis's condominium just as he arrived following him. He didn't want to alarm Caryl by telling her the investigation had taken on a sinister aspect.

When he finished telling her about Aunt Elvira, the sweet old woman he'd met at Dayton, Caryl challenged him. "Stannard…"

He kept talking, instinctively knowing she was about to press him for details he didn't want to discuss.

"Stannard, stop babbling and listen to me." Her tone of voice had the edge he remembered from his childhood. It was the same tone his mother had used to get his attention, and after that, it was the same tone used by his elementary school teachers.

"What?" He waited.

"I want you to tell me what it is that has you so uptight. What happened? And, I don't want to hear about cornfields and walks along the Gulf of Mexico."

He did not immediately answer. He knew he would have to tell her some of what he'd learned, but he couldn't decide what to tell her and what to leave out.

Before he could begin, Caryl eased his pain. "I know you won't tell me everything, Stannard, but you need to talk about this and I need to hear it. You are keeping things from me. That is the problem. Something is bothering you, and you need to get it out. Just tell me what you can."

He decided to tell her about Florida and leave it at that. "There is something about Erin Kasalaitis that bothers me," he began. "In the first place, she didn't seem to be the sort of person Dr. Parlous's widow portrayed her to be. When I called her on the phone, she was pleasant and agreeable. She agreed to meet me at her home that evening." He stopped and considered whether to say anything about the tough-looking man or not. He once again decided against telling her. "She didn't express any remorse at the death of her son's father. I really didn't expect her to do that, but I was surprised at just how ambivalent she seemed. I expected aggression. Instead, all I got was a calm and patient insurance claimant."

"So why did that bother you?" Caryl wanted to know.

"Well, don't we have some emotion when a distant relative dies? You would expect something. After all, Parlous fathered her son. Besides, it surprised me because when I asked her about whether she'd been in Kansas City the day before the incident on the road, her tone changed. It almost seemed like she was reciting from a script."

"In what way?"

"The story she told me was identical to the story Lorelei Parlous told the police. The only departure from it was she said she changed her ticket and left Kansas City the same day—on the last flight out to Florida. She said it was a real milk run, stopped in Dallas first. She ended up spending the night in a hotel in Houston."

"So?"

"She had the ticket and the boarding passes! She even had a receipt from the hotel. Who keeps those things? I don't. When I get home, I toss them. What's the point of hanging on to them unless it's to provide an alibi? Marjorie doesn't want them or need them for her records. So why did Erin Kasalaitis keep them? She wasn't traveling on company business; this was a personal trip. And, they were at her fingertips. She didn't even have to look for them, although she made a show of doing so. She had them so she could show them to me."

"I guess she wanted to prove she wasn't in Kansas City when her ex-husband was tortured. But if that is the case, then…" Caryl stopped before going on. "So then, she didn't deny sending the threatening letters?"

"Oh no, she denied that all right. She said the only reason she came up here was to tell her ex-husband and his sexy new wife what she thought about them."

"But you said she seemed to be ambivalent toward him."

"Well, that was then. By this time she sounded downright vengeful."

"So what do you make of it?"

"I don't know. One thing is certain. Erin Kasalaitis was not in Kansas City that night. Since the terrorist attack on 9-11, no one gets on a plane without identification. She has the tickets and boarding passes to prove she was out of here on the 7:20 American Airlines flight to Houston. She even had the receipt from the airport Doubletree Hotel on JFK Boulevard to prove she spent the night there." Stannard's eyes suddenly widened. Time was important to understanding what happened. Erin Kasalaitis had taken the Continental Airlines flight that connected through Houston and arrived in Kansas City at half past noon. There is no question she left at 7:20 after arguing with Dr. Parlous and his wife just minutes before six. They were on 39th Street, a block east of the Kansas University Medical Center in a medical student hangout. She had to drive to the airport, check in her car, and then change her ticket. Or did she? Airlines wouldn't answer questions about scheduling from an insurance investigator, but they would from a police officer. He would ask his old pal, Lieutenant Pezzati, to find out when Erin Kasalaitis changed her ticket. The airline would have a record of it. Why would she do that? If all she intended to do was have a brief confrontation with her ex-husband, she could've booked the earlier flight to begin with—unless. Unless what? Maybe she never intended to stay but wanted to make it appear she did. *If so, it brings me back to my first question. Why would she do that?*

The following morning he called Lieutenant Pezzati, who in turn called the airline. An hour later Pezzati returned the call. Erin Kasalaitis had changed her ticket at the airport ticket counter just minutes after her flight arrived in Kansas City. She never planned to spend the night in Kansas City. Why then did she originally book a ticket with a return flight the next day?

Chapter Ten

The questions mounted but still Stannard felt no pressure to wrap up the investigation. He'd been on the case for only a few days. There was plenty of time, or so he thought. In most cases his job ended where the police responsibility began. He made a determination of what had happened from an insurance standpoint, and that finished it. In a case of fire loss, he frequently had to investigate to see if the property loss had been the result of arson. Once he made that determination, police worked the case to identify the perpetrator. In a property loss case, he looked for proof of ownership. Only where precious jewels were involved did he have to consider the possibility that the owner had arranged for the jewels to be stolen so a double payday might be realized. For that reason the financial stability of the owner generally resolved the issue of an arranged theft. In arson cases, you looked for an accelerant. Of course people did torch their own property, but the financial stability of the owner normally resolved that case as well.

But in life insurance cases, the issues of accident or suicide frequently determined whether the company paid out or not. Murder seldom played into a case, but when it did resolution became more difficult. In those cases he looked for motive, means, and opportunity. If a beneficiary became a person of interest—and that couldn't be discounted here—he worked with the police. To further complicate the case, the Parlous policy had an unusual rider that excluded murder from the double indemnity payout. *Odd—I wonder why they put that in there. No one plans to be murdered. It generally fell under the category of accidental death.*

Two full weeks had passed since the filing of the claim, and a week since the file had been referred for investigation. It troubled him that he still did not know whether he had a murder or accident. If it turned out to be an accident, how would self-inflicted injuries play in a determination of benefits? *That's not my concern. I just find the facts and give them to the company lawyers.*

Of the three alternatives—suicide, accident, or murder—suicide or accident seemed the most likely. The only evidence he had that suggested murder came from Lorelei Parlous, and that had been answered by his trip to Florida. His efforts to connect the letters Dr. Parlous received with his ex-wife had been a dead end. She hadn't even been in town when the emotionally disturbed psychiatrist drove his car into that bridge. Even if she had been in Kansas City, how could she make him do such a thing? Stannard's mind raced with speculation. *What about the statement in the letter alleging Dr. Kasalaitis not only wanted Dr. Parlous dead, but wanted it to look like an accident? Could someone else be involved?* His mind raced to the man who had followed him in Florida.

He arrived in the office at his usual time, dropped off his dictated notes for Marjorie to type, and drove back north to Lake Quivira. A surprise visit to Lorelei Parlous might prove interesting. After the interview she staged at the swimming pool, he wanted to see how she'd react when she didn't have time to set up the meeting. He stopped at the Lake Quivira entrance and waited for the guard. No one came. *No matter,* he thought, *the surveillance camera will catch my arrival. I wonder if that thing works.* He turned toward the camera and waved then got back in his car and drove on. He typed in his destination on the Garmin GPS device and turned left at the fork. He followed the instruction it gave until he reached the hairpin turn that went down the hill toward the lake. *Oops, is this thing right?* Relying on it for accuracy, he drove to the parking spot where only the garage stood. He parked beside the silver 2005 Toyota MR2 Spyder and thought, *Nice car, but where's the house?* As the police had before him, he considered the strange appearance of the property. He'd never seen a place developed with only the garage showing above ground. It looked like the fortress he'd heard about at the military installation on Johnson Island in the Pacific. There, the only thing above ground was a runway and concrete bunker that led to an underground and undersea facility. He took a few minutes to look around, peering over the edge of the embankment to see the shape of a concrete roof and wall protruding toward the water. From this vantage, he heard the indistinct sound of voices but could see nothing. As he walked around the garage and parking pad, the sound of the voices grew louder. He stopped at the corner of the deck leading to the entry of the house and listened. The excited voices continued, a man and woman, neither apparently paying attention to what the other was saying, although Stannard still couldn't make out their words. The wind blowing off the lake through the trees and the insulating properties of the building muffled their voices.

When he rounded the corner, he heard the woman's voice, Lorelei Parlous's voice, saying, "Not now. I'll let you know when it's time."

The young man stood facing Stannard's direction. His eyes gave away the presence of the intruder. Lorelei Parlous, dressed in tight-fitting white shorts and pressed cotton top, stepped away from the man. Both people's faces flushed with embarrassment. The shrill edge went out of Lorelei's voice. "Stannard Jackson, what a surprise. You should have called ahead." She smiled. "What brings you out my way?"

"I was in the area—" he didn't like lying, but he fumbled for something to say "—and you called the office. I thought I'd stop by and let you know about my trip to Florida." He looked at the young man. *Nothing!*

"I need to be going," the man said as he began to brush past Stannard. The man stood a head taller than Stannard. *He's about the same age Russell would've been. Now, why did I think of that?* The statuesque woman did not move.

Stannard moved clumsily to his right, as if trying to get out of the way, but chose the wrong side to do so. He blocked the man's exit and stuck out his hand. "I don't think we've met. I'm Stannard Jackson." As he did so, he noticed the slight discoloration by the right ear. A crescent moon on his neck below the ear. *That looks familiar, but where've I seen it before?*

The young man took his hand in a weak grip, his hand cool and clammy—almost a disembodied hand.

Odd—for the time of year. "Willsson Parlous." He did not say more; there was no need. The man bore only a slight resemblance to his dead father, but the age and name said all that needed saying. He slid by and hurried up the walkway to where he'd parked his car. *He says his name with all the sibilance of a snake.* A moment later, the muffled sound of the powerful engine of the Toyota Spyder reached the two people on the deck.

It must've been some heated conversation. You can hear the sound of a car down here, yet they didn't seem to hear me drive up, park, or walk around the side of the house. "Dr. Parlous's son, I take it."

Lorelei led Stannard into the house. "Yes, he wanted to get some of his father's things." She motioned to the chair where Pezzati had sat during her interview with him.

"I guess they look a lot alike." He didn't really think so. The boy had his mother's eyes.

"Not a lot. I think he looks more like his mother. It never bothered me before, but it does now."

"He was mentioned in the obituary but not by name. Did you fill out the form for that?"

"Yes, I did. They weren't close, at least not after I married Loren. I, we, didn't have much contact with him. He and his father had a falling out. I don't know what it was about. I didn't think he wanted to be included as one of Loren's survivors."

I, we, interesting slip. "I thought he would be younger. Dr. Parlous was what, fifty-eight, when he died? With all that schooling, you would not think he had time to marry and start a family. I always thought medical studies took precedence."

"Well then, you are in for a surprise. Wills is older than you think."

Wills is a pet name, an interesting choice of words for someone to use, especially with reference to someone who didn't approve of her marriage to his father. "He must not be much younger than you."

"Really, I never thought about it."

He saw just the slightest show of embarrassment. Oh, really. "Does he live near here?"

"No, not close. He hardly ever came over when his father was alive. I can't imagine what he would want with any of his things. They did not get along well. At least they didn't after I married Loren."

Evasive. I didn't ask all that, and she is repeating herself. I wonder why she is trying to convince me of that fact. "If you don't mind my asking, Mrs. Parlous, how old are you?"

"Well, no, I don't mind. I am thirty-four. How old are you, Stannard Jackson?" She shifted her body to intentionally strike a provocative pose.

There it is again, flirting. "Old enough to be your father," he stretched the truth. "And how old is—" he feigned forgetfulness "—what's his name again?"

"Willsson. His name is Willsson, but we called him Wills. He is twenty-six or twenty-seven now, I suppose. Maybe a year or two older, I don't know."

So, the father named his son after himself. Wills was his middle name, so Willsson is Wills's son. I wonder what else they had in common. "Has he lived here with you and his father?"

"No, he was away at college when I married Loren."

In school until he was what—at least twenty-three, could be. "Where does he live now?"

"He lives in Kansas City, but I, we, seldom saw him. He is an investment counselor. He helps people put their money offshore where Uncle Sam can't tax it. He has nothing to do with medicine."

There it is again, that I and we problem, and too much information. I didn't ask about that. "Was there a problem with any investments?"

"You'd have to ask him about that, wouldn't you?"

Evasive now. Stannard made a mental note. "What about from your point of view?"

"No, I'm all right with him. His mother did all she could to poison any relationship I might have with him though."

He noted that also. *Why would a woman want to have a relationship with her stepson, especially one only six or seven years younger? Could it be for the obvious reason maybe? They are both attractive, and she is a lot closer to his age than she was to his father. Then there is that business about the open marriage.* He changed the subject. "I wanted to talk to you about my trip to Florida and Dayton, Ohio."

"Go ahead. I doubt there is much I can help you with there. I've never been in Florida."

Stannard's antenna was now on full alert. *My impromptu visit has Lorelei Parlous rattled. Is it the visit or the fact she was here with someone who isn't supposed to like her? I didn't ask her if she'd ever been to Florida.*

Lorelei Parlous continued, "Florida I can understand, but Dayton is a bit of a mystery."

"I know you believe your husband was murdered, but the company is more of the opinion it was a suicide. I wanted to get more background on him."

He watched as Lorelei's eyes widened in disbelief. "Suicide? You've got to be kidding." *No flirting now. Is that anger or something else in her eyes?* "You've seen the pictures of his body. I can't believe anyone in their right mind would think that was a suicide."

"Well, that's just the point. I've talked to the first Mrs. Parlous and an aunt by marriage of your husband. They both paint a different picture of Dr. Parlous than you. I went to the University of Dayton and actually found his faculty adviser. Guess I was just lucky there. He was still on faculty."

Lorelei tried to stay calm, but Stannard could tell she was agitated. "And what is it they told you that has you going in this direction?"

"Just this, your husband appears to have been a deeply troubled young man. From what they tell me, he had been troubled from the time he was a small boy."

"What do you expect? Loren told me his family turned on him years ago. That's why he never went back there. As for his college experience, I imagine they are all jealous of his success. After all, what does a man have to brag about if he stays at the same university for thirty years?"

"You may have a point there," Stannard conceded. "His old faculty adviser didn't appear to be a world beater, but then he didn't appear to be someone who really cared about what the world thought of him. He had his tenure and the obvious affection of the student body. If I have him sized up accurately, that is enough. He'll stay put until he retires. Why would he lie about Dr. Parlous? As for Dr. Parlous's aunt, I don't see any reason for her to lie."

Lorelei became defensive. "You're going to tell me about that business involving some retarded boy, aren't you? Loren told me all about it. He said after he left town everyone got together and changed their story about what happened."

She seems to know a lot about Dayton. So what was the phony surprise about my going to Dayton all about? "That may be true, but it just doesn't make sense either. You say Dr. Parlous hadn't been back to Dayton. Are you certain of that?"

"He told me he wrote them all off years ago. He wanted nothing to do with them. They were all a pack of liars who just wanted to bring him down to their level. I think those were his exact words, 'They just all want to bring me down to their level.' "

"And he never went back?"

"He said he hadn't been back there since his mother and father died in the fire that burned down their house. He said the people in that little town outside Dayton blamed him for that too."

He made a mental note. *Did Parlous have anything to do with that?* Shifting to another topic, he continued to probe. "It seems a lot of folks believe Dr. Parlous was something of a manipulator. That's quite a combination, a manipulative personality with a touch of paranoia."

Lorelei chafed at the comment. "So now you're a psychiatrist too, I see."

"No, ma'am, far from it, but I do recognize the obvious when I see it."

"Okay, so he wasn't perfect. I never said he was. But I can tell you one thing with certainty. Loren

Parlous did not commit suicide—Erin Kasalaitis killed him."

He tried to diffuse the conversation that now bordered on confrontation. "Look, I get your point. You don't want his first wife to inherit anything or receive the proceeds of the insurance.

Fine, either way, suicide or murder, she doesn't collect. You'd rather it turned out to be an accident? If the evidence ultimately rules out murder and suicide, accident is all that's left. She collects then!" He looked for a reaction but did not get one.

Calming, Lorelei answered, "Stannard Jackson, I like you. You seem to be a nice man who is trying to do his job, but I don't want to leave you with the impression I don't care about the truth. Erin Kasalaitis killed her ex-husband, my husband, and I want to see her pay for it. If I can't get the police to investigate, and it appears I can't, then I don't want her to profit from her actions."

He heard her and sympathized with her plight. "I really do understand, but you're going to have to help me. It just doesn't seem possible. She told me she was on her way back to Florida hours before Dr. Parlous drove his car into the bridge. She even has the plane tickets and hotel receipts to prove it." He watched to see her reaction to this revelation.

Lorelei did not disappoint. "I don't know. All I can tell you is she's behind this. If she didn't do it herself then she got someone else to do it for her."

"I suppose that is a possibility. She may have planned her sudden departure before she arrived. She changed her ticket minutes after her flight arrived. If so, it still doesn't explain how you get someone to intentionally drive his own car into a bridge abutment."

Lorelei looked resigned to the facts. "I don't know. I'll help you any way I can, but please, please don't just assign this case to the suicide pile. He was murdered and I believe Erin Kasalaitis is behind it." She paused, then thinking of something else, she started, "The letters…"

"She denied any knowledge of them, but that's just what you would expect. If I'd sent them, I wouldn't admit to doing it. I didn't accuse her of sending them, of course. That isn't the way to get information. When I told her about the letters, she just looked at me at first."

"He always told me she could present a stoic face but underneath there seethed a hot-blooded Greek."

"When she did respond, all she said was, 'You don't think I had anything to do with them, do you?' I told her I had no way of knowing, but the police had the letters and they were postmarked from down there."

"I'll bet she had an answer for that too."

"Not really." *What she did tell me was that you'd probably sent them and had them forwarded on up here.* "That's when she just out and out denied knowing anything about them."

"She is good. I told you that."

"She has some interesting friends too. I guess if you work in a drug rehab facility that's likely to be the case."

"Drug rehab? I didn't know that. She worked in anesthesiology up until the time she moved from here."

"How well did you know Dr. Kasalaitis?"

"We actually had been casual friends at one time. In fact, I knew Erin before I knew Loren."

"Did you ever get a sense of the hot-blooded Greek when you were around her?" He wanted more about the early relationship but knew he wouldn't have to ask. Lorelei Parlous wanted to talk now.

"I can't say that I did. I wasn't around her all that much. We worked in the same building. It was next to the building where Loren worked. I just ran into her from time to time at the little food court on the lower level. We ate together a few times. There weren't many tables and everyone just shared the space."

"You don't get to know anyone well in that setting."

"I suppose not. I did see her getting in the face of the blind couple who ran the place once. She said she had given them a twenty and they only gave her change for a ten. Her temper was pretty wild then."

"That happened to me once too. I don't see how those blind people can tell the difference in the denomination of bills unless you tell them."

"The guy wasn't totally blind. If he held a bill close to his eyes, he could see a little bit. At least we all thought he could. He always held the bills up that way. Erin was convinced he tried to cheat her intentionally. She really pitched a fit, told him she would contact the agency that set them up in our building and get him fired."

"Nice lady!"

"When she came over to the table, she acted as if nothing had happened, all sweetness and light. Two weeks later the blind couple was gone."

"Anything else?"

"Shortly after that, we were walking out of the building to our cars at the same time and we ran into Loren. He always had an eye out for a good-looking woman. He was giving me the once-over, and Erin didn't like it."

"Did she say anything?"

"Not then. She just looked at me queerly. You've seen her. She is about fifteen years older than I am, and she's not all that good-looking. She must've had a good body when she was younger, but it'd gone to seed. Anyway, he liked what he saw—but she didn't."

"She did say something later, right?"

"She left notes under my wiper blades."

"How do you know it was her?"

"I can't prove it, but the notes were nasty—making veiled threats, calling me all sorts of names. No one else had cause to do it. Besides, after that she never sat at the table with me. She just got her lunch and went back to her office or somewhere else to eat it."

"Do you still have the notes?"

"No, I threw them away. After I married Loren, I didn't see any point to keeping them."

"When did you start seeing Dr. Parlous?"

"Almost immediately. He had a talent for accidentally running into a person. It wasn't long before we started going out for a drink. Then, one thing led to another. I think Erin knew about it from the very beginning. She followed us in her car one day. When we stopped she came up to Loren's car and threatened us."

"Threatened you how?"

"She said that with her knowledge of drugs, we had better both watch out."

"You don't have any proof of that, I don't suppose?"

"No. Shortly after that they separated."

"What about any friends or associates, do you know anything about them?"

"No, just doctors and nurses I imagine. She just had one partner in her practice, but she moved away from Kansas City shortly after she did."

More unsubstantiated accusations against Dr. Kasalaitis—accusations she can't prove. She could've told me all this before I went to Florida. Why now? "What about her former partner, what was his name?"

"It wasn't a he, it was a she, and I don't know. After Erin moved to Florida, she closed up the practice and moved too. I imagine the medical association can tell you where she is now."

Stannard marked the evasive answer in his memory. He changed the topic. "I've read Detective Pezzati's report. Can we talk about the meeting you and your husband had with his first wife the night before he died?"

"Okay, what do you want to know?"

"As I recall, you told Pezzati you met Erin at Jimmy's Jigger at about five o'clock on that afternoon."

"That's right."

"I seem to recall from years ago that the Jigger was a jumpin' joint most nights."

"Well, yeah, it was crowded when we got there, so?"

"Had you ever been there before?"

"No, it is a med student and nursing student hangout. I was surprised at it when we got there. There isn't any parking on the street, so we had to park at the KU Med Center lot and walk a couple of blocks."

"It seems like an odd place to meet. I mean, why there, especially considering the nature of the meeting?"

"It was where Erin wanted to meet. She and Loren used to go there when she was a student and he was on the prowl for female med students or nurses. We had suggested the bar at the Rafael Hotel on the Plaza. It would've been a lot quieter."

"So who got there first?"

"She did. It surprised us. She'd been there for a while holding down a table near the back. If it hadn't been for that, we would've had to go somewhere else. As it turned out, I guess the Jigger was the best place for the meeting after all. You know those places, everyone self-absorbed, on the make. No one pays any attention to what's going on in the next booth. A quiet place like the Rafael would've really drawn attention when the conversation turned nasty."

"What was Erin's mood when you got there?"

"I would say she was in a good mood. She'd been there long enough to have a couple of drinks. She was relaxed, certainly not angry. She even made a show of getting up when we arrived and hugging both of us. That surprised me."

Stannard considered the strange behavior he had observed from Erin Kasalaitis, first ambivalence then aggression. "She showed me both sides of her personality too. She was pleasant on the phone and congenial when I arrived at her condominium, but she got a little on edge before I left. I think she had some tough-looking fellow follow me while I was there as well."

Lorelei visibly blanched at those words. "She did what?"

"She had me followed. The guy who did it looked like a beach bum of some sort, maybe one who'd battled drugs or booze a little too long. He wasn't very good at being a tail. I had him spotted almost from the minute he began."

Lorelei now became the questioner. "Did you get a good look at him?"

"I actually did. He wasn't the sort of man you would be likely to forget."

"When did you first notice him?"

What is this all about? Why all the interest in a man I only casually mentioned? "He came out of her building just as I arrived. He walked right past me, looked right at me with a questionable smile on his face."

Lorele waited to see if Stannard would add anything more. He did not. "You don't suppose he had anything to do with Loren's murder, do you? After all, if she left town when you say she did then it doesn't seem possible she could've been directly involved. Maybe he was up here with her or came ahead of her."

To be entirely honest, that thought hadn't occurred to me. So why is she bringing it up? "I don't suppose you have any idea who he may be," he asked.

"No, why should I? As I said, I've never been to Florida. One thing is for certain, whoever did this to Loren had to have some physical strength. Loren may not have been a big man, but he wouldn't have willingly submitted to something like this unless it was his own idea."

There it was again, Florida. "I wish I had gotten a good picture of him. All I got was one from my cell phone through the window."

Stannard showed the picture to Lorelei. She shook her head no. "I've never seen that man before."

"You said Dr. Parlous 'would not have willingly submitted to his own mutilation unless it was his own idea.' That is quite a statement."

"He was a difficult man to understand. You never knew him. He got a real kick out of manipulating people. You could really go wrong by underestimating what he was capable of doing."

I don't get it. A while ago you bridled at the suggestion your husband had a manipulative personality. The two people sat with an awkward silence for a moment then Stannard spoke again. "The afternoon you met Erin

Kasalaitis at Jimmy's Jigger, were you there for a long time before the disagreement? What'd you talk about?"

Lorelei answered, "If you have read Lieutenant Pezzati's report, you already know the answer to that. We tried to buy her off."

"Well, yes, I did read that. But it doesn't take the better part of an hour to just irritate someone so they walk out on you in a huff."

"No, it doesn't. When we first got there Doris, the woman tending bar, came over and talked to us. She must have stayed for about fifteen minutes. She kept going on about how good it was to see Loren and Erin. Apparently, they'd spent a good deal of time there years ago. Doris knew them, but she didn't know about their divorce."

Stannard made a mental note to check with Doris. "What is this Doris's last name?" he asked.

"I don't have a clue. That is the first and only time I have ever been in Jimmy's Jigger. I don't suppose I'll ever have a reason to go their again. It's a dump."

"Anything else?" Stannard inquired.

"Just this, before he left Wills told me his mother had been having some money problems. It seems closing up her practice here and taking that clinic job in Florida hadn't worked out very well for her. I gather the twenty-five grand we sent her had bailed her out of a hole."

Clinic job; a while ago she knew nothing about where Dr. Kasalaitis worked. Stannard thanked her for her time and stood preparing to leave. "Did Wills find what he was looking for?"

"No, he wanted access to Loren's computer. I wouldn't let him have it. We were discussing that when you came up on us."

"Oh." *From the sound of it, I would have used the word arguing.* "One more thing—what was Dr. Parlous wearing when you met with his former wife?"

"Khaki slacks and a blue shirt and loafers. Why?"

"Could he have changed clothes somewhere between when he left you at Jimmy's Jigger and when he crashed his car?"

Lorelei didn't answer immediately. Stannard watched her closely. *Something is wrong. She doesn't know how to answer or why I asked that question.* "I don't think he could have changed clothes. He didn't come home, and he never kept a change of clothes at the office."

"What about cotton sweats? Did he ever wear them?"

"No. He wouldn't be caught dead in something as shabby as that."

Stannard tried not to smile. *Oh, but he did wear them, and he was caught dead in them. At least that is what you said when you identified his body. Of course, the corpse you saw was unclothed, so there was no way for you to know what he wore at the time of the car crash.* "Oh, yeah, I almost forgot. You called the office while I was gone. What was it you wanted?"

"Nothing really, I just wondered how you were coming with your investigation. I guess you've answered my question. Thanks."

Stannard stood looking at her for a moment. *Really!* He noticed she seemed to fidget, shifting her weight from one foot to the other before turning ever so slightly in profile, showing off her figure. *There it is again. Every time she is uncomfortable, she gets flirty.* Without any comment, he turned to walk toward the massive front door. At the entryway he glanced to his right and looked into what must have been Dr. Parlous's private study. What he saw hanging on the wall to the side of the desk sent an electric shock through his brain. *What's that?*

Lorelei Parlous, following closely behind him, noticed his reaction. "The painting has that effect on just about everyone. It is something Loren purchased about ten days before his death. I hate it. It seems to have been some sort of twisted joke or something."

Then why didn't you have it removed? After all, weeks—months—have passed.

"He said that if anything ever happened to him and I moved it…he would come back and haunt me."

"You believe that, don't you?"

A faint shiver told Stannard that she did. He took a step into the doorway to get a better view of the picture. The perspective came from behind the barefoot image of the artist, partially revealed in the painting. *It's a monk. He's wearing a brown robe and cowl. Or is he a monk? I've never seen a monk like that before.* He continued to stare at the painting. Over the monk's left shoulder, a picture on an easel drew his attention. *It's a picture within a picture.* The monk appeared to be about to put the final touches on a portrait of what appeared to be the pope. The man sat on his throne with a golden chalice of red wine setting on an ornate table to his left hand. The pope had an inscrutible expression. *No, it's not the pope. The man is clearly intended to be a religious figure—but what kind of religion? Good or Evil?*

As he viewed the painting, his eye moved toward the upper left-hand corner of the painting. He now saw the model for the painting in the picture. He sat slumped on his throne, his face ashen and twisted in agony. The man was dead and the chalice had been spilled onto the table. Red, bloodlike wine dribbled across the white lace tablecloth and over the edge of the table. *Poison!* The image sent a shudder through Stannard. *Why would anyone want such a macabre painting? Why did Dr. Parlous purchase it when he did? And, why hang it here? Who is the artist? The painting isn't signed, yet it is clearly an original. Maybe Parlous is the artist, but if so does the imagery have some special meaning? We have been missing something. Things aren't what they appear to be. Maybe the solution to whether this is murder or suicide is like the painting. Does it depend on my perspective?*

"You can have it if you want." Lorelei broke the spell.

Stannard said nothing—just walked out of the house, up the steps, unlocked his car, and started his predrive routine. The scent of Lorelei Parlous lingered in his nostrils. *That is one sensuous, troubled woman.*

Lorelei had retreated to the security monitor and watched him sitting in the car on the concrete pad at the top of the hill. She smiled. Then worry lines appeared on her forehead. *I should have removed that picture,* she mused. The time was 3:25 p.m.

Chapter Eleven

Stannard paused at the entrance to Lake Quivira Estates and waved to the guard, who eyed him suspiciously, recognizing him from the image captured by the security camera and the flippant manner he had entered. Stannard then called his office. "Marjorie," he said when she answered the phone, "I'm just leaving the Parlous house and going over to Jimmy's Jigger by the KU Med Center."

"Really, so now you're a drinker too," Marjorie chided. "First you're playing around with that Parlous woman, and now you are heading for a bar. It must've been some hot meeting."

"I'm not and you know it. Mrs. Parlous says a woman by the name of Doris working there may be of some help. Let Big Ed know, okay?" Flipping the cover to his phone shut, he turned right onto Holiday Drive. As he did so, he noticed the surveillance camera mounted on top of the guard building. *I'll have to check that later.* By the time he was finished with the case, he would wonder where that thought had come from, and why.

Holiday Drive East ran along the south bank of the Kansas River. He followed the road until it reached the rock quarry. There he veered left and followed Inland Drive, a deceptively attractive-sounding but isolated and depressing road leading to the Turner Diagonal. He turned east on Kansas Avenue through more heavy industry, twice crossing the Kansas River. His mind wandered through the labyrinth of conflicting information as he took the twisting, turning route toward his destination. *Lorelei obviously intended for me to go to Jimmy's Jigger. Why didn't she just come right out and say it? Why drop the name of Doris? She said she'd never been to the Jigger before that day. How likely is it that she would recall the name of some barmaid? Why the game?* His mind drifted away from the case to Lorelei Parlous. *She is flirty; I like that. No one has paid that kind of attention to me in a long time.*

Momentarily lost in thought as he approached the busy and confusing intersection at the 7th Street Trafficway and Southwest Boulevard, he saw the vehicle race toward the changing traffic light at the last moment. He stomped on his brakes to avoid being

T-boned by the driver of a uniform-company panel truck. *What a senseless way to die—a traffic accident. Loren Parlous died that way. No, Loren Parlous was killed that way; there is a difference.* He regained his composure and turned on West 39th Street. Just ahead on the corner of West 39th and State Line Road, twenty feet into the state of Missouri, sat Jimmy's Jigger.

The ten-mile trip had taken a half hour. He smiled as he thought about all the doctors, nurses, and students who, during the long dry decades of Kansas's self-imposed prohibition, fled the stress of the medical profession after a hard day and walked across the street to have a drink at Jimmy's Jigger. *Sometimes the law doesn't make much sense. You draw a line on a map and make believe it's day on one side and night on the other.* He drove around the block twice. *In the old days, back in the seventies and eighties, parking was difficult, but this is ridiculous. With the expansion of the medical center, it's become almost impossible.* At last he gave up, parked in the covered hospital parking lot, and walked back toward the bar. The afternoon sun beat down on the concrete and blacktop. Sweat stained the underarms of his shirt by the time he reached the bar.

He opened the door to the darkened room, blinded by the contrast between the bright heat generated from the sun and the cool darkness of the dimly lit interior. The room had the familiar smell of all old buildings, especially bars. Smoke, from the days when smoking was lawful, permeated the paint and wood. Spilled booze mixed with the stale odor of other aromas too disgusting to recall wafted over him, settling on and in his senses. As his eyes grew accustomed to the light, he moved forward, noting that the room was remarkably empty for the time of day. His gaze found the woman behind the bar.

"Kind of quiet, isn't it?"

The woman smiled. "Yes it is, but you can forget the clock here. Our day is driven by activity over at the med center, class schedules for nurses and grad students. The day doesn't really begin in earnest until the evening shift change at the hospital."

He perched on a bar stool. "I'm looking for someone named Doris," he said with an inquiring tone.

"I'm Doris. What can I do for you? You are?"

"Jackson, my name is Stannard Jackson." He eyed the woman. *Fifties, small, sort of mousy, not at all what I expected. Women working in bars are normally a little rough around the edges, bluesy, blousy, and blonde. This lady could pass for someone's grandmother.* He considered handing her one of his business cards but then thought he would ask questions first and give her the card later. "I was wondering if you knew a doctor by the name of Loren Parlous." He startled himself with the directness of his question. *Okay, Grandma, you got me.*

Doris flashed a big, open smile.

I'll bet people tell her things they won't tell their own grandmother. That look and expression certainly got me.

Doris answered, "I do! I have known Loren ever since he arrived in KC and became associated with the med center."

Something in her voice told him there were deep waters here. In the moment he paused to consider his approach, Doris continued to smile, welcoming his inquiry. She spoke first. "Why do you ask, and why'd you ask for me first?"

He recovered quickly. "A mutual friend told me you might know where I could find him. I just came from Dayton. I know his aunt Elvira." He felt a twinge of pain at the half-truth, but then what he'd said was true, sort of.

The expression on Doris's face fell. "I am sorry. I can't tell you where you can find him. His personal number is unlisted, I imagine. Have you tried his office? That shouldn't be too hard to find."

Stannard felt hard-pressed to keep up the lie. "I did. But you know, when I called the office, all I got was a recording that they were closed and giving me some office hours."

Doris smiled again.

I don't think she bought that for a minute. "Well, I was just hoping he stopped in here once in a while."

"He was a regular in the early days, but we don't see much of him anymore. In fact, it had been a couple of years since we last saw him, then, lo and behold about two months ago, he was here with his wife. I hadn't seen them together since I don't know when." She looked at him expectantly.

Stannard took the bait. "It's hot out there today. How about a beer? Draft, make it red."

Doris smiled again. The smile was beginning to irritate him. *Real or phony, I can't tell.* She turned and drew off one of Boulevard Brewing Company's best and poured tomato juice into it. As she set it before him, she smiled again. "Okay, Stannard Jackson, who are you? I don't for a minute believe you're an old school chum of Loren's from Dayton. In all the years I've known him, there's never been a single person from Dayton in here looking for him."

He drew out the card case from his pocket and handed her his business card. She looked at it and said, "That's more like it. You're an insurance investigator. Now then, what's this all about?"

I don't think she knows what happened. Stannard told another half-truth. "Sorry, I should have been more up-front with you. You said he and his wife were in here about two months ago.

There was an accident the next day. I'm investigating the accident. I'm trying to trace Dr. Parlous's activities before that accident."

"Well, you should've just said. I'll tell you what I know. Ask away."

No, he thought, *let her tell the story.* He would ask questions afterward. "Why don't you just tell me what you recall?"

The door opened before she could begin. "Hello, Ralph," she said greeting the twenty-something customer who bolted through the door. A medical or doctoral student in one of the allied science disciplines. The young man continued past Stannard and settled in a booth near the back of the room. "The usual?" she called after him. He nodded. She drew a beer and took it to him. When she returned, she addressed Stannard's question. "As I recall, his wife got here first. I can't tell you how long it'd been since I last saw Erin."

She doesn't know they are divorced.

"I chatted with her a little. We were beginning to get busy, so I had to keep working. Loren came in later with some—" she hesitated, groping for the word before finally settling on "—bimbo. Erin didn't appear to be particularly happy to see them together, but she was gracious. She gave them both a hug. It was more than I'd have done." She looked at Stannard, imagining what he was thinking before adding, "No, the answer is no, they didn't have too much to drink, any of them. They did have a couple of drinks, as I recall, but nothing that would have contributed to an accident." She stopped.

"How long were they here?"

"Not long, less than a half hour, I suppose, maybe a little longer. They seemed to be getting into some disagreement and Erin left. I can imagine what that was all about. The bimbo seemed to be causing some sort of fight."

"Did you hear any of it?"

"Not that I can recall. After Erin left, Loren and the...I shouldn't be calling her a bimbo. I don't know anything about her. He and the woman who accompanied him continued to argue for a few more minutes, and then Loren left. He seemed upset. I suppose he was going after his wife."

Stannard considered how best to get what-ever additional information he could from Doris. Settling on full disclosure, he said, "I should tell you that Loren Parlous died early the next morn-ing in the auto accident, if it was an accident. There is a question whether it was that, suicide, or a homicide."

"Well—" Doris furrowed her brow "—if you ask me, that woman who came in with him was not right, not that Loren was either though."

"What do you mean by that?" he wanted to know.

"Just that she had a smug look on her face after he left. She made a big show of calling for a taxi, but I don't think she waited around for one. She left way too soon. I've never seen a taxi arrive as quickly as that, not in this neighborhood anyway. It couldn't have been more than five minutes."

"What about Dr. Parlous? You intimated there was something wrong with him."

"It wasn't just a matter of bringing that woman with him to meet Erin. There was more. He was always a little odd. He certainly had some weird friends. Shortly before he stopped coming in here, he started hanging out with that weirdo who owns Roberto's 17th Century Bazaar Bizarre over on Broadway at 39th or 40th."

"Anything else you can tell me?"

"Just one thing. Dr. Loren Parlous was a man you remembered. It may have been he was a psychiatrist, but he was odd. No, more than odd, he was creepy. He was always friendly but in a creepy sort of way, always on the lookout for something or someone."

Stannard rose from the bar stool and turned. The red beer sat untouched on the bar. "Thanks, Doris. One more thing I should tell you. That bimbo is, was, Dr. Parlous's wife. She apparently broke up his marriage with Erin years ago."

Doris nodded knowingly. "What did I tell you? He was always on the lookout..."

"Oh yeah, one more thing. Can you tell me what Dr. Parlous was wearing that evening?"

"What he always wore—khaki pants and a blue shirt. Why?"

"He didn't have on cotton sweats?"

"Good grief, no. Loren Parlous was a ladies' man. He would never wear anything like that. If he wore exercise clothing, it would be something from Ralph Lauren or Tommy Hilfiger."

"What makes you so certain of that?"

"I hadn't seen him for a long time had I? If that dapper Dan had been wearing sweats I would remember it."

Stannard waved his hand as the door closed behind him. "Thanks, Doris, you've been a big help." *Nice woman, but not one I'd recall necessarily. It seems strange that Lorelei would recall her name. I am being led, but by what?*

Under normal driving conditions, the one-mile trip from Jimmie's Jigger to 39th and Broadway in Kansas City, Missouri, would take just over four minutes. By the time Stannard collected his car from the med center parking lot and headed east on 39th a quarter hour had already passed. Heavy traffic through the Westport entertainment district delayed him another ten minutes. He noted the high-dollar cars—BMWs, Jags, and Lexuses—parked on the street outside sleazy joints intermingling with twenty-year-old Japanese- and Korean-made cars. In his mind he could see the vintage Corvette parked in the same location. At the corner of 39th and Broadway, he waited for the light to change and looked for a sign that would announce the name Roberto's 17th Century Bazaar Bizarre. The name meant nothing to him beyond the obvious. Doris had offered little help other than to say the owner was a weirdo, whatever that was supposed to mean. *Okay, bazaar means market, and bizarre means weird. So, what do we have? Some sort of market for weird and bizarre stuff, I guess—might be some sort of an antique store.* He guessed south and drove slowly, looking on both sides of the street for some sort of business sign. He almost missed it. The shop was tucked around the corner from Broadway off 40th Street on the diagonal connecting to Washington Street. The small, two-story building also housed a used bookstore. The upstairs appeared to be occupied as a small apartment.

He parked a half block back up Washington and backtracked to the business, which had a cheap sign painted on the glass storefront. Wearing a white shirt and tie with his chinos, he looked nothing like the young people on the make or the druggies who hung around the doors and street crossings panhandling. *I'm glad it's summer; this place could get rough after dark.* He stopped at the entrance to Roberto's 17th Century Bazaar Bizarre. *Wacky place!* Voodoo, witchcraft, and warlock paraphernalia, shrunken heads, bongs, incense burners, and fragrances, and literature on how to start a coven littered the shop window. He viewed the contents with disgust. He saw the magazines and posters with images dressed like the painting in Dr. Parlous' house. *If the painting and this entire affair has anything to do with Roberto Bertonelli then it has to do with the occult.* His eyes then fell on the games. *Covens of Death. Forget it, Stannard. Let it alone. It's in the past. It's information you want.* He pushed on the door and heard an eerie electronic groan summon the owner. Lighting inside the shop was intentionally dim, adding to the sense of otherworldliness about the place. Burning incense mingled with a ten-year layer of dust that coated everything in the store.

He stood waiting. *Okay, in a joint like this, I suppose atmosphere is everything. Whatta I do—call out or wait?* He opted to wait. A minute later he heard the sound of shuffling feet coming from somewhere behind a chain-strand curtain. Each strand was made of unicursal hexagrams enclosed in a circle, the symbol of a warlock. He was on the verge of calling out when a voice came from behind him. "I greet you in the name of the ruler of the world." The words were spoken with a melodious, almost feminine voice.

Stannard felt his body seem to jump in place as he wheeled around. Facing him was a person who was more apparition than human. *Is this a man or a woman? Whatever it is it is creepy. The person* extended its hand, its eyes drawing Stannard forward.

Stannard felt his body tense. He stepped back and looked. *It's a man.* He looked at the hands, which had long fingernails beginning to curl. *What an entry. How did he—get behind me?* He looked up into the face again. The pasty complexion, squinting beady eyes electric magenta in color, and greasy long gray/white stringy hair gave the impression that the person did all he could to avoid the light of day. A shudder went through Stannard, and he felt the hair on his arms begin to stand and goose bumps rise. Repulsed but still somehow compelled to do so, Stannard reached out his own hand.

The fleshy, soft hand enveloped his. "My name is Roberto. It is my desire to help you find your way in this world of misguided souls."

The man's words broke the spell. Stannard pulled back his hand, and as he did so, the long, dirty fingernails scraped his palm. Stannard had the distinct feeling the man was trying to scrape away part of his soul with the raking of nails across flesh. He felt violated by the sense that somehow the man had gained a measure of control over him. He took a step back, putting distance between himself and the man. *If this is showmanship, it's first-rate. If it's for real then ask your questions and get out of here as fast as you can.*

Stannard's face showed his unease.

Roberto appeared to take delight in what he saw. "What is it I can do for you?"

"Information. I need some information." It was then he noticed the gallery of pictures, all young boys. *A gallery; but a gallery of what?* Stannard felt himself getting sick. Then, pulling himself together, he continued, "I'm looking into the death of Dr. Loren Parlous. I think you knew him?"

Now it was Roberto's turn to recoil. Seeing Stannard's gaze had fallen on the picture gallery, his eyes squinted with suspicion. His voice dropped, no longer melodious and now filled with suspicion. "What are you—a cop?"

Stannard's instinct told him Roberto was a man who would know a cop when he saw one. "No, I used to be, but that was a long time ago. I work for insurance companies now."

"Well then," Roberto said, his expression once more amiable, "I knew him. It is a terrible thing about his death."

He knew he was dead before I told him. "How well did you know him?"

"Quite well. At one time he was a valued customer and friend. We weren't only friends. We were colleagues, you might say. At one time I mentored him in the arts. He was a novice then. We had mutual interests that we pursued together."

He's holding back. He's lying. There is a lot more to it than that. "What might those be?"

Stannard felt compelled to inquire but feared he would get an answer.

Roberto looked at his hand, the one he'd dragged across Stannard's palm. "An interest in the occult. We had a common interest in human psychology."

"I take from your comment that something happened."

Roberto's expression revealed nothing. "Not really. We just sort of drifted in different directions."

"In what way?"

"He and his son, Wills, came in together. That was before Loren's wife, Erin, objected. He said she thought coming here was bad for Wills. She insisted that the shop had some sort of satanic purpose. She even accused me of casting spells on Wills so he would come around. Can you imagine?" He laughed. The sound made Stannard's skin crawl. *Why is he telling me this? He's toying with me.* "She wouldn't let up, and in the end they stopped coming around."

Changing the subject, Stannard asked, "Was Loren Parlous the sort of man who would commit suicide?" As he asked the question, he maneuvered himself between Roberto and the door to the shop.

Light reflected off the windshield of a passing car and into Roberto's eyes. They seemed to glow red in the light. Stannard shuddered again. *Something is wrong. Ever since he got hold of my hand, I've felt strange… almost like he had cast a spell over me. Nah—it's just this creepy place.* "Who knows what people are capable of doing. I could tell you things that would…" He stopped without completing the thought.

"Is that a yes?" Stannard wanted to know.

"If you want it to be."

"What about self-mutilation? Could he, would he do that?"

"Oh my, yes, without a doubt. If he thought he could gain something by it—some advantage over someone—yes, he would do that."

Stannard eyed the man. The spell was momentarily broken. "What about you?"

"What about me?"

"Would you consider suicide, or murder, or self-mutilation?"

Roberto smiled and moved back between his visitor and the door. "Why, of course. Where do you think he learned those things?"

"So, when was it that Dr. Parlous stopped coming around?"

Roberto paused to give the impression of having to think. *What a phony; he knows exactly when it was.* "Let me see, it must have been about fifteen years ago. There was an... unpleasantness...Of course, he didn't stop coming in altogether. He still came in—but infrequently."

"And you continued to mentor him?"

"Oh no, by then he believed he had become quite my equal. I permitted him to engage in the fantasy." His eyes narrowed. *Here it comes, more theatrics.* "But don't get me wrong. My powers have not diminished even though his have grown. Excuse me, I should've said his 'had' grown."

"Meaning what?" *He used present tense. He doesn't think Dr. Parlous is dead! What does he know? This entire conversation is a lie.*

"Only that I am the supreme warlock of Kansas City." The small, overweight, pasty-complexioned man seemed to be taunting him, but why?

Is he saying he would kill to regain his position? Stannard nodded toward the picture gallery. "I take it the picture gallery is still up there from the days when Loren Parlous and his son were regulars."

"Yes, those were exciting days." He sighed. "I guess we all move on."

Stannard stepped toward the gallery hanging on the wall, but Roberto insinuated himself between him and it.

"When did you last see Dr. Parlous?"

"A few months ago. We had a minor disagreement, and he broke off the relationship. I don't want to talk about it. We were friends and now he's dead. I don't see any reason to dwell on the past."

"What about his son?"

Roberto's appearance seemed to change. He seemed to grow in stature, and his eyes flashed with the light Stannard had noticed earlier. "Oh, I see Wills from time to time."

Stannard was late getting home that evening. The investigation had begun to play havoc with his otherwise staid routine. He wanted to tell Caryl about his day, what he had heard and seen, but it would have to wait. Caryl's sister and husband were coming for dinner that evening. Normally a warm and friendly person, Stannard bordered on rude as the evening wore on. He played Shanghai, the progressive rummy game they all enjoyed, but he was distracted—frequently discarding a card that his sister-in-law needed to win the hand. The game pitted the men against the women, and his brother-in-law grew more irritated as his play deteriorated. At last, Jim and Alice said good night.

Their car had not cleared the driveway before he began. He related his conversation with Lorelei Parlous and the woman named Doris at Jimmy's Jigger. He told her how that had led him to the shop in Westport where he discovered evil existing on a busy street in Kansas City directly under the eyes of the police and concerned citizenry. Caryl did not show any surprise as he related this information until he told her how the man Roberto had by use of his voice and eyes virtually compelled him to take his hand.

As he talked he felt a jolt of recognition. It passed through his body like the shock from an electric wire. *One of the boys in the gallery of youths was Wills, Dr. Loren Parlous's son. The birthmark by the right ear—it was the birthmark of a crescent moon that drew me to the picture gallery. If Wills's picture is up there, I wonder whom else I might find? Russell? Russell had been withdrawn in the days before his death.* He wracked his memory for some clue about the game Covens of Death. Had Russell been involved with Roberto's 17th Century Bazaar Bizarre and the game Covens of Death? All he could recall was that rumor said that boys who engaged in the game became obsessed with death and dying, even killing. It had been that last bit of recollection that worried him. *You are letting your imagination run away with you. Forget it. Get a grip on yourself. If you let this case get under your skin, you'll be back on a psychiatrist's couch or worse.*

Caryl understood where the narrative would end. "Don't, Stannard," she began. "You know this will only upset you."

"I know. It worries me too. All these years I have blamed myself for not preparing Russell for the kind of people he would encounter. I was trained to do better. I've enforced my will on criminals in the past but never had the feeling they had any influence over me. What I saw today was evil personified. Worse yet, I couldn't seem to resist." He stopped, searching for words. "I failed Russell. What's wrong with me? How could I have prepared him for someone like Roberto and his 17th Century Bazaar Bizarre when I too was powerless before it for a moment? Evil exists in the world, and we must all find our way to deal with it." He thought about what he'd said. "No, we don't just find our way to deal with it. I just don't understand how that kind of evil found Russell. Maybe I never will." He lapsed into silence. *Oh, Russell, I ache for you! Did God fail you, along with me?*

He saw pain reflected in Caryl's eyes. She wanted to talk about her loss. Russell had been her son too, but he stopped her. "I don't want to talk about it anymore. Let's go to bed now."

He did not get up in the middle of the night to look at the scrapbook. He slept fitfully, his dreams taking him back in time to the days following Russell's death.

He awoke at 2:30 and remembered the events as if it were yesterday. He recalled the conversations with the investigating detectives. The two boys convicted of the crime had been part of some sort of warlock coven, but they refused to say more, fearing the power of evil more than the punishment of the law. *Warlocks, Covens of*

Death, Roberto's bizarre bazaar, that picture gallery. I wonder.
No matter how much he wanted to talk to them now,
it could never happen. Both boys had been sent to the
prison in Lansing just a few miles northwest on Wolcott
Road. They both died just a few years later. One died of
AIDS, having contracted HIV before his incarceration.
The other died in a prison stabbing three years later.

He got up and went to the kitchen. He brewed
some chamomile tea and sat thinking. His mind
reeled from what he had learned about Dr. Loren
Parlous. When the man had nearly hit him on the
freeway, he'd thought it was just a crazy driver. After
that the man had had a fatal car crash. Accident they
said. Then when the case came into their shops for
investigation, the coroner and police suggested that
it might be suicide. After all, Parlous was a psychiatrist and something of a manipulative character. Even
Aunt Elvira was afraid of him. The stories the doctor's
family, classmates, and professor all told suggested
the man would do just about anything to get his way.
They seemed to support the idea that he may have
inflicted the injuries on himself in order to manipulate someone—but whom, and what about the claim
by the "grieving" widow, Lorelei? She insisted it wasn't
an accident or suicide; she was positive it was murder.
He'd originally been slow to accept that theory, but
now…after meeting Wills Parlous and that weirdo

Roberto, he wasn't so sure. Most of all he couldn't shut off his brain when it came to Russell. What was he investigating, Dr. Parlous's death, or did it have something to do with Russell? Why did he continue to think about Russell after all these years? It was bad enough dealing with the signs of mutilation of Dr. Parlous's body—so similar to those on Russell—but the picture on the wall in Roberto's 17th Century Bazaar Bizarre wouldn't go away. He was certain he'd seen Wills Parlous's photograph in that picture. He had to find out if Russell was in it as well. *I need to go back to that weird shop and look at the picture gallery again.* He knew it would be too late. Roberto had seen his interest in the gallery and would surely remove it.

The word *evil* continued to run through his brain. Parlous was evil. Maybe not as evil in the beginning as Roberto Bertonelli, if the man was being honest, but even Bertonelli said Parlous had grown much stronger over time. Did Roberto Bertonelli kill Dr. Parlous out of jealousy because of the man's dark powers? Why? So he could be the prince of darkness in Kansas City? That would be too much. What about Dr. Erin Kasalaitis? She had motive but no opportunity.

The long night passed slowly for Caryl. She lay awake listening to him toss and turn. She heard him get out of bed and waited for him to return.

Hours earlier and ten miles away Lorelei Parlous replayed the video. She had watched Stannard from the hidden security camera monitor as he drove away. Shutting off the machine after watching the tape again, she retired to her bedroom, where she unclothed, put on her best silk nightgown, and, smiling to herself, settled down for a much-needed rest. Drifting off to sleep, she thought, *I like Stannard Jackson. He's sort of cute for a guy who was once a cop. He works hard, but how smart is he? I can't help but wonder what he will conclude. Loren's death is a riddle that gets more complicated all the time. Will he just follow leads that take him to a dead end? I've done what I can; now it's up to him.*

Chapter Twelve

Stannard did not rise early the next morning. When he did get up, he was in no hurry to leave home. There were places he wanted to go in Wyandotte County before going to his office. The events of the day before, coupled with his troubled sleep, had left his mind unsettled. Did any of these people pose a danger to either him or his wife? He said little that morning before he left the house. When he did finally leave, he stopped the car by the side of the road as soon as he thought he was out of sight. He wanted Marjorie to know where he would be and how to contact him. She answered her phone on the third ring. "Marjorie, Stannard here. You remember where I told you Dr. Parlous nearly sideswiped me?"

He listened.

"That's right. He came up the Leavenworth Road ramp onto the interstate."

"Where are you? You're never this late." Marjorie sounded disturbed by the few phone calls she'd received from him since he left for Florida.

"I'm just leaving home. I think I'll do some poking around the area where he came onto the road before coming to the office."

"Didn't the police do that?"

"No, Pezzati said it was out of his jurisdiction, and no one apparently bothered to trace the incident back to Leavenworth Road." He thought for a moment. "How could they? I'm probably the only person who knows that's where he got on the freeway."

"So what is it you plan to do?"

"Look around. I just want to have a look around. Parlous had to be coming from somewhere west of I-435. I want to see if there's anything suspicious out that way. It isn't far from my house. I should've done it before now."

"Fine, I'll tell Big Ed where you are. He was worried something might be wrong. Any idea when you'll get in?"

"Can't say. It depends on what I find or don't find. You can always reach me on my cell phone if you need me."

He put down the phone and considered his route. The direct way would be to take 123rd Street south off Wolcott Road. He rejected that, opting instead to begin his search by attempting to back-track the path Dr. Parlous had taken as he raced toward his death. He drove slowly down the freeway toward Leavenworth road, looking off to his right for anything visible from the four-lane road. He saw nothing. At the Leavenworth Road exit, he drove down the ramp even slower. Still nothing. *I don't even know what I expect to find down here.* Even though the location was only about four miles from his home, he had never been in the area before. He drove about aimlessly for several minutes. For the most part, he found the location to be sparsely developed. Small residential developments marked the expansion of the city away from what the locals called the War Zone. They called the inner city the War Zone because of the spreading violence that made it unsafe for law-abiding people to live there, especially the aged and infirm who had the appearance of even modest wealth. At 110th Street, he noted a ten-acre new housing development. He turned there and followed the curving roads. *Nice homes; some have pools in the backyards. Dead end. There's only one way in and one way out. Besides, what would Parlous be doing in a residential neighborhood like this?*

He drove up Canaan Valley Drive. *Same thing— one way in and one way out with more nice homes.* He backtracked to Leavenworth Road and drove farther west. Still nothing; he soon found himself in farmland and pasture. His thoughts turned once again to Russell. His son's mutilated body had been found not more than twelve miles directly west of here. He shuddered then turned around and drove back toward the city. At Hutton Road, he turned south and discovered that the development off Parallel Road had extended well to the north. *This whole area is too well developed.* Whatever happened the night of the June 22 or morning of the 23rd had to have taken place somewhere more isolated than this. He went back up Hutton Road and crossed Leavenworth Road. Just beyond Fox Meadows Drive, the road changed name to 107th Street. There he found what he was looking for, a self-service storage facility. *Isolated and lonely; no reason for anyone to be around at night or early in the morning.* He spent the next few minutes observing the facility. He then drove down the road for a half mile before turning around and coming back. *If I were going to mess with someone, this would be a likely place. Nothing nearby that isn't closed up with air-conditioning, and not much of that. The isolation is right.* He drove to the locked gate. *No indication of the owner; no name to call; just a phone number.* He wrote it down then dialed the number on his cell phone.

The voice at the other end answered, "Hyde Property Investments. What can I do for you?"

The person answering was a woman, her voice thick and raspy from smoking. Stannard imagined her, overweight and fifty, maybe sixty, sitting at a metal desk somewhere answering the phone all day or harassing some poor slob who hadn't made his rent payment. He answered, "I'm at a storage facility off Leavenworth Road near I-435 and got your number."

"Well, that'd make sense. We own the place. Like I said, what can I do for you?"

Stannard considered his response. She didn't sound like the sort of person who would give away too much information over the phone. "Well, I may be in the market. Got anything for rent?"

"You are in luck, mister. We got two units. One is empty now. It's the smallest unit we got—a four-by-six box. The other one is larger, but I don't know about it. Some guy rented it a couple of months ago." He heard her rasping cough and imagined an ashtray full of stale butts from the day before. He could almost smell the room. "He paid for two months. He paid cash for it, but he ain't come back and he ain't paid for another month neither. He's still got his key, but the box could be empty. I don't know. It's bigger, eight by ten feet."

His heart beat faster. *Bingo!* "Can I get a peek at both of them? I'm not good at visualizing things, so maybe you could have someone meet me."

The voice on the other end hesitated. "Yeah, that'll work. I'll give Wally a call and have him meet you. You gonna be there for a while?"

He did not want to sound too eager. "Depends on how soon he can get here. I want to look at something right away."

The raspy voice at the other end answered, "Hang on there. I'll call him on the bag phone and get back to you. Don't hang up now, and what's your name?"

Stannard stifled a laugh. *No one calls a cell phone a bag phone anymore.* "I'll hold the line. The name's Jackson." He listened while the woman phoned the man she called Wally. He tried to hear what she said, but her voice sounded muffled. She must have turned around to use the phone. She was back a moment later. "Mr. Jackson, Wally can be there in about ten minutes if you'll stay put."

He thought for a second. *Ten minutes—right—I'd just bet he'll be here in ten minutes.* "Okay, I'll wait." Stannard would have waited even if it had taken much longer than that. He wanted to get inside the storage facility, especially the larger one, the one rented for two months, the one for which the key had not been returned.

He pulled his car to the gate located at the center of the facility, got out, and walked around the perimeter while he waited. A seven-foot-high chain-link fence topped with barbed wire surrounded the one acre storage area containing four rows of low-profile concrete buildings separated by gravel paths. At the back right corner, he saw a security camera perched on a pole. At the front of the facility, he noticed a second camera mounted on a pole at the left front corner just a hundred feet from his car. Both were old models, and he couldn't tell if either camera worked. Neither camera rotated. At best they appeared to provide only a fixed view of the one-acre facility; not much security for such a large place. *I wonder if either camera shows anything worth seeing? Certainly not much at the front gate.*

Eighteen minutes after the woman who called Wally hung up the phone, a pickup with a sign that read Hyde Property Investments came down Hutton Road and parked behind Stannard's car, which was blocking the road. The driver had the squinty-eyed expression of a man possessing above-average intelligence, the sort frequently underestimated by those who mistook education for intelligence. He stood half a head taller than Stannard, wore thin khaki work clothes and a NASCAR ball cap, and spit tobacco juice when he got out of the truck. "You must be the guy who called the office," he said, stating the obvious.

"Yeah, I almost left. You're late."

The man answered, "Traffic was bad. They were doing some work on Parallel. A utility truck had the street blocked. It looked like some idiot ran into one of the poles or something." He looked Stannard over and then motioned to his car. Whatta you want with a storage unit up here? You got Wyandotte County tags. Why don't you just store whatever it is you got at yer own place?"

"Are you kidding? The place is already full of junk, and the old lady just keeps piling more stuff into the house," he answered.

"Yeah, I know the type, hanging out at garage sales every weekend. Come on, I'll show you what we got." With that, he punched in the code to unlock the gate and led the way down the gravel path to the storage units. Which unit is it you wanna look at? We got two."

"The larger one, I think."

The two men walked about forty feet down the row of doors and stopped. Stannard looked over his shoulder at the security camera on the left front pole. "I see you have security cameras, but I doubt the one over there can see this location. The camera doesn't swivel."

The man looked. "I don't know, maybe it does, maybe not. It was workin' fine a couple of months ago, but somethin' happened to it. I've been meanin' to get it fixed. The one in back is even worse. It gets great shots of nothin' but that grass over there." He waved a sun-burned hand in the direction of grass off the property.

"This place is isolated. It would be easy for someone to break in. I want to know my things are secure—" he paused for effect "—if I rent a unit here."

"What's wrong? Afraid some of your wife's junk is gonna get stolen?"

"Yeah, something like that. We can't have any of her precious stuff go missing."

"No problem," the man called Wally said. "Like I said, if there's somethin' wrong with it, we'll get it fixed." He unhooked the wad of keys from the clip on his belt and paused. "I guess this is okay. The guy who rented this box hasn't paid for it." He turned the key and opened the door.

Both men stood in the sunlight unable to see anything until Wally flipped on the light switch. Wally said nothing, but Stannard drew in his breath ever so slightly. In the center of the small room was a heavy, wooden old-fashioned desk chair. A pair of old, worn-out sneakers lay in the corner. Strips of torn duct tape lay on the floor beside the chair, bits of it still clinging to the armrests and the rear chair legs. Nearby he spotted two Heath candy bar wrap-pers on the floor. Each had been neatly tied in a slipknot and tossed aside. A dark stain on the concrete floor in front of the chair told Stannard he had found what he suspected when he first saw the storage facility location. Blood!

An hour later, he'd taken a one-month rental on the storage unit. He called Lieutenant Pezzati from his car in the parking lot on 78th Street, just off Parallel. "Pezzati, St Jack here. I found something on that Dr. Loren Parlous automobile incident you should see. How fast can you move your Irish-Italian fanny up to where you were born? If what I saw is what I think I saw, this Parlous investigation just got moved away from suicide or accident."

"Really?" The tone in Pezzati's voice sounded interested. "Give me a half hour to get out of here. Where is it you want to meet?" He reached in his desk drawer and pulled out a CD. Mike Pezzati was a complicated man. As he pulled away from his parking spot at police headquarters, he slipped the CD into the player and turned up the volume. A moment later the car was filled with the sound of Andrea Bocelli signing a Verdi aria. Pezzati's rich tenor voice blended with that of the famous blind Italian tenor.

By the time the sun set that evening, the crime scene investigation unit had completed its work. Pezzati and his boyhood friend, the man he thought of as St Jack, stood off to one side as the cooperative units from Overland Park PD and the Kansas City PD prepared to leave.

"It's a good thing you followed your hunch and came out here," Pezzati said.

"Yeah, as anxious as these people were to rent out the place, whatever we get here would've been lost." For an instant, the image of Russell flashed in his mind, but then it passed. Sure, there was a similarity, but maybe this case would help put those nightmares to rest. The adrenaline rush he felt by working an insurance claim only to discover it was a murder connected him to the world in a way he had not felt for over a decade. He knew he had much to offer the investigation. But excitement and doubt nagged him concerning his role now that the case had become a homicide.

"I suppose you'll want me to back off and let your detectives take charge." It wasn't a statement. It was a plea for a role in the investigation.

Lieutenant Pezzati recognized the words for what they were. He also knew that connecting the apparent auto accident to a homicide wouldn't be easy. Motive, means, and opportunity were the key ingredients in a criminal case, but so far, they had none. "Not necessarily. After all, at this point you know more about the case than anyone else. I don't see any reason why we shouldn't continue to cooperate."

"I had hoped you'd say that. I don't want to over-step my role, but I do believe I have a lot to offer. This case has elements of the murder of my son years ago. I won't let that interfere with my judgment; just wanted you to know about it up front."

Pezzati smiled. "I already knew about it, St Jack. You had quite a reputation. You still do, even if you aren't aware of it."

He swallowed to hold down his emotion. "Thanks, that means a lot to me."

As the men followed the technicians out the gate, Stannard turned to Pezzati and, motioning to the stationary security camera, said, "You might want to see if they still have any of the electronic imagery from the night of June twenty-second and twenty-third. The camera in the back won't pick up any-thing in the front, but this one might get something, even though it is stuck at the wrong angle."

"Good idea."

The following morning Lieutenant Pezzati and Stannard Jackson met in the parking lot of the two-story brick building on 78th Street housing the office of Hyde Property Investments. The neighborhood was still marginally safe. The area known as the War Zone hadn't yet extended far beyond 40th Street, although individual tentacles reached well beyond that. They waited. At a quarter past the nine o'clock opening time, they saw Wally and a woman drive up in the pickup and unlock the door. The two men followed them into the building and up the half flight of stairs to the office on the landing. Neither person appeared happy to see the two law enforcement types.

"Oh, it's you two," Clara said, laying down her cigarette and standing, legs apart and braced, as if to say I'm spoiling for a good fight. "We just came from the storage facility. When're you gonna to take down that yellow crime scene tape? It ain't good for business, you know."

Lieutenant Pezzati, not wanting to antagonize Clara and Wally, answered, "I can't say. We didn't put it up. I'm with the Overland Park PD, and Mr. Jackson's an insurance investigator. We'll do whatever we can to help you though."

Clara was not mollified. She looked at Stannard. "You lied to me. You rented that space from me under false pretense."

"I'm sorry, truly I am. It's just that I didn't want to run the risk that someone else would rent it when it had all the appearance of being important to my investigation."

"Doesn't matter, you lied!" Then turning to Lieutenant Pezzati, she continued, "And you don't have any jurisdiction here."

"True enough," Pezzati replied. "Still, we need your cooperation. That's why we're here instead of the KCK police department. I understand your concern, but the sooner we finish our work, the sooner that yellow tape will get removed. We work faster than the KCK police can. We don't have the same workload they do. Less crime in the Golden Ghetto, but—" he paused for effect "—I can call them if you like…" He let the unfinished comment hang for effect.

The comment irked Stannard. *They had me working on this because they said they were too busy. At least that's what they told me.*

Wally, who'd been standing aside all this time, spoke up. "No need to get in a hurry here. My wife didn't mean nothin'. It's just that we got a business to run. Empty spaces and police tape don't mix, if you get my meaning."

Get your meaning; I'm way ahead of you. I wonder how many of those storage spaces just hold household goods. I'd be willing to lay odds some of them also hold stolen property. Stannard thought it. He didn't say it. "I didn't lie to you, Clara. Check the phone book. I live where I said I did. I live just up the road from your storage unit. As for my motive in renting the space, well, it was important to secure the site."

Lieutenant Pezzati didn't want the conversation to stall. "I, we, need to see the paperwork on the man who rented the unit from you." Then turning to Wally, he continued, "We also need to see what your security camera captured."

Clara and Wally exchanged glances. Clara spoke, "I can pull the paperwork, but I don't know anything about the security camera." She got up and walked to the dented metal file cabinet.

While she looked for the file, Lieutenant Pezzati turned back to Wally. "How about it, Wally, can we have access to your security record?"

Wally looked like a man caught between two equally unpleasant choices. At last, he answered, "Yeah, it's on VCR tape. I can look, but I can't say how far back it goes. We recycle those tapes every month or so. I may have something taped back to when he rented it; I may not. When was that anyway, Clara?"

Stannard felt as if his eyes had rolled back into his head. *Tape! What kind of antiquated security system do they have?*

Clara had now returned to her desk. She sat down and opened the used file folder. She extracted a single piece of paper and handed it to Lieutenant Pezzati. The paper bore the handwritten title Unit 8.

Below the title, someone had provided the following information:

Name: Joe Smith

Address: Kansas City

Phone Number: None

Method of Payment: Cash

Rental Term: Month to month

Date: June 21, 2006

The form did not bear a signature.

Pezzati handed the paper back to Clara. "Is that all you've got?"

"That's all."

"Is that his handwriting?"

"No, it's mine."

"You don't have them sign the contract?"

"No, why should I? They either pay or they don't. For us, if it's a cash deal, we don't care. We honor the deal. After the month is up, if he don't come back and pay for another month, we just open the door, auction it off, and get the stuff out so we can rent the unit to someone else." She stopped to throw another snarling comment Stannard's way. "Someone who is more honest than you."

Lieutenant Pezzati started to say something but caught Stannard's eye. Stannard answered, "It's okay; business is conducted a little different up here. I don't suppose you took a picture of his driver's license?"

"You're right, Mr. Jackson, I didn't."

"About that electronic tape," Lt Pezzati asked expectantly.

"It's in the truck," Wally answered.

Convenient, Stannard thought. "Let's get it," he said then thought, *Before something happens to it too! I wonder what you really had in mind to do with it.*

Pezzati wrote out a receipt for the rental document and the tape. They followed Wally to his truck, where they retrieved the small piece of ancient magnetic wizardry. Stannard and Pezzati then drove around the corner to a Wendy's restaurant, where they stopped for coffee. Once inside, Lieutenant Pezzati took the lead. "St Jack, I'll begin by looking into this tape at our lab and have the forensic boys get over and take a look at what's left of the Corvette. Can you keep following the personal leads; you know, with that cold fish Mrs. Parlous and wherever that leads you?"

"Can do," Stannard replied, "and thanks, Pezzati. It isn't every detective who'd let me keep working the case with him." *You have Lorelei Parlous all wrong. She is not a cold fish. That is one hot woman.*

"No problem. Like I said, you had quite a reputation a few years back. From what I've seen, it was well deserved."

Chapter Thirteen

The shattered and fragmented remains of the yellow Corvette lay near the back fence of the police vehicle compound located at the junction of Interstate 35 and old Highway 56. The car driven by Dr. Loren Parlous sat caked with dust, crowded by other wrecks and abandoned cars inside the locked chain-link fence of a salvage yard set aside for that purpose. Lieutenant Pezzati had arranged for the police forensic team to meet his boyhood friend at three o'clock that afternoon. Stannard arrived first and sat in his car parked in front of the small office shack. Ten minutes later, the team of forensic specialists arrived. Two men got out of the vehicle. The passenger unlocked the gate.

"You Jackson?" the driver asked when Stannard approached the panel truck.

"Yes."

The men exchanged names and the driver, impatient to start at what he considered a waste of his valuable time, said, "Let's get on with it."

Stannard had no official capacity in this part of the investigation, and so far as the others were concerned their involvement constituted little more than an unnecessary diversion from more pressing matters. They nevertheless went over the smashed remains of the Corvette rapidly and efficiently. Little of the fiberglass body remained. Force of the impact had pushed the engine back toward the driver's seat, making access difficult to the location where Dr. Parlous died. After the first hour, they began grumbling as they made notes of their observations. Nothing they discovered suggested the incident was anything other than a routine traffic accident. When Stannard asked about the possibility of homicide, the men looked at him with disbelief. After that, he didn't speak but observed the level of efficiency diminished as the time passed.

The lead forensic officer halted the investigation at a quarter till five. "That's it. Let's wrap it up and analyze what we have. We'll have to move the car again so we can look at the steering and brakes. Other than that, I'd say this's all we can do here."

Stannard watched as they packed their gear. *Pezzati believes the car is evidence in a crime, but these yahoos are only interested in getting out of here. I don't see that they've been much help in the investigation. For whatever reason they showed up believing this was a waste of their time. The bloodstains should match Dr. Parlous' blood, but there may be more.* He paused to look into the wreck. He always said later that what happened next was his single-biggest break in the case. The angle of the car against the chain-link fence, unobstructed by the building next door, caught the sun as it moved across the southern sky, cloudless and bright. Something caused his eye to catch the reflection of an object previously unnoticed. "What's that?" he asked.

The lead officer stooped. A large fragment of glass lay on the floorboard, mostly hidden by the seat and the crumpled interior. "Looks like it's a piece of the rearview mirror," he opined. "I doubt if it means anything. It just got knocked off the windshield by the impact."

"Just the same," Stannard insisted, "let's take a look at it."

The officer frowned. He wanted to get home. "My son has a Little League baseball game, and now I'm going to miss the first inning. There'll be trouble in paradise if that happens." Nevertheless, he put on another pair of latex gloves and picked up the glass.

Stannard moved in behind the officer, and as he did so, something grabbed his attention. *Eyes, there are definitely eyes in that mirror.* He exclaimed, "Now that's interesting."

The officer didn't see what it was that Stannard found so fascinating. As he moved the piece of glass ever so slightly, his expression changed. Slowly, he drawled out the words, "Yeah, I see what you mean. Someone has stuck one of those transparent holograms on the mirror." The new discovery now had the officer's full attention. All concern for his son's ball game disappeared. He would just have to take the verbal abuse he knew would come from his wife and son.

"It's a what?" *Holograms I know; stick-on transparent holograms I never heard of.*

"A transparent hologram. They are used on identification cards, driver's licenses, passports, that sort of thing. It appears someone has found a more creative use for them. But why'd anyone want to glue something like that on a rearview mirror?"

Stannard did not hesitate, "Fear, they'd put something like that on a mirror to create fear."

"I don't get it, how can this create fear?

"It is easy if you know something about Dr. Parlous. Take a close look at those eyes. Tell me what you see."

"Well, first of all I see more than just the eyes. Part of the nose and forehead framed by brown hair are there."

"Yes, but the eyes, whatta you see in the eyes?"

"Intensity, I see intensity. The gaze is fixed." He held the mirror so it would have the same approximate position in the Corvette. He looked again. "Well, I'll be…"

"Now you see it, don't you?" Stannard smiled.

"Yeah, I do," the officer answered. "From this angle that face looks absolutely menacing."

"Bingo." A sardonic chuckle erupted from deep within Stannard. *Mutilation, taped wrists and ankles, wild and erratic driving, panicked expression according to the trooper, and now this. Malevolent eyes pasted to the rearview mirror. Dr. Parlous was frightened to death, maybe not literally but certainly figuratively, and you two didn't believe the car had any evidentiary value when you first arrived. If we hadn't found this, you would've been no help at all.* "Where can someone get a thing like that made?"

"Lots of places; you can order a machine over the Internet. I would imagine there are dozens of places in Kansas City where you can have 'em made to order for a small fee."

Stannard considered the last comment. "I seriously doubt this one was made that casually." *Roberto's 17th Century Bazaar Bizarre; I'll bet you can get one made there.* "Everything about the death of Dr. Parlous points to careful planning and execution." He looked at the cracked mirror. *We got lucky. The glue used to put the hologram on the mirror probably reinforced the glass just enough to keep it from shattering.* He stared at the image in the glass. *I know those eyes, but where...* Then it hit him. The eyes, the face—they were on the table in the condominium on Opa-Locka Lane. The eyes appeared to be those of Dr. Erin Kasalaitis, the ex-wife of Dr. Loren Parlous. *I don't know how she did it, but maybe Lorelei Parlous is right. Maybe the doctor's ex-wife is behind his death. One thing though is for certain, this's no suicide. It's a homicide. Now all I have to do is figure out how Erin Kasalaitis pulled it off. Those airline boarding passes and the hotel receipt are going to be difficult to overcome.*

Stannard spent the next two days following up leads and examining evidence. His first call was to Allied Security Systems, located at the corner of 58th Terrace and Kessler Lane in Merriam. The company provided security for Lake Quivira Estates. The small building surprised him when he arrived. It was not much bigger than the guard building at the entrance to the lake-view development. It occupied a triangular-shaped lot adjacent to the railroad tracks, and like most of the buildings in old Merriam it had been there since the early days of the last century. He wanted to look at the security record for the evening before and morning of Dr. Parlous's death. It was a loose end and unlikely to lead to

Erin Kasalaitis, but he believed in tying up loose ends. Besides, who knew what he might find? The owner was a lawyer who had decided there was more money to be made in operating a security company than in chasing ambulances in a city already overrun with ambulance chasers. He laughed at Stannard before refusing to give him access to the company's digital records. A quick call from Lieutenant Pezzati changed the man's attitude and his mind.

"Come on," the chastened man said after returning the telephone to its pedestal. *The smart ass isn't so smart now! It's amazing what a badge can open.* "There's a computer back here that you can use." He shrugged. "You must have a lot of time on your hands. You know that if it takes twenty-four hours to record something, it'll take twenty-four hours to watch it. Of course, you can always speed it up, but you probably won't catch what you're looking for. Speaking of that, what is it you're looking for?"

I don't know. I just have a nagging feeling there may be something on that tape. Maybe

Dr. Parlous did come home and leave; maybe someone followed him when he left. "You can never be sure what'll grab your attention."

"Suit yourself, it's your time." The one-time lawyer showed him how to operate the high-tech machine. *This's no jerry-rigged security system like the one Hyde put together. This is the real thing. Whatever*

227

happened that night at Lake Quivira, it's going to show up on this. "You'll have to be out of here by four-thirty. That's when I close up the office. Enjoy yourself." He turned to walk back to his office.

"Thanks," Stannard rejoined. "I doubt it'll be enjoyable, but hopefully it will be enlightening." He maneuvered the mouse to the date on the index and clicked on the icon. The date and time appeared in the upper right corner of the image, beginning at midnight on the morning of June 22. He used the fast-forward button to advance the image through the early hours of the day, slowing the image down only when a vehicle approached within range of the camera. Beginning at half past six, he slowed the image repeatedly as residents left for work. He saw Dr. Parlous's yellow Corvette leave the development at seven. He couldn't tell who was driving; he could only see the back of a man's head. An hour and a half later, he saw Lorelei Parlous's car leave.

Once the morning traffic ended, he fast-forwarded the image without pause for much of the afternoon. Lake Quivira didn't attract many visitors during the day. The FedEx and UPS delivery trucks made entrances and exits, as did the US Postal Service truck. He began to develop a headache from watching the fast-forward pace of the machine. He saw nothing of interest until around four, when both Dr. Parlous and his wife returned home in their cars. Fifteen minutes later they both left in his yellow Corvette.

Traffic picked up again in late afternoon when the residents began returning home from work. Then, at nine minutes before seven, he saw something unexpected. A silver sports car came into view. He backed up the image to take a second look. There it was, a 2005 Toyota MR2 Spyder; the same make and model of car driven by Dr. Parlous's son, Wills. He stopped the machine and went into the owner's office. "Can you give me a hand with the computer? I found something of interest but can't make it out. Is there a way to zoom in on the image so I can see it more closely?"

"Yeah, but I'd better get one of the techs to show you how to do it." The man punched a button on his phone and said, "Rex, come on over here. I need you to do some fine-tuning on the security tape. When? Now—what did you think, tomorrow? Okay." He turned back to Stannard. "Give him a couple of minutes. He's in the yard."

Rex proved to be something of a surprise. He was not your run-of-the-mill techno-nerd. The name Rex should have been a clue. The man was a T. rex. At over six feet tall and weighing at least two hundred and twenty pounds, he looked more like someone you expected to find at Gold's Gym just a few blocks down the road. Nevertheless, the man had an engaging personality. "Here, le' me help you with that thing," he said in a gravelly voice clearly altered by steroids.

Moments later, the image of the car that had been little more than a speck in the picture now filled the screen. "Can you sharpen that a little?" Stannard asked.

Rex adjusted the focus, and the image cleared. "Wow," Stannard exclaimed, drawing out his words. "Now, that is a surprise."

"Yeah?" Rex responded. "How's that?"

"It's just that I hadn't expected to see those two people together."

Rex made a noise that passed for a laugh, throaty and raw. "I know. We hear that a lot; not so much in the security side of our business but on the private surveillance side."

"I wondered about that. You don't look like the private security type. Those guys and gals are mostly a little overweight, people you can hire for less than I'd guess you make."

"Hey, man, don't knock 'em. They're good people; good at what they do. No one expects them to get into a fight. They watch and if things get hot, they call me...or the police...You through here now?"

"No," Stannard answered. "I want to watch a little more tape." He winced when Rex stared at him for using the word *tape*.

"Think you can operate this thing now? I got someplace to go."

"No problem. I believe I have a handle on it."

Rex started to leave.

"One more question—is this the only way in and out of Lake Quivira?"

"Nah, there's another way. The members have their own entrance. It's private. It comes in off Renner Road. You gotta have an electronic remote control to access the gate. There aren't any cameras over there. The residents like it that way." He left and Stannard settled back in the chair. His headache had mysteriously disappeared with the image of Lorelei Parlous and her stepson driving past the Lake Quivira Estates security camera. An hour later when Wills still had not left, he pressed the fast-forward button, slowing it down only when a car approached within the range of the camera. It was dark when the Toyota Spyder passed through on its way out into the night traffic. Nighttime and the lack of lighting at the Lake Quivira gate prevented him from seeing anything other than the car as it sped out of the development, not bothering to slow at the guard building, ignoring the stop sign, and proceeding west toward the interstate highway. The time was 9:50 p.m.

The rest of the tape took only a few minutes to watch. As the images rolled past in fast-forward, he slowed the process four times. The first three times because of residents arriving home from late engagements, the last time when he received another surprise. At 5:38 in the morning, a dark blue BMW sedan drove out the gate. Registration on the car he already knew would belong to Loren and Lorelei Parlous. The next time he saw the car was when it arrived back at Lake Quivira. The time then was 7:05 a.m. on the morning of June 23, just minutes after Dr. Parlous had nearly sideswiped his car.

Chapter Fourteen

Stannard met Lieutenant Pezzati at the Santa Fe Café on 87th Street in Overland Park at noon the following day. Both men arrived at the same time, pulling off the busy street into the strip mall housing not only the home-style café but also a body-piercing establishment, an Indian restaurant, and a Mexican cantina. The hostess at the cash register greeted the two men as they entered, calling Pezzati by name and asking what he had done with Pollard. "Who's this—your new partner, Detective Pezzati?"

"Nah, just an old friend who doesn't know where to eat in Overland Park." She seated them at a table near the back where they could have some privacy. Stannard had driven by the eatery many times on his way to the Johnson County Central Library to do research but had never stopped. It surprised him to find a down-home place with plastic-covered table-cloths and a 1960s décor. The patrons all appeared to be what most people would call regulars. Several said hello to Pezzati then looked inquisitively at Stannard.

Once seated and coffee poured, the men began talking at the same time. Stannard stopped and said, "You go first?"

Pezzati drank down a slug of the hot coffee, making Stannard wince. *How can anyone drink coffee like that? It'd take off the roof of my mouth if I tried that.* Pezzati didn't seem to notice the pained expression on his friend's face. "I think you're in for a surprise. We got quite a bit of info off the security tape Hyde gave us from the storage facility. Not as much as we would like but enough to fill in some pieces. The location of the storage units with reference to that stationary surveillance camera prevents us from seeing what was happening just outside the unit. The tape must've filled up just at the worst possible moment too." He stopped and took another swig of coffee as the waitress, Stacy, arrived to take their orders. Stannard waited impatiently for his friend to tell him more. Pezzati didn't appear to notice. He ordered his usual, steel-cut oatmeal with a side order of sausage and whole wheat toast.

When Stacy left their table, Pezzati picked up his narrative. "The quality of the picture isn't too good.

That's no surprise though. Wally went cheap on the equipment. Our lab guys shook their heads when I took the VHS tape in. They initially told me they doubted that he got anything from a homemade system like that. They speculated the whole setup was more for show than anything. It's obvious that computerized technology has marched right on past Wally."

"Yeah, yeah, but what did you get off it?"

"The yellow Corvette arrived at the storage facility at 12:17 a.m. There was only one man visible in the car, but we can't make out his face. You know the lighting at that place is terrible. The fact that the Corvette was a vintage model is the only thing that makes it easy to identify."

Stannard interrupted, "I know. I just spent several hours looking at the security tape from Lake Quivira."

Lieutenant Pezzati paused with a wry expression, the light in his eyes dancing. "Really? I'd be willing to bet you something about that!"

"Okay, what do you think?"

"Lorelei Parlous left Lake Quivira sometime early, just about sunrise."

Stannard's eyes widened. "How did you know?"

Pezzati looked triumphantly at his friend. "Part of it is observation, but a lot of it is intuition. Something you're famous for. About an hour after the Corvette pulled into the storage lot, another car, big one, looked like an old Cadillac, pulled in. Shortly after that it left. It was all quiet after that until a dark-colored car pulled up at the storage facility gate at 5:59. It just turned around in the entry drive and went back the way it came. We can't make out the make of the car from the angle of the picture, but Lorelei Parlous drives a dark blue BMW sedan. It could've been her."

Stannard nodded. "Maybe, maybe not. I don't think I'd go that far. All I can say for certain is that she, or someone driving her car, left Lake Quivira exactly twenty-one minutes earlier."

"We may never know for certain," Pezzati answered. "The tape stops at six a.m. Have you asked her about where she was going that early in the morning?"

"No, I haven't had a chance to talk to her. I just found the security recording yesterday. I wanted to get with you first. It makes sense to have her explain her whereabouts though." He stopped and considered what he said next. "There's more. She lied to me about the meeting with Parlous's ex-wife. She said she took a cab home, even made a big show at Jimmy's Jigger about ordering one, but she came home in her stepson's car."

Pezzati couldn't restrain a grin. "Really, and what time did he leave?"

"That is another strange thing. They're not supposed to get along that well, but he stayed for over two hours."

Lieutenant Pezzati probed his friend for more information. "I don't suppose you saw a car like Mrs. Parlous's coming up the ramp after Dr. Parlous nearly sideswiped you?"

"No, I was just angry. It's the nearest to road rage I've ever been."

"And while you came on down 435, did you see her car then?"

"I don't know. After I calmed down, I just watched the Corvette until it was out of sight. Now I wish I'd paid attention to the other cars, not that I would've necessarily recalled any one car unless the driver was doing something suspicious." He stopped and thought, then he asked, "Are you thinking Lorelei is responsible for Dr. Parlous's death? What about his ex-wife? We have information that points in both directions."

"I don't know. I don't even know whether Lorelei had anything to do with it. We are getting lots of circumstantial evidence, but it still doesn't lead us to a murder. As for Dr. Kasalaitis, why would she put that hologram on the rearview mirror? Why do something that would lead back to her?"

Stacy brought their food. Neither man spoke while he ate, each one thinking about the information they had exchanged.

"So," Pezzati asked, breaking the silence, "what's your next move?"

"I'm going to the office now. I'm uncertain. Whatta you think? Should we let Lorelei in on what we know or not?"

Pezzati did not hesitate. "We will eventually. For now, let's just play it along. There's a lot of security tape to examine now. Who knows what we'll find."

When Stannard left his office that afternoon, he drove to the building located at 78th Street and Parallel in Kansas City, Kansas. He wanted to talk to the woman named Clara at Hyde Property Investments. He arrived at the office a few minutes before five. Clara and Wally were preparing to leave.

"Oh, it's you," Clara said, not trying to disguise her distrust. "Whatta you want now?"

"Don't take long," Wally added, "we got tickets for the T-Bones doubleheader that starts at six—two for the price of one. We had tickets for a game with the Winnipeg Goldeyes that got rained out."

"Not a problem. This won't take but a second," Stannard answered, pulling his cell phone from his pocket. "I just wanted to see if either of you could identify a picture for me." He scrolled down the pictures until he found the one taken on Opa-Locka Lane. He held the phone out so Wally could see the image.

Wally took his hand and moved it so the picture on the tiny screen pointed directly at him. He frowned. "You ain't too good with a camera, are you? And no, I never saw that guy before. Who is he?"

He held the phone out so Clara could see the image.

"Anybody but you come in here with that picture and I'd tell 'em I didn't know him either. But since you aren't just anybody, and since you were in here asking about a particular man, I'd say he looks familiar. Can you zoom that thing in on his face?"

"Sure," he answered and adjusted the picture. The man's face now filled the screen, but the image lost some of its clarity.

"You're in luck, mister. That's the man who rented the storage box you now got."

"Are you certain?"

"Yeah, I'm sure. He talked funny—had an accent. Sounded like he come from somewhere down South. Where'd you get his picture?"

Stannard assumed his best aw-shucks attitude. "Come on, Clara, you know we have our ways." He reached in his pocket and took a twenty out of his billfold. Handing it to Wally, he said, "Thanks guys, have a couple of those dollar dogs and a beer on me."

They parted company in the parking lot, friends now. "You said you live close by Village West. Why don't you get your missus and go to the game with us?" Wally insisted.

Stannard didn't hesitate. "Thanks, I believe I will. Where are your seats?"

"We're on the first baseline about ten rows up."

The Canadian national anthem had just finished when Stannard and Caryl spotted Wally and Clara. The two couples found seats together just beyond first base and back another seven rows. "I love this place," Stannard commented after they were seated. "The Bones play a good brand of ball, and the price is right. Eight bucks for a ticket, parking is free, and the food is good. A night out here doesn't set you back thirty dollars. You can't even get in the game for that price across town, and that is per person."

He had barely finished when a foul ball sailed high over the stadium followed by the sound of breaking glass—the advertisement for Kryger Glass. The games finally ended five hours later. The T-Bones lost the first game, the completion of the rainout game stopped in the top of the third, by a score of six to five. They had blown a two- run lead when their pitcher consistently fell behind in the count. The pitching staff did better in the second game, shortened to just seven innings, giving up only one earned run in a five-to-two victory.

On the way home, Caryl asked, "What was that about? You never want to go anywhere on a workday night."

"No one ever proved to me you can't mix work and pleasure. I like baseball, and those people had information I needed. I don't mean to say they were holding anything back. A lot of times people simply don't know what they know."

"Like what?" Caryl wanted to know.

"For one thing, Wally told me they live across the road and just under a quarter mile from the storage facility. He said they're early risers because of their black Lab. She starts raising a ruckus by a little after five each morning, wanting to go out. Wally saw a car approach the facility just before six. He didn't recognize the vehicle. He said whoever was driving didn't have the code to open the gate, so someone on the inside opened it. He said it was a dark-colored sedan. That's all he could tell from where he stood waiting on Mandy to do her thing."

"Could he identify the driver?"

"No. He said he didn't get a look at the driver."

"I wonder why he didn't he tell you that when Lieutenant Pezzati and you talked to them."

"I asked him that. He said they didn't want the police snooping around that facility too much. He didn't say it, but I think he knows I already guessed they have some of those units rented to the wrong sort of people."

"Did he see who opened the gate?" Caryl prodded.

"No, he said it was too far away. All he could say was he thought a man had done it."

"Did he tell you anything else?"

"The rest of it was the same thing he told me when Lieutenant Pezzati was there."

They rode along in silence for a minute before Caryl reached over and touched him on the arm. "Stannard." She stopped.

He hesitated before answering, "What is it, Caryl?"

"I'm proud of you."

"You're what?" He nearly chuckled.

"No, Stannard, I mean I'm really proud of you."

"Well, thank you, Caryl. What brought that on?"

She squeezed his arm now. When she relaxed her hold, she continued. "There've been times this last month when I've thought this case has been good for you. Something's happening. You seem more like your old self."

He knew what she meant. He had felt a spark of the old confidence rekindling. It was as if some part of the old Stannard Jackson, the one everyone called St Jack and expected to someday become chief of detectives, had found its way out of the labyrinth where he'd languished for so many years. It frightened him just a little. What if he failed? "I feel it. After all the years of working easy cases, maybe I'm ready for this chance. I could be lost forever if I don't get this one right. I intend to see it through. There is something evil about what happened. There is so much manipulation; so much that's not what it seems; so much similarity in the psychology of the people that matches…" He gulped.

"You were going to say, so much like Russell, weren't you?"

"Exactly, I don't mean to sound paranoid, but it's almost like seeing his face in the rearview mirror. It's like seeing death approaching and driving me forward. Maybe, just maybe, looking at it backward that way will give me the peace I haven't had since then."

Caryl slid across the seat as they turned into the driveway to their house and kissed his cheek. "I believe. I hope you will. This case will be your redemption." Caryl wanted to believe the words. She doubted she would be able to withstand another bout of depression if her husband descended into that black hole again, absorbed in self-pity.

The following morning he called Pezzati to report what he'd learned. "Pezzati, St Jack here. I have some information for you. Those folks who run the storage facility identified a picture of the guy who rented the unit from them."

Pezzati's response revealed the surprise he felt. "You had a picture? How in the name of all that is holy did you get a picture of him?"

"It's a guy I saw outside Erin Kasalaitis's condominium while I was in Florida. He was eyeballing me, so while he was getting in his car I took his picture with my Blackberry." Another pause, "Nah, he didn't see me take his picture. After that he did follow me around town for a couple of days though. Maybe the doctor saw me. She had been standing on the balcony when I did it."

He listened to Pezzati talk for a minute then replied, "I didn't talk to him. Maybe I should have. He was at the airport when I left for Dayton." He listened to the response Pezzati made. "Yeah, I'll send you his picture as soon as we end this conversation. Maybe you can get the PD in Fort Walton Beach to ID him for us. It can't be too difficult if he's hanging around the clinic where Dr. Kasalaitis works."

A week later Lieutenant Pezzati called Stannard just as he prepared to leave his office with the news. "The PD at Fort Walton Beach made a positive ID on that guy in your picture. His name is Richard Simmoni. He goes by Riki for short. You were right—he does have a drug history, and a rap sheet too. It seems Mr. Simmoni has been in and out of prison since he was a teenager."

"What for?" Stannard wanted to know.

"That is the interesting part. His last brush with the law was for something he did not serve time for."

"Yeah?"

"Yep. He cooperated with the police in Saint Petersburg on a murder for hire. It seems someone wanted to pay him to kill a lawyer in Tampa. He didn't like the deal and helped make a case against his principal."

"He sounds like a real sweetheart. I don't think I'd want to put much reliance on a guy like that. How would you know when he might turn on you?

"My thought exactly."

"Is there anything else?"

"Yes, the Fort Walton Beach PD can't find him. He was last seen three days ago, the same day they made the ID."

"Did the police talk to Dr. Kasalaitis?"

"They did at that. She acknowledged he'd been a patient at the clinic on and off for several months. They said she seemed a little uncomfortable when they asked her about him. She volunteered that he did some work around her condominium some-times—said she felt sorry for him; he seemed like a nice fellow who just got mixed up with drugs."

Convenient. "Is that it?"

"Not quite. She must've given them a bad time about how long it was taking to get her insurance proceeds."

Stannard chuckled. "As if they had anything to do with that, huh?"

"That's it. Have a nice day." Lieutenant Pezzati rang off.

Chapter Fifteen

Stannard had been working on the case for more than two months. Labor Day had come and gone. Early signs of autumn were in the air, cool nights and shortened days. The yellow tint of scrub trees came first then the reds and orange of the oaks and maples. The deep red of the burning bushes edging the Jackson property in Wyandotte County came last. Stannard loved the season; it gave the homestead a Currier and Ives appearance, the hills ablaze with color, dotted with rustic buildings, and carved by the twisting curve of the roadway winding its way to unseen destinations.

When he awakened, the recollection of his conversation the day before with Lieutenant Pezzati was foremost on his mind. *A glimmer of light at last.* He looked forward to getting back to work on the case. The pressure from management for him to finish the investigation had increased as the deadline set by the policy approached. He had no doubt Dr. Loren Parlous had been murdered, and he suspected that one of the wives had something to do with it. Intuition told him to look at the doctor's first wife. The information provided by Pezzati about Riki Simmoni seemed to support the assertion of Lorelei Parlous that Dr. Erin Kasalaitis had been behind her ex-husband's death. A killer for hire may not work for one principal, but a drug head may be willing to work for someone who can provide a legal supply of drugs. *If I can make the connection between them and put Simmoni in Kansas City at the time Dr. Parlous died, maybe I can save the company a bundle. Pezzati may need evidence beyond a reasonable doubt to make a charge stick, but all I need is a preponderance of evidence to uphold a wrongful death case.* Stannard would save the company $4 million, and that would mean a nice bonus at the end of the year.

When he arrived at his office an hour later, he got an even greater surprise than he had so far experienced. Settled behind his desk, he began opening his mail. The gray-colored "Confidential" envelope on top of the interoffice mail caught his eye. When he opened it, his eyes opened even wider. He read a cover memorandum.

Claim for Life Insurance Benefits.

Claim date: September 11, 2006

Policy Type: Ten-year Term expiring June 17, 2016.

Southern Metropolitan Life Insurance Company.

Name of Deceased: Loren Parlous, Lake Quivira, Kansas.

Name of Claimant: Lorelei Parlous, Lake Quivira, Kansas.

Amount of Claim: $1,500,000.00, with double Indemnity for death through accident or misadventure.

Nature of Investigation: Cause/Method of Death

He stopped for a moment to consider the information contained on the cover sheet. *Dr.*

Loren Parlous was not worth $4 million dead. He was worth $7 million dead, but only if suicide wasn't the cause of his death. Hello, Lorelei! That explains why you've been so adamant about his death not being suicide. He kills himself and you don't benefit. Why not just tell me so?

Flipping pages, he found the policy application, dated six weeks before the day the doctor died. The agent had delivered the policy to Dr. Loren Parlous's home, but it didn't indicate whether the policy had been delivered to Dr. Parlous or his wife. The owner of the policy was Dr. Loren Parlous. He checked the address of the agent. Now that's interesting—the agent's office is just three blocks from the doctor's office. *What does Lorelei Parlous know about the issuance of this policy? Had her husband discussed it with her prior to making the application? Why not have it delivered to his office rather than his home? Wouldn't that be more convenient? Why file the claim at this time?* The questions came fast; the answers remained obscure.

In the modern world, revenge, money, sex, or drugs accounted for the vast majority of premeditated homicides. He now had two people in Kansas City with a motive to want Dr. Parlous dead, even more if you counted the ones he may have abused but who hadn't yet surfaced. Unfortunately, in this case all four motives could be loosely in play. His ex-wife, Dr. Kasalaitis, had revenge and money as motives. Money could also be a motive for Lorelei Parlous. What about the man he'd seen leaving Dr. Kasalaitis's condominium? He had the appearance of a man who'd do anything for a reliable supply of drugs, and he had a history of being a man willing to hire out his unique talents.

The thought of Riki Simmoni jolted him. Okay, so now I have three reasons to make a call on Lorelei Parlous. He picked up the telephone on his desk and dialed the cell phone number Lorelei Parlous had given him weeks before.

"Mrs. Parlous, Stannard Jackson here. I was wondering, would it be convenient for me to stop by if you are home? There are some things I'd like to discuss with you."

He waited while she answered. "That would be fine. Besides, there's something I want to show you."

Another pause.

"Fine, I'll see you then." He returned the phone to its base. The stack of routine paper on his desk beckoned, but he was in no mood to shuffle paper. He looked at his watch, a quarter after nine. He had seven hours before his appointment with Lorelei Parlous.

Stannard could not explain later why he did what he did next. He would always insist it was nothing more than an investigator's hunch. He left his office in Corporate Woods and drove north up Interstate 35 to the Johnson Drive exit in Mission. At the offices of the company handling security for Lake Quivira Estates, he asked the one-time lawyer in charge for access to the security video. He wanted to see the tapes for the period two days before and two days after the date when Lorelei Parlous filed her claim for benefits under this second policy.

"I suppose you're still snooping into the death of that doctor out there," the man remarked.

"Yes. It seems like this one will never go away."

"I don't suppose you want to tell me what you're looking for."

"No, not really, but if you have a problem I'm certain Lieutenant Pezzati will be happy to vouch for me. Here, I'll get his number for you."

"That won't be necessary. You know where to go!"

Stannard could not help but smile inwardly. He'd often heard it said that telling someone to go to hell in a polite way was the ultimate indicator of breeding. Five hours later, his eyes numb and itching, he saw something that interested him. The Toyota Spyder belonging to Wills Parlous passed through the gates and left an hour later. He looked at the date and time. The date was the same as that on the beneficiary claim, September 11. That makes four things to discuss with the doctor's widow. He watched to the end of the tape but saw nothing more of interest.

At five minutes before the hour of four, Stannard stopped at the security building at Lake Quivira and told the guard on duty where he was headed. After being waved through, he rounded the corner, heading for the fortress home of Lorelei Parlous. He parked on the concrete pad above the house and wondered if Mrs. Parlous had watched his arrival. He was sure of it when he walked around the house and onto the deck. The oversized front door stood open, and a dazzling Lorelei Parlous greeted him.

He stammered out his greeting. "I...I...I hope I'm not interrupting. We had an appointment at four, remember?"

"Of course I remember. I was expecting you. Did you think I was looking for someone else?"

Trying to recover, he responded, "It's...Well, it's just that you appear to be dressed for an early evening out."

"No, no," Lorelei answered, "I was only expecting you." She smiled and her dark eyes sparkled.

Stannard was now more flustered than ever. *She's flirting with me again. What's that all about?* Then he noticed. *Her eyes; I hadn't noticed before. Her eyes are eerily like those of Erin Kasalaitis.*

"Won't you come on in? Now, what is it that is so important? I haven't seen you for weeks."

He could smell her perfume as he moved past her. *Exotic.* She moved toward the open door as he entered, making certain their bodies would brush. He felt the smooth silk blouse against his arm and the warmth of her body. She moved beside him, slipping her arm inside his as she led him into the living room.

"I was planning to have a cocktail. Can I fix you something?"

"No, but you go ahead."

She crossed the room to a Mediterranean-style cabinet, where she opened the doors and lifted the top, exposing an ornate bar. Moments later, she sat on the sofa beside him with her long, bare legs crossed, exposing more flesh than he thought necessary.

There it is again—that coquettish look. "I believe you had something you wanted to show me," she purred.

Regaining some of his lost composure, he answered, "Yes, I do." He reached in his shirt pocket and extracted a copy of the cell phone photograph. "The quality isn't too good, but I wondered if you could identify who that man is?"

Lorelei paused to look at the picture. She didn't answer immediately, and when she did, all she said was, "No, I don't believe I've ever seen that man before. Who is he?"

Stannard felt the presence of the man St Jack as his long-lost police senses now kicked in.

The death of Dr. Loren Parlous had brought back so much, and now this. *She's lying. I can tell she's lying. No one who had never seen someone before would take that long. She was considering her answer.* "It's the man who rented a storage unit up in KCK. It was the same storage unit where we believe your husband was tortured." He looked at her closely to see what her reaction would be to the news that they'd found the location of the surgical procedures.

Lorelei Parlous did change expression; she no longer smiled, but she still sat close to him.

"You didn't tell me the police had found out where Erin Kasalaitis did that." He could feel the heat of her body.

"We just found out about the storage unit the other day. I haven't seen you since then. Besides, I keep telling you, we don't have any evidence that Erin Kasalaitis did anything..." He started to say something more but stopped, waiting for Lorelei.

He felt certain Lorelei intended to respond, but she did not. An awkward silence ensued.

"So then," she said at last, "I suppose you are going to pay out on her claim for the insurance?" She stopped again, just long enough to draw a deep breath. "And what about my claim?"

Stannard didn't hesitate. "That's another matter I wanted to discuss with you. You didn't tell me you were beneficiary on a life insurance policy."

"I didn't tell you because I didn't know about it until my lawyer got a court order to open Loren's safe-deposit box."

"I thought as much." The little white lies were coming more easily to him now. He waited for the comment to sink in before continuing. "What really made me wonder about your claim was the timing of a visit your stepson paid to you the day you filed the claim."

Lorelei got up from her seat and walked away. At the liquor cabinet, she took her time fixing another drink. "Are you certain you don't want anything?" she asked.

"Positive."

She walked back, this time sitting on the other side of the large coffee table. *Interesting body language—defensive.* "Well, I have never had three million dollars before, and I didn't know what to do with it, so I called Wills. I told you he handled large investments for private clients."

"So you said, but the policy is not for three million dollars; it's for one and a half million."

"I know, but Erin Kasalaitis killed Loren. I'll gladly spend all of the three million I may get just to prove she did it."

Stannard responded, "That won't be necessary. We have an interest in this as well." They sat for a moment, each waiting for the other to speak. He broke the silence at last. "One more thing. I've been looking at security tapes from the front gate. There have been some surprising guests coming and going, some real surprises for me." He waited for what seemed another eternity.

Lorelei Parlous was a good actor, but her eyes gave away the stress. When she finally answered, the words were noncommittal. "What have you seen that concerns you?"

"I've seen Wills Parlous entering and leaving Lake Quivira at some disturbing times. I can only suppose he was coming here." He waited again. "And on the morning your husband died, I saw what appears to be your car leaving at a highly suggestive time."

Months later he would recall her eyes seemed to moisten when she said, "Wills has been here, but I can't talk about it. I would like to, but I simply can't. Will you believe me?"

Stannard rose from his seat. "You realize how this looks. Only you can explain it; or should I go talk to Wills?"

Lorelei looked devastated. "He won't talk to you; you know that."

"And what about you driving out of here on the morning your husband died?"

Silence! At last she answered, "I went looking for Wills, but I can't say why."

At the door to the fortress house, Stannard stopped. "One more thing." He saw the fear and uncertainty in her eyes.

"What's that?"

"We found a transparent hologram stuck to the rearview mirror on your husband's car."

He heard an audible gasp escape from her as she looked away. She didn't answer. "I wondered why Dr. Parlous didn't come home instead of continuing on past Holliday Drive. This house is a fortress and it has security provided by a retired police officer. Dr. Parlous must have been terrified. Why didn't he come here, where he'd be safe?"

Her voice trembled as she answered, "I don't know."

She is upset. This caught her off guard. Why? Was she expecting something different? For that matter why should she expect anything? Is she being forthright with me or is she holding back? The conversation ended in a jumble of broken sentences. Neither person knew what more to say.

Lorelei watched Stannard from the security monitor. He stood beside his car and looked up at the camera mounted on the corner of the garage. His stare frightened her. Her reaction to the news about the hologram had bothered him. She was sure of that. She continued to watch until Stannard was out of sight then she called her stepson, Wills Parlous.

Chapter Sixteen

Caryl Jackson no longer watched out the window of their house for her husband to arrive home at six fifteen. It would be St Jack who came home now, not Stannard Jackson. She felt a mixture pride and relief intermingled with a sense of loneliness and despair watching his confidence grow as the case progressed. He was pulling away again but this time from confidence, not depression. The years since Russell's death had molded him into a plodder, a man who found comfort in routine. In a way she found that comforting as well. The compulsive behavior had slowly sloughed off like the skin of a snake. What remained was new and comfortable. Still, she had to admit there was much to like about what she saw. The excitement had spilled over to every aspect of their life together. Caryl still watched for him to come home but now it was not for reassurance that he was safe. Now she watched for his arrival inwardly with a tingling excitement that her husband and lover, the father of her only child, would soon be home. He talked more about his day than he had for years. She enjoyed that. The years of darkness had been a strain not only on him. They had threatened their marriage. For that reason, she was concerned when she saw him step out of the car. His furrowed brow spoke of doubt and worry. He didn't park in the garage but stopped on the driveway. He trudged back to the mailbox at the end of the pavement. He opened the box, took out the contents, and examined each envelope. She watched from the window and saw the distraction etched on his face. He walked slowly back to the house, bypassing the car that he left in the driveway.

"Are you all right?" she asked as he came through the door. She'd watched the mood swings before; she knew how fast they rose and how completely they crashed.

"Yes. I just came from a meeting with Lorelei Parlous. You know, the case gets more complicated all the time." He suddenly reached out to her, not so much hugging her as clinging to her. "I am sorry," he said with feeling. "I wouldn't have you worry for anything in the world. Things have become so much better for me, us, since I started working on this case. I'm just perplexed, that's all." He stepped back. "Enough of serious talk, okay? Let's just have a nice quiet evening. No, better yet, let's go to Wellborn Barbeque for dinner."

"I would like to, but that isn't possible."

"And why not?"

"You old coot," she chided. "Wellborn Barbeque changed names years ago. It's the Hickory Log. If you want to take me to Hickory Log, the answer is yes."

Stannard feigned mortification. "Okay, okay, so I'm living in the past. Whatever the name, they still have the best burnt ends in town, and the Croatian coleslaw is to die for!"

Five minutes later, they left the house and drove east toward the city. It wasn't until they had gone almost all the way around the west side of Wyandotte County Lake that he noticed the dark green Ford Focus. When he reached Leavenworth Road, he turned east. The Ford Focus had dropped well behind him, but when it reached the stop sign he noticed it too turned east.

As they drove he continued to watch the car in his rearview and side mirrors. Caryl noticed. "Is there something wrong?" she asked.

"I don't know. There's been a car following us. It may be coincidence, but..." He slowed down as he approached 77th Street, wanting to time his arrival as the light turned yellow. He watched to see if the car following him would pass. It did not. At the light, Stannard sped up, going through the intersection as the light turned red. He looked back. The Ford Focus had gone through behind him. *He ran the light. He is following us.* The car once more dropped back a half block but continued to follow. *Whoever is driving that car is either stupid or not very good at tailing someone.* He said nothing to Caryl, who appeared irritated. "Stannard, whatever has come over you? You never drive like that."

"We're being followed," he answered. "I wanted to be certain."

"What are you going to do?" Caryl seemed worried now.

"Nothing. I'm not going to do anything. We don't want to get into some sort of confrontation or road rage incident."

He continued to drive slowly until he reached 51st Street. A short block later, he nearly stopped as he looked down Wellborn Lane. A sigh of relief escaped from him when he saw a place to park in one of the handful of parking spaces adjacent to the entrance.

The Ford Focus continued down Leavenworth Road.

"Who was that?" Caryl asked as they sat in the car.

"I don't know. The sun was low enough in the sky that I couldn't identify the driver in the rearview mirror." He considered calling the police, then decided against it. What could they do? Nothing had happened.

Fifteen minutes after they had ordered their meals, one of the regulars entered the restaurant. "Anyone in here own that 2005 Taurus?"

"Yeah," Stannard called back, "I do. Is anything wrong?"

"No, but there mightta been. When I came around the corner there was a man lurking around the front of the car. He dropped down between it and the building when he saw me. I made eye contact and he took off."

"Did you see what he looked like?" Stannard asked.

"No, he ran across the street to the parking lot at the muffler shop. I can tell you this—he's not in very good condition. He seemed to have trouble running. He headed toward a dark green car. By the time I parked and got to the front door, he was long gone."

An hour later, Stannard and Caryl were back at their house. Caryl took a bath. Stannard used the time alone to pull down the box hidden behind some books. He opened the box and removed the .38-caliber Bulldog. He groped farther back until he felt a small, dust-covered box. He pulled it out.

I wonder if these are any good. They've been there for what, fifteen years? He loaded the pistol with five cartridges, placed it out of sight in the magazine rack beside his chair, and turned on the television set. He sat reclining in his chair when Caryl entered the room and took her place in the dual recliner separated by a built-in table. She reached across and touched his arm.

"Are you all right?" she asked. "You've been a little tense ever since you noticed that car following us."

"No, it's okay. It's probably nothing. You just never know. At first I thought maybe it was someone planning a bump and rob, but there was only one person in the car." It was a lie, but he did not want her to worry.

After the weather forecast ended, Caryl announced she was going to bed. Stannard followed once the sports report ended, but he didn't go to sleep. He waited until Caryl had fallen into a deep sleep before getting up and sitting quietly in the den with the lights out. *Whoever followed us, it was no random act. They were after something or...* He didn't want to continue with the thought. *...or else they're after me!* Regardless of everything else, he would not allow his wife to be hurt; he would stay awake all night listening, watching. After that, he made a quiet reconnaissance around the house every fifteen minutes or so.

At a little after one in the morning, he heard a noise outside and tiptoed to the farthest door away from where he heard the sound, thankful that door was at the far end of the house from where Caryl lay sleeping. Once outside, he crept around the house, using the shadow of the dwelling to conceal him from the full moon. The autumn night sky was clear and cool. He shivered. *Is it the cold or fear?* Coming around the corner to where he heard the noise, he became even more alert. He felt the weight of the pistol in his hand, an unfamiliar feeling after all those years.

He stepped out. "Hold it right there, fellow." It was nothing more than a hoarse whisper.

There was no answer, only the sound of running.

He realized he was now perspiring as he lowered the hammer on the .38. The deer had bolted, giving him a brief glimpse of something white as it high-tailed it into the trees. Only the nibbled leaves of the hosta plants remained as evidence of the intruder.

After that, the night passed peacefully.

The following morning he told Caryl what he had done and reminded her that living in the country came with a certain amount of risk. He asked her to call her sister to come stay with her; better yet, she should go there. She promised to do so.

At six thirty Stannard backed his car out of the garage and proceeded to the end of the driveway, where he turned right toward the city. He had gone only a hundred yards when he saw the dark green Ford Focus backed into a field entrance. He slowed as he passed. He saw a man slumped against the driver's side door. He reached across to his briefcase and removed the pistol. *It ends here! If you are who I think you are, it's going to end here and now!* Stopping the car just beyond the row of trees along the side of the road, he walked back to the entrance, making certain to keep the trees as a shield. At the last tree, he stopped. Twenty feet of open ground separated him from the Ford. He stood and watched. The man appeared to be asleep. He moved cautiously forward around the back of the car, coming up on it along the driver's side, the pistol in his right hand. He reached for the door handle with his left hand. Then he saw the man's face. It had an unhealthy bluish hue.

Riki Simmoni. It was you following me last night, but what're you doing here? Why didn't you come to the house? That had to be your plan. When he yanked open the door, he expected trouble. Instead, Riki Simmoni tipped out, coming to rest head down, still held inside the car by his legs. Stannard reached out with his left hand to feel Simmoni's carotid artery. His pulse was faint.

No matter what his feelings toward the man, Stannard did the decent thing. He dialed 911 and called for an ambulance. He then called Detective Pezzati on his cell phone.

The voice that answered sounded sleepy. "Pezzati here. Whatta you want? I had a late night, and now I have an early morning thanks to you, whoever you are."

"The 'whoever' is the guy you call St Jack, and I have some very interesting news."

"This had better be good. What is it?"

"I have news of the whereabouts of one Riki Simmoni."

"Okay?"

"He's here. He is about a hundred yards from my house, and he's barely breathing."

"You didn't do anything stupid, did you?"

"No, I would have but didn't need to. I found him that way when I left for work. The paramedics and KCK police are on the way now. If you want in on this, you'd better hurry."

"You haven't touched anything, I hope."

"Come off it," Stannard answered. "I'm a former cop, you know."

Two days after the discovery of Riki Simmoni in the field entrance off Wolcott Road,

Stannard Jackson—St Jack—had still not heard anything. Caryl had been emotionally distraught when he returned to the house after the police and first responders finished their work. She understood what it meant. The man in the car had come to kill her husband and, if she was in the way, to kill her as well. She had cried while he tried to comfort her. Later they argued. She had been proud of the way her husband came alive early on in the investigation. Now she worried. No, she was afraid. He in turn responded to her fear with anger, not at Caryl but at whoever it was behind the sudden appearance of a man who had to be an assassin.

The afternoon of the second day, Stannard called Lieutenant Pezzati to find out what the police had learned.

"Early days, I am afraid," Pezzati answered. "We know a lot, and we don't know anything. I'll tell you what we do know."

Stannard waited.

Not hearing a response, Pezzati continued. "First of all he hasn't been able to talk to us. He was practically dead when they got him to Providence Hospital. He has been on a ventilator the whole time."

"What about the car? It had a rental car sticker."

"Yeah, he picked it up at National Car Rental out at KCI. The airport car rental agent actually remembered him."

Stannard considered the odds of that happening. "He must've made quite an impression. What'd he do, cause a scene?"

"No, nothing of the kind. They thought he was drunk or something. His speech was slurred and he looked sleepy—you know, his eyelids were droopy. He was polite and convinced them he was just not feeling well and taking medication. They insisted he take out all the extra insurance."

Stannard couldn't help but notice the insurance dig. "Nice one, Pezzati."

"Yeah, I thought you'd like that. Anyway, it isn't anything against the insurance business. They just wanted to be certain they were covered in case he went to sleep and had an accident."

"What time was that?"

"About eleven o'clock the morning before you found him."

"I saw him about six-thirty that evening when he followed us from the house to a barbecue place on Leavenworth Road. He'd been in town for about seven hours. I wonder what he'd been doing?"

"I don't have a clue on that, but I can tell you one thing that will ring your bell."

"What's that?"

Pezzati waited, wanting the full dramatic effect, before answering, "He caught a flight out of KCI on the afternoon of June 23 going to Florida."

Stannard's voice had a note of urgency. "Great news, we've got to talk to him…"

269

"Hold on a minute," Pezzati interrupted. "There's another call coming in. I'll have to take it, but don't hang up."

Stannard stayed on the silent phone line for at least five minutes.

"St Jack, you still there?"

"Yeah, what took so long? I thought you intended to get rid of whoever it was."

"I couldn't; it was the KCKPD. Riki Simmoni died about an hour ago. Whatever he'd been doing, I don't suppose we'll ever know now."

Stannard wanted more information but understood his responsibility to Caryl had priority. "Pezzati, I need to go home and be with my wife. She's still in a bad way over this. Can we meet tomorrow at the Santa Fe Café and talk?"

"Sure, what time?"

"Early. They open at six. Whatta you say we meet there at six thirty?"

"Fine, I'll see you then."

Stannard left the office early that day, arriving at the field entrance while it was still light. He wanted to make a search of the area on his own. He had no idea what he was looking for. All he knew with certainty was that if any evidence remained, he would have to be the one to find it. All he found was the filter from a Marlboro cigarette in the ditch a good ninety feet from where Simmoni had parked the car. He turned it in his hand, examining it in detail. In the center he thought he could see a small hole. *What if there is a hole in the filter? I don't even know for certain it came from a cigarette smoked by Simmoni. It could just as easily been tossed there by one of the investigators after they finished their work.*

Stannard arrived at the Santa Fe Café ten minutes early for the meeting with Pezzati the following morning. Caryl had slept through the night for the first time since he'd found the unconscious Riki Simmoni in his rental car. He felt relief when she kissed him good-bye; she no longer trembled, and her voice no longer had the frightened sound of a child afraid of the dark.

The breakfast special was French toast with eggs and bacon. He ordered that. Pezzati studied the menu, apparently more concerned with ordering his thoughts than ordering breakfast.

The waitress cleared her throat. "What would you like to order?"

"Huh? Oh yeah, give me the oatmeal. Eggs do funny things to me."

"Well...," Stannard left the word hanging in the air along with the smell of coffee and bacon.

"Right," Pezzati responded. "First of all, Simmoni had a bad case of what the doctors at Providence Medical Center called botulinum poisoning."

"Never heard of it."

"Sure you have. I didn't know it by that name either. Simmoni died from botulism."

"So, what does that mean?"

"No one seems to be certain. The guy was a picture of health for a man in his midforties with a drug problem. The drug use hadn't limited his physical prowess in any way, according to the medics."

"How does someone in that state of health come down with botulism?"

"From eating tainted food, usually. You know, we've all heard about eating something out of an old can, one with a lid that's bulged. You can also get it through an open wound, but we can rule that out. He didn't have a scratch on his body. In rare cases, people have contracted botulinum toxin in the air. That is so unlikely...well, there's no point in even going there."

"Were there any food wrappers in the car, anything that would tell us where he'd eaten? I don't believe either of us thinks this is an accidental death."

"I just don't know," Pezzati answered. "There's nothing to say it was anything other than an illness. The forensic boys didn't get a chance to go over the car. The car rental company had cleaned it all up. They weren't very happy though. Simmoni was a smoker, and he'd been smoking in the car. The car stunk of cigarette smoke. He'd even stubbed out a cigarette in that coin box they put in cars now instead of ashtrays. Simmoni must've been a real 'throwback' not to know the difference."

Stannard recalled the car Simmoni drove in Florida. "It makes sense to me that he'd been smoking in the car. You should've seen his car. I didn't see inside it but it had to be a mess." He thought for a moment. His mind began to connect the rental car to the point about Simmoni smoking in it. "I found a cigarette butt on the ground not far from where we found his body." *Could there be a link?* He stopped again to consider the cause of death. "So what killed him was botulism. But how does that kill you?"

"That's part of the problem. The docs say it takes at least a couple of days for botulism to kill you. He hadn't been here that long, so he must've contracted it before he left Florida. Botulinum toxin is nasty stuff. It causes muscle problems that end up in paralyzing the muscles controlling inhalation. You suffocate."

Stannard thought for a second before answering. "That would explain why the man at the Hickory Log said the guy he saw messing with my car seemed to have some sort of problem when he ran away."

Pezzati said nothing.

"I guess the police are satisfied this was a simple case of food poisoning, then?"

Pezzati nodded. "That seems to be the official position."

Stannard bristled. "Well, that doesn't make any sense to me. It's way too much of a coincidence."

"Hey, buddy, don't get upset with me. I said it was the official position. I didn't say it had anything to do with what I believe."

"Sorry, pal; it's just that with Simmoni dead, I don't know where to go next. I have one more lead to follow, but I don't hold out much hope it will lead anywhere. Lorelei knows more than she is telling me. When I pressed her about her stepson, she clammed up. I told her maybe I should just talk to him, and she said, 'He won't talk to you; you know that.' "

"I could bring him in and have a sit-down session with him in an interrogation room, if you think it would do any good."

"It can't hurt anything. The worst thing that can happen is he refuses to answer or lawyers up." Stannard didn't know what more to say. His corporate home office pressured him more every day to conclude his investigation. The company wanted a finding of suicide on the Parlous death. He knew that would never hold up. He'd pinned his hopes for denial of the claim on proving Dr. Kasalaitis had been behind the death. Simmoni had been his only link, and with Simmoni dead that hope dwindled. "What about the criminal case?" he asked.

Pezzati shook his head. "It's an open file, but all the leads are proving to be dead ends. If something doesn't happen soon, it'll probably move to the bottom of the stack. You know what that means—cold case."

"That's too bad. I thought we were about to get somewhere with this when we got an ID on Simmoni. I'm not ready to give up, even if you fellows don't know where to go." *That sounded tough, but I don't have any idea where to go now either, except to pressure Wills Parlous.*

Lieutenant Pezzati proved to be as good as his word. He did bring Wills Parlous in for questioning after receiving a detailed briefing from Stannard, who watched the interview on the closed-circuit TV monitor and listened to every word. Lorelei Parlous had been only half-right; Wills would not talk to Stannard, but he also refused to talk to the police. Pezzati did all he could to pressure the young man into telling them whatever he knew about the incident. He refused to talk and refused to ask for a lawyer. In the end, Wills Parlous walked out of the police station with a smug grin on his face, got in his fancy sports car, and raced out of police headquarters.

With that failure, the official police investigation moved from active to cold.

An hour later Stannard arrived back at his own office. Marjorie collared him the moment he walked through the door. "The boss wants to see you."

He didn't like the tone of her voice. "Okay. Anything I should know about?"

"I am afraid so. The home office is getting pressure from some lawyers to pay out on the claim filed by Dr. Kasalaitis."

"But I'm not finished with my investigation. Here look at this." He held up a Heath candy wrapper tied in a slip knot.

"What's that supposed to be?"

"Just what it looks like; we found one like it in the storage unit where Dr. Parlous was tortured."

"That doesn't prove anything." Big Ed reached in his waste basket and pulled out a candy wrapper he had tied in a knot. "Lot's of people probably do it. Where'd that one come from?"

"The parking lot at PD headquarters. It was on the ground next to where Wills Parlous was parked."

"Sorry, Stannard, you can save it for the boss. I got my orders and you know that we gotta follow them. We may be an independent investigative company but we are also a wholly owned subsidiary of the insurance company. They call the tune and this one is over."

He walked down the hall to the corner office. The meeting with Big Ed lasted only about five minutes. In the end, by agreeing to the payout on the Kasalaitis claim, he wheedled a promise that he could have another week on Lorelei Parlous's claim. After that, the company would pay it too.

Chapter Seventeen

Stannard and his boss met with the company lawyers a week later at corporate headquarters in Omaha. He knew he was beaten. When the case review ended, he received the decision he dreaded. They would pay out on the claims by both Lorelei Parlous and Dr. Erin Kasalaitis. He'd never believed he had enough evidence to prove Dr. Kasalaitis's involvement beyond a reasonable doubt, but it galled him to hear the conclusion that there was insufficient evidence to deny her claim based on a theory of wrongful death. The lawyers insisted they simply didn't have enough evidence to prevail in a civil lawsuit. They were very nearly brutal in announcing he hadn't been able to amass even a preponderance of evidence.

The company issued the check a few days later then sent it by registered mail to Fort Walton Beach for delivery to Dr. Erin Kasalaitis. The agent reported the doctor appeared to have a smug expression as he secured the appropriate receipts.

Three days after that, Stannard received a letter bearing a postmark from Peculiar, Missouri, one of the many small towns on the south side of Kansas City. The three-and-a-half by six-and-a-half-inch envelope was addressed to Stannard Jackson at his home. It had no return address. Inside the envelope was a single sheet of common multipurpose paper, the sort you bought at any Walmart. Upon reading the note, Stannard Jackson collapsed in his chair, the note falling to the floor beside him. When Caryl picked it up, she understood why. In bold-face, four-teen-point font, she read the following words:

"I know you St Jack, and you know why!

You lost years ago, and you lose again!

Why not end it all yourself, you cowardly cripple!

If you don't maybe I will take care of you and your wife, Caryl!

You remember, just as I did Russell."

The envelope and letter were tested by the Kansas City police forensic laboratory. The envelope had prints of so many people who handled the mail, including the Jacksons, that it would never be conclusive. The envelope had been moistened using tap water. When the residue on the envelope was tested, they found it came from the Kansas City, Missouri, water department, indicating the letter had probably been typed in KC and taken to Peculiar for mailing as some perverted joke. The letter itself had fingerprints and DNA only from Stannard and Caryl Jackson. After that, Caryl worried about her husband's state of mind. He began to sink back into the shell that had been his refuge for over a decade. Slavelike adherence to his routine once more became the norm. The spontaneity he had shown during the investigation disappeared. The people in his office observed his listless behavior. Eventually, his employer suggested he see a doctor. A prescription for a mild dosage of Paxil to offset the debilitating depression and anxiety attacks failed to have the desired effect. His doctor prescribed the stronger Prozac, but it dulled his ability to work effectively as an investigator. In the end, his employer insisted he take temporary medical disability leave.

Autumn turned to winter; a cold, wet Kansas winter. Rain fell, soaking the fallen leaves.

Wind blew from the north, driving the damp, thirty-degree air through coats. As the weather worsened, so did Stannard's depression. He obsessed over the death of his son and the threat they had received in the mail. With the depression his marriage suffered. Caryl had worried during the weeks of near-manic devotion to the investigation that with the highs the lows would soon follow. She wondered if she would be able to survive another incident.

In January, he left the house and drove to the Westport area in Kansas City, Missouri. He went to the location of Roberto's 17th Century Bazaar Bizarre intending to confront Roberto Bertonelli about the pictures he'd seen on his first visit. He found the building locked. Bertonelli had closed the business one night and not returned. His mind confused by disappointment and the pain of failure, Stannard wandered in and out of the adjoining shops. No one seemed to know anything about Roberto Bertonelli. To a person, they were all delighted the strange man had gone. That fact only added to the pain he felt.

Lieutenant Pezzati continued to phone. The two had rekindled their old friendship during the weeks of collaboration, but Stannard no longer wanted to talk to him. Only Marjorie at the office maintained personal contact. The loneliness, the isolation he experienced pressed down on him like a heavy weight. He entertained thoughts of suicide, but when he looked for his old service revolver, he discovered Caryl had hidden it.

February gave way to March. The weather moderated; spring seemed to promise warmth and light.

Caryl took a job working at one of the new retail businesses at Village West. Stannard's temporary medical disability leave would extend only another few weeks. After that she would be the sole breadwinner. It had been years since she had last worked out of the home, but now he looked forward to having her gone. As the weeks passed, she left for work earlier and came home later. He could see she looked for ways to avoid the black mood that permeated the house. It was fine by him.

Finally, on March 28, Stannard received his first piece of good news in six months when Lieutenant Pezzati called him on the phone. "St Jack, Pezzati here. I have some news for you about the Parlous case."

"If it's good news, go ahead. Otherwise, just let it lay."

"It is good news. They're dead."

"Who? Who's dead?" Stannard sat upright, seeming to come alive.

"Dr. Kasalaitis and Lorelei Parlous; they're both dead."

He struggled to grasp what his friend had said. "I don't understand. Whatta you mean they're dead? How can they both be dead? Do you mean they died at the same time?"

Lieutenant Pezzati heard the spark of a soul emerging from the darkness. "That's precisely what

I mean. If you're free I'll come over and tell you about it."

He could hardly contain himself. "You bet I'm free. I'll put on some coffee. Come right on out."

Five minutes later he saw the unmarked police car turn into his driveway. A new tan-colored Crown Vic. *Oh, well. I don't suppose a detective is trying to sneak up on very many people.*

The car pulled to a stop and Lieutenant Pezzati got out as Stannard exited the front door of the house. "I guess I should've picked up on it when you said you'd come over instead of come up. Where were you anyway?"

Pezzati smiled. "On my way up here. I'd just passed the I-70 cloverleaf when I called."

"Really? I thought you guys had been told to stay off the cell phones while you were driving."

"Yeah, but don't tell anyone, okay?"

The effort to stay lighthearted in the conversation had already begun to wear Stannard down. The news that justice was meted out in the death of Erin Kasalaitis could go only so far at this point. "So, what's this all about?"

Pezzati wanted to blurt out what he knew but decided to let it play out slowly so his friend could absorb all the news. "Not so fast; you promised me coffee."

Stannard realized what Pezzati was trying to do and so made a concerted effort to play along. "I did at that, but it isn't ready. It takes more than five minutes, you know."

The two men entered the house and settled at the country-kitchen table, where they stared at the pot as it gurgled.

"Come on, St Jack, you know what they say, 'A watched pot never boils.' " The effort at humor fell flat.

"Enough already, what happened?"

"Okay, okay, so I'm not as funny as I thought. They're both dead, just as I told you. What's more, it looks like they were murdered."

"Where, when…"

"They were on Grand Cayman Island in a guest-house. We had a fax from the police down there asking us for some information on them." Pezzati paused. "Somehow I get the impression that they aren't too interested in pursuing the case unless it has a local connection."

"But they hated one another. Why would they be together in the Caribbean, unless…"

"Unless…," Pezzati let the thought hang in the air. "Yep, you're thinking what I'm thinking. Are you up to talking about it? Maybe seeing if there's something we missed?"

"I would like nothing more. I know you're a believer in the Good Book. It says to be patient, stay the course, and you will see the evildoers punished, or something like that."

The conversation didn't take long. Information about the incident on Grand Cayman was sketchy. When Caryl arrived home from work that evening, she knew something had happened.

When she opened the garage door to the kitchen, she could smell dinner cooking. Music played on the Bose radio, and Stannard made a noise that only he could have equated to singing.

"Well, aren't you chipper today?" Caryl remarked.

"You don't know the half of it. I feel better than I have in months. In fact, I called the doctor. I have an appointment for tomorrow morning. I want to talk about backing off the anti-depressant meds. I want to go back to work."

Caryl stared, her mouth agape. She had stood by her husband throughout their marriage, but she instinctively knew what he had in mind. He planned to go back to work on whatever was left of the Parlous case. Surprise slowly gave way to shock then anger as she contemplated the effect another failure might have on him. She had gone through everything he had, and she stayed beside him. But how much more could she be expected to endure? She started to argue then decided it would be futile. What could she say? In the end she just stood still for over a minute before finally blurting out, "Whatever!" She turned, walked out of the house, and drove away. She did not return until after ten that night.

Over the following week, Pezzati learned more and shared what he learned with his friend, hoping it would lead to some forgotten piece of information. *I wasn't beaten. I only hit a roadblock. All the anguish I've felt, and for what? I should've remembered what I told Pezzati about being patient. 'Vengeance is mine,' that's what God says. I should have remembered that.*

Pezzati and Stannard met for lunch on April 6, Good Friday, three days after Stannard had gone back to work. In his old police days, he would have considered the work light duty. They were working him back into the operation, watching to see how he handled himself. He was bored with light duty, but when he was honest, he admitted he tired easily. The months of inactivity had weakened him physically as well as mentally.

They met frequently now at the Santa Fe Café. On the sixth the two men arrived simultaneously at the parking lot. Pezzati spoke as he saw Stannard get out of his car. "Glad to see you're back at work, buddy. I wondered how long you'd be able to milk the system."

His sense of humor had returned since Pezzati's last attempt at levity. "You know where you can go... or do you need directions? I've heard it said that the sign of real tact is being able to tell someone the go there and have 'em ask for directions." He laughed.

Lunch lasted until the restaurant closed at two o'clock. During that time, the two men reviewed all they'd learned about the deaths of Erin Kasalaitis and Lorelei Parlous.

Stannard listened as Pezzati summarized what the investigation had turned up. The two women had arrived on Grand Cayman by air a few days before their murder, landing at Owen Roberts International Airport in George Town. Both women made an impression on the customs officials, who were accustomed to the arrival of wealthy visitors, many carrying illegal drugs. Dr.

Kasalaitis had been rude when questioned about the contents of her luggage, providing evidence of her profession and literally bulldozing her way past the clerks. *A complete opposite from what I observed when I visited her in Florida.* Lorelei Parlous had been just the opposite and would not have drawn any particular attention if she hadn't been accompanying Dr. Kasalaitis. The Parlous woman would otherwise have struck the officials as just another sexy single woman possibly on the make, though nervous. The fact that the two women were traveling together didn't raise any question but rather served to confirm the belief of the clerks.

Suddenly Stannard blurted out, "I don't believe for a minute that the relationship of those two was a lesbian liaison, regardless of what some island clerk thinks." For the first time he realized the impact Lorelei Parlous had made on him. He blushed.

Pezzati noticed and continued his narration. What came as a surprise to the island police was the local destination listed on both passports, a house off Frank Sound Road between the Breakers and Old Man Bay, not the sort of place two wealthy women would choose when there were five-star resort hotels less than six miles from the airport. The house they rented was something of a dump. It stood near an isolated and lonely bog at least twenty miles from the party spots. The lease agreement, handled by an island estate agent, identified Dr. Erin Kasalaitis as the lessee. Nevertheless, the agent was emphatic the person who'd arranged for the lease had been a man.

Stannard appeared confounded by the news.

He continued. Erin Kasalaitis rented an English Ford from one of the car rental companies at the airport and apparently drove straight to the house. What they did there is anyone's guess. Several credit cards were found in the purses of the two deceased women. There were no charges made against any of the cards when police checked the records, other than for the rental car. They had apparently just stayed in the house. No one saw them until they arrived, in the company of a younger man, at one of the banks specializing in international accounts. The police did get an official at Island Private Bank & Trust of Cayman Limited to acknowledge they'd been there. That was the third day they were on the island. The man refused to discuss their business without a warrant. Not even the war on terror or the US Patriot Act could persuade him to do otherwise.

The bodies were found in the house by the leasing agent several days following the deaths. Both bodies were in an advanced state of decomposition when the police coroner arrived on the scene. The coroner said they'd been dead for at least three days. In the tropical heat, the bodies had…well, they were in bad shape. They found the rental car in the parking lot of a small hut-style restaurant specializing in conch stew a couple of miles away.

The cause of death was obvious, cyanide poisoning. Residue of the potassium cyanide had been found in a bottle of California pinot blanc. The nutty, almond-flavored wine disguised the cyanide. Their death hadn't been an easy one. Both women had suffered terribly. Cyanide gas kills quickly, but cyanide ingested takes much longer, up to an hour. The police immediately ruled out murder/suicide.

No one would intentionally commit suicide in such a manner, especially not someone with medical knowledge. On the other hand, whoever did it had some knowledge of chemistry. Potassium cyanide is unstable around acid. They had to have known that would be a problem when the bottle was uncorked. It would be safe to assume the killer uncorked the bottle and put the poison in the wine, then recorked the bottle. When it came time to kill the women, the killer would have to decant the wine ahead of time, being careful not to breathe any of the fumes.

When Lieutenant Pezzati and Stannard finished reviewing the information, Pezzati asked, "Does any of it suggest something to you?"

"It does. The killer must've known the women and had their trust. You don't let a casual stranger open a bottle of wine for you unless that person is the wine steward at a restaurant." Stannard paused.

"What're you thinking?" Pezzati wanted to know.

"I don't know for certain. Do you suppose they were moving the seven million dollars offshore to avoid taxes?"

"Possibly, but we'll have to wait for warrants to be issued so we can get more information on that."

"Looks like we're in a waiting game again." Stannard considered the news. *Or moving the money could have been part of a more diabolical plot.*

"Yeah," Pezzati answered. "It seems like a lot of police work is just waiting around."

They left the restaurant and drove off their separate ways. Then it hit. *Wills. Wills Parlous is an investment counselor specializing in offshore investments.*

Chapter Eighteen

The investigation at Grand Cayman came to an abrupt halt at the end of the following week. Warrants to search the bank files were not issued for the reason the attorney general's prosecution office did not pursue them. The island government was more concerned with maintaining an image for tourism than in publicizing the murder. Stannard didn't see it as an indictment of Grand Cayman; it was simply a fact. Whoever committed the crime had undoubtedly gone. The entire affair had been an imported crime, for imported motives with imported victims and an imported perpetrator or perpetrators. Only the money remained on the island, and that was just the way the locals wanted it. The prosecutor and business community, even the governor and attorney general, refused to press the investigation.

When Stannard asked about the bank records, Lieutenant Pezzati told him that too had come to naught. The bank would not cooperate. It had far too much to lose by allowing access to the records. No one believed these murders had anything to do with terrorism, and without the terrorism connection, nothing could force the banks to cooperate.

The memo Stannard wrote to the home office asking for authority to investigate in Grand Cayman received prompt approval, to everyone's surprise. He arrived at the Grand Cayman airport less than a month after the murders. To his surprise, the government officials were open to his inquiries once he assured them his interest was corporate, not public, in nature. They had much more information than they had been willing to share with Lieutenant Pezzati.

The young man who accompanied the women to the bank had been, in fact, Wills Parlous. He arrived on the island the day after his mother and stepmother. The immigration arrival card gave the guesthouse off Frank Sound Road as his residence while on the island.

While the two women had rented an English Ford, Wills had opted for a more luxurious car. The red Aston Martin drew attention. The owner of the conch shack recalled seeing it parked behind his building out of sight for a whole day but couldn't state whether it was the day of the murder. The police found the English Ford behind the same conch shack after the murder. The owner confirmed that the Ford had been there for at least two days. He wondered why someone would leave a rental car at that location but had nevertheless said nothing to anyone.

When he checked at the immigration office, he learned Wills had departed from the island two days before the Ford was reported missing by the rental company.

At the customs office, he examined the declaration form signed by Willsson Parlous. *He'd declared two bottles of wine in the place marked for spirits. Why bring wine to a party island... unless...*

The full police report recorded finding two bottles of California pinot blanc, but only one of them had poison residue in the bottom. A small fingernail scratch on the label had identified the bottle containing the poison. That bottle had been kept for DNA analysis.

The guesthouse had the appearance of being the scene of a party that police surmised must have preceded the murders. Three wine glasses along with a plate of fruit and cheese were on a table. Two of the glasses contained traces of potassium cyanide. The police speculated the killer had participated in drinking the wine. If they were right, he would've made certain to be the one decanting and pouring the drinks. Only after seeing that the two women were slightly intoxicated did the killer begin pouring from the poisoned bottle. Once he saw their distress, he could leave the house, taking the Ford Focus. The two women, trapped without a vehicle and in the throes of cyanide poisoning, were unable to get help.

When questioned about the rental agreement, the estate agent recalled the man arranging for the lease specifically asked for a house without a telephone. The police did not find any cell phones in the house, or among the dead women's possessions. When Stannard met with the chief inspector to go over his findings, it didn't surprise him that the man seemed to know all that he'd discovered. At the conclusion of their meeting he asked why, with all that evidence, they were not pursuing the crime. The man answered, "Business, it wouldn't be good for business. Besides, the man we believe is responsible has departed and will probably never set foot on the island again. Whatever his banking requirements are, the transactions will not require his presence. I imagine he knows that. He wouldn't be the first person to set up an account like this. You do understand an island like ours requires a certain amount of tolerance and discretion to maintain our lifestyle." There was nothing more for Stannard to say or do. He left on the first flight to Miami.

The inch-thick, nine-by-twelve package arrived at his home two days after he returned to Kansas City. He felt the weight of the envelope and noted the ten first-class stamps affixed in the right-hand corner. A shipping label, hand printed, had his name misspelled, "Jakson" instead of
Jackson. There was no return address. The package bore a postal stamp from Kansas City. *Odd way to mail a package. I wonder what's inside.* Before opening it, he thumbed through the other mail quickly, two bills and a letter from Caryl's mother, who was living in a Des Moines assisted residence facility. *I'll bet she's complaining that Caryl hasn't been up to visit her. Maybe Caryl should move her to The Manor in KCK. Nah, that place in Des Moines is nice. Besides, Caryl would feel obligated to be over at The Manor all the time.*

He went back inside the house, poured coffee, and using a paring knife he found in the kitchen drawer, opened the mystery package. Reaching in, he extracted a stack of mismatched paper roughly a quarter inch thick and a second envelope. The stationery on top of the inner envelope bore the embossed name Lorelei Parlous. He could smell her perfume. He began reading the typed letter.

Stannard,

I hardly know how to begin this letter. Let it be enough that when you receive it, you will know—I am dead. I can't help but wonder if receiving such a letter is as strange as writing one. At this point my life is clouded by uncertainty. As you read this you will know why. I have left instructions with Maria, my housekeeper, to mail the envelope to you in the event I don't return from the trip I leave on tomorrow.

I like you Stannard, but either way you will never see me again. If my intuition is wrong, and I get back alive, I intend to disappear—destroying this letter first. You were always honest and thoughtful, even when I suspected you were holding back what you knew. You have been badly used in this affair. You deserve to know the whole truth, but where should I begin—there is so much to tell you.

Let me start by telling you where I am going and why. I fly out of Kansas City tomorrow morning on my way to Grand Cayman. I will meet up with Erin Kasalaitis and Wills Parlous. Wills is moving the insurance proceeds to a bank there. I don't trust either of them, I never have, but I am as guilty of murder as they are. The entire plan was one of Wills's devising. He is so much like his father—a manipulator—but even more than that, he is like his father in a more awful way.

In the margin she had written is her precise penmanship, "Loren not only named him after himself, but he tried to literally turn him into a duplicate of himself."

The body of the letter continued:

Wills is involved in satanic ritual just like his father. Loren dragged him into it as a boy, but Wills has gone far beyond anything his father did. I only recently learned about their involvement in this; but more of that later.

Much of what happened to you was truly an accident. Your involvement from the time Loren nearly sideswiped your car, even his escape, was accidental. It may be that *accidental* is the wrong word. It may have been providential. By the time you finish this letter, you will know what I mean by that.

Loren was supposed to die at the storage unit. That was Wills's original plan.

Only Wills and Riki Simmoni were at the storage facility, so I suppose we will never know the truth about what happened there. Maybe you will be able to get the truth from Wills. I only had a bit part. I was supposed to set up Loren so Simmoni could kidnap him; that is all.

I had to improvise as the facts came out during the investigation. Can you imagine my surprise when the cops came to the house and told me Loren had died in an automobile accident? He was supposed to be lying dead with his throat cut in that storage unit. Wills planned to make it look like a ritualistic killing. For some reason that he never shared with me, he must have dreamed up some other idea. Either that or maybe it was always his plan to have it work out the way it did. Otherwise, why put that foolish hologram on the mirror? *Wills Parlous is unpredictable and dangerous.* As for Simmoni, he was just some drug head Erin picked up in Florida to do the heavy work.

I can only surmise what happened at the storage unit. Wills must have drugged his father and put the hologram on the rearview mirror to terrify him. After that, he let him escape, trusting the narcotic-cocktail hallucination and those eyes in the mirror to terrify him to the point he would wreck the Corvette. In a high-speed accident, he would be sure to die. Wills told me he followed down the road behind his father but was too far back in traffic to see the accident.

Stannard paused to consider that. *The Cadillac! He may have been sitting on the road right beside me for all I know.* He continued reading.

Wills is such a snake. I think he always planned to blame his mother for the killing. I believe he hated both of his parents. He wanted me to suggest his mother was behind the killing as a way of making her squirm. He insisted I accuse her. He knew the police would never be able to prove she did it. I just did what he wanted. After that I had to keep repeating it. He did his best to avoid having any suspicion coming his way. As time passed I became more afraid of him. I now think he plans to kill both Erin and me. That way all the insurance proceeds would go to him.

He never planned on you getting involved. He was shocked when you caught us arguing outside the house.

Again she had scribbled in the margin. "That argument about him wanting access to some files is the truth. He may have been after the file I have enclosed with this letter. I do know this, he wanted access all right, but what he wanted was access to me. He wanted to supplant his father in every way."

Stannard returned to the body of the letter.

When you discovered the security tapes, he became paranoid. He got even worse when I told him you had questioned me about the timing of our coming and going the night and morning of the murder. I told both him and his mother that you didn't believe me when I said I had gone out early that morning looking for him but didn't find him. It was true though. I didn't know where they planned to torture his father, but I wanted to stop it.

Well, that's a lie, Stannard thought. *She is lying. I wonder how much of this is a lie?*

In the margin she had scribbled once more: "The dark blue car at the storage unit belonged to Simmoni; it must have been his rental car, not my car, that the owner of the storage unit saw. You can probably check that out. He used the name Peterson and a phony driver's license when he rented it." *She is truly distressed. This is a stream of consciousness.* Stannard turned his attention back to the typed letter and read:

I almost got you killed when you asked me why Loren didn't come home instead of driving on down the interstate highway. I called Wills after you left and told him I was afraid you were making a connection between the two of us and the murder. That was when he insisted his mother send Riki Simmoni up here to get rid of you. I think you were the only person he really feared. He knew your reputation from a long time ago. You were relentless, and it scared both of them.

Erin called me on the disposable phones we used for contact and told me Wills wanted you killed. Neither of us thought it was a good idea, so Erin devised a way to get rid of Simmoni. After all, he was the only connection between her and the death of Loren. We could kill either you or Simmoni. I convinced her Simmoni was the greater threat. She was afraid to cross her son, so she hit on the idea of making it look like he died from natural causes up here. If Simmoni died down there, Wills would surely catch on. Do you have any idea how easy it is to come up with botulism material? All she had to do was go to a food pantry and rummage around until she found a can that bulged out. She got Simmoni's cigarettes away from him while he was at her clinic and injected the botulism into the filters. He was such a chain smoker he didn't even notice the hole in the filter of the moist tips. He just sucked the poison directly into his lungs. The beauty of the plan is that even though heating botulism kills it, there is not enough heat when you first light up to do that. It worked.

It may not count for much, but I did my best to save you, Stannard. Erin sided with me on that but not because she cared about you. She sided with me because Riki Simmoni was the only unstable person besides her son who could connect her to Loren's death."

The cigarette butt. I had it in my hand. We will never know whether testing it for botulism would have found the poison. Stannard turned back to the letter.

The rest of us were so entwined in this we couldn't say anything without drawing attention to ourselves. It may be that when Wills discovered his mother had left Kansas City earlier than planned, he lost his temper and that is when he pushed me into implicating her. After all she was the one with the motive. As her only heir, he would inherit if the murder was pinned on her.

You know I lied when I said Loren and I had a good marriage. It was a nightmare of deceit. Loren and Wills are so much alike. You can't trust anything either of them says. Stannard, I am afraid for my life. I want so much to call you and tell you the truth. Maybe you could protect me, but why should you?

Stannard felt a lump rise in his throat. *She is up to her neck in murder, but there is a vulnerability that I can't shake. However she got into this, she is way out of her league. She should have called. I would have done what I could for her.* He read on.

I would like to think I would have turned on Wills and Erin at some point and told the truth, but we both know I wouldn't. The promise of money was just too great. I was going to be rich, $3,000,000 rich, only now I'm not so sure. The trip to Grand Cayman may have as much to do with killing me as it does moving the money into an untraceable account.

The last thing I want to tell you has to do with your son. I just found the material in the white envelope when I was going through Loren's papers. They were in a box he had hidden away. There is more, but only what I enclosed pertains to you. The papers will be painful, but having them may help you close a difficult time in your life. As you know, Loren was involved with that creep Roberto who runs a shop in Westport. So was Wills.

So the kid in the picture gallery was *Wills Parlous.*

What you see will tell you the rest. I went down to that evil shop on Broadway the other day. Roberto has disappeared. I can't say for certain, but I suspect that Wills has done away with him. The material in the envelope will tell you why. If so, the police are not likely to find the body. Roberto knows too much about Wills and is the only living person with enough firsthand knowledge to put him away for years in the penitentiary. That is not likely to happen. Wills is very tidy and will tie up all the loose ends if he can.

What I did, I did for money. Erin acted out of revenge. Wills is simply evil.

Stannard, I am sorry, truly sorry! Watch yourself!

Stannard looked at the signature. Her hand had quivered when she signed the letter. He opened the inner envelope, this one faded almost yellow. He removed the mismatched sheets of paper, but before he began reading, a photograph caught his eye. He stared at the images on the black-and-white picture. He wept uncontrollably for the next half hour. Each time he thought he could continue, the picture brought another wave of sobbing.

The photograph showed a young boy held down on a crude altar in the woods, his arms and ankles held in place with duct tape. The boy was nude, his nipples removed. He had been emasculated and a hexagram was sliced into his torso, all of it clearly done before he died. The boy,

Russell Jackson—the only child of Stannard and Caryl Jackson—was dead when the picture had been taken, his throat cut. Standing beside the gruesome sight were three boys, the two who had died in the Lansing prison and Wills Parlous, their expressions twisted with ghoulish satisfaction. It didn't take a genius to name the photographer. Stannard knew it would be one of two people, Roberto Bertonelli or Loren Parlous.

When he gained control of his emotions, he began to read the faded documents. Loren Parlous and Roberto Bertonelli had used the latter's shop in Westport to lure young boys, using the game Covens of Death as bait. Loren Parlous made notes and carefully laid out the details of how Russell, once caught, was initiated into—no, sacrificed in— Satanic worship.

The man's sick diary detailed the capture of Russell by the two boys from Piper. What followed was detail only a police officer or a killer would have. Sick with disgust, he held the documents in his hand and began plotting his revenge. This had nothing to do with the law or Lieutenant Pezzati, or who he now was, or who he'd once been.

He walked to the desk where Caryl kept their household bills. He turned on the shredder and held the photograph over the grinding whirr of the machine. He pulled the picture back and replaced the entire file Lorelei had sent him in the envelope. He then retrieved the scrapbook and began feeding the pages that caused so much pain through the angry-sounding machine. Each page that disappeared into the jaws of the machine removed a piece of the shame of failure from the burden he had carried. Never again would he look in the scrapbook that chronicled his shame. He made it in despair, and it had been a prison cell for him. The first page to disappear into the machine unlocked the door. Each page after that took him a step closer to freedom, to forgiveness, and he never again wanted to look back. By the time the last news article was gone, he felt the fulfillment of the awful task. *Why did I wait so long? Maybe I just needed to know the rest of the story. It was so much more than just two boys acting out some silly game. It was evil beyond anything I could have imagined.*

Sure, the pages in Lorelei Parlous's envelope were much worse, but they were someone else's records. Those records existed for another reason. They were evidence that he would pass on to Pezzati if the plan he slowly saw taking shape in his mind failed to come to fruition. He walked to the garage, where he put them in the trunk of his car. He would tell Pezzati but not Caryl about the envelope and its contents. He would merely tell Caryl he had destroyed the scrapbook. It was time to move on with life, and he knew what he had to do.

A few days later, he applied for a private-carry license. Lieutenant Pezzati questioned the need for him to have the license but deferred to his friend and smoothed the way for its issuance. "You know the law. The fact that you can carry a firearm doesn't give you any special right to go looking for trouble. I truly believe you are in danger from this young man. It looks like he is guilty of murder, but we don't have the evidence yet to prove it. You and I both know that without corroboration that letter isn't going to be admissible, and those folks down in the Cayman Islands aren't interested in pursuing this. From what you say, he is just paranoid enough to come after you or Caryl, maybe both. If what Lorelei Parlous wrote you is half-true, he already has. That guy Simmoni was Wills's hit man."

Stannard agreed. He had to get Caryl out of harm's way. She had nothing to do with the investigation and was in no position to threaten Wills, but the young man didn't think like a rational human being. "Maybe I should suggest she go to Des Moines and visit her mother. She wants her to come for an extended stay."

Lieutenant Pezzati considered the comment. "That's a good short-term fix. What about in the long term? Wills Parlous doesn't seem like the sort who, once he is threatened, goes away quietly."

"I just don't know. Living in the country seemed like such a good idea when we moved there, but all this has me worried. First Simmoni, now Wills. The house is not exactly isolated, but there are not any neighbors within several hundred yards. We already know how devious Wills can be. I feel helpless…" *I feel guilty lying to a friend this way, but I want that murderer to pay, and I don't want it to be without a lot of fear.*

"Well, you can't leave Caryl alone out there, and you can't be home all the time. Not with a killer on the loose. If I were you, I'd send her to Des Moines and try to figure something out while she was gone. After that, drop it. It's a police matter. We will watch him and protect you."

He nodded in agreement. *I'll move Caryl, but I will not leave it to you. I will not have that threat hanging over our heads for the rest of our lives, until he decides to strike.*

The memo to the company legal department outlined some of the facts. Stannard felt certain there was sufficient evidence to file suit against the estates of Dr. Erin Kasalaitis and Lorelei Parlous for the recovery of the insurance proceeds. There may not be enough proof to sustain a criminal prosecution, but a civil suit required a much lower standard of proof. Depriving Wills Parlous of the fruits of his most heinous crime, patricide, would be a good start on his revenge. He tried to recall other cases where someone had killed both mother and father. The only name that came to mind was Lowell Lee Andrews, "The Nicest Boy in Kansas" the headlines of the day had read. He shuddered to think what the headlines would read if the papers found out about the murder of Wills's mother and father. This was no nice boy. He wondered how they would cast their headline, perhaps "Depraved Demon Tortures Then Kills Parents."

His memo revealed too much of his underlying motive. The lawyers persuaded management to remove him from any further involvement in the matter while they pursued the civil action. Seven million dollars were at stake, and no one wanted to jeopardize the case because of some vendetta that Stannard Jackson had against Wills Parlous.

One of the lawyers from Omaha flew down the Kansas City to hand deliver the memorandum removing him from the case. He took the news stoically, not saying anything.

Fine, they can do whatever they want. They can reassign me to other work, but after hours, my time is my own. If I want to pursue Wills Parlous, that's my business. It was not, of course, and if they discovered what he was doing, they would fire him.

The following Saturday Caryl left for Des Moines. It had taken her a few days to arrange to be off work. There was none of the loving relationship in their parting that had characterized their marriage. The anger Caryl felt had built to the breaking point. She wanted to be away just as much as Stannard wanted her to go. As she drove north out of Kansas City, neither knew if she would return. Nevertheless, Stannard tailed her in a rental car. He didn't want her to know he was following. More important, he wanted to make certain no one else was following her. Watching her in Kansas City was one thing. It would be impossible in Des Moines. By the time she passed Cameron, satisfied no one was following, he turned around and returned to Kansas City. Night had fallen. The overcast sky obscured the moon and stars. It was a perfect night for what he planned next.

At that point, Stannard Jackson did something everyone who knew him would say was completely out of character. He called Wills Parlous on the telephone. Caryl was safely away, where the evil son of an evil father could not reach her. He could now allow his seething rage to push its way to the surface.

The voice on the answering machine sounded flippant. "Hi, you have reached Willsson Parlous. If you think anything you have to say is worth my time listening, do so after the beep, and maybe, if I agree, I'll return the call."

The letter from Lorelei and the pictures and narrative written by Dr. Loren Parlous alone were enough to enrage him, but the arrogant voice provided what little impetus he needed for the message he wanted to leave. "Listen, you little creep. I know what you did and how you did it. I know it all. I know about the boys years ago. I know about Russell, and I know what you did to your father, your mother and Lorelei. If…"

Wills Parlous picked up the receiver. "Really, now, aren't you the clever one? You don't know anything."

Stannard shouted into his cell phone, "You won't get away with it. I'm going to see to that. One way or another you're going to pay for all you've done." The phone connection was dead. Wills had hung up, and Stannard didn't know if Wills had heard the threat. He hoped he had. His hands shook as he pocketed the phone and began making plans for the next step in his revenge.

He drove the rental car back down the road to the place where Simmoni had parked and waited. Eleven o'clock became midnight. Another hour passed, and just when he thought Wills Parlous wouldn't come, he did. Stannard dumped the cold remains of his coffee out the window and watched as the Toyota Spyder crept along the silent road, its lights off. *I knew he would come.* The car pulled into the driveway. The driver edged around to the side away from the road and the bedrooms. *He's been out here before. He knows his way around.* Stannard waited. He couldn't see the Spyder from where he sat, but he didn't need to. Wills Parlous intended to break into the house and kill him and his wife. For that reason he had intentionally left the door unlocked. He did not have long to wait. Fifteen minutes after the Spyder pulled beside the house, he heard a gunshot. Shortly thereafter the Spyder drove away toward the city with its lights on. Stannard smiled; then he laughed aloud. He recalled the words of Andy Rooney, "If you laugh when no one is around, you really mean it."

He sat alone in the car for another forty minutes before returning to the house. Upon entering he saw the object of the gunshot. The family portrait that hung in the den, the one taken years ago with Russell, its glass shattered and a bullet hole through Stannard Jackson's forehead.

That night he left two more calls on Willsson Parlous's answering machine. He knew there was nothing to fear by a complaint for harassment. The last thing Wills wanted was police involvement in any of his activities. The next day he mailed a note, marked "Personal," to his office in the Commerce Tower.

After that, the stalking began. Stannard followed him from his home in the San Francisco condos to his office on Monday morning, making certain Wills would see him. He left a note under his windshield, telling him he was armed and looking for him. The note, printed on a friend's printer, was untraceable and unsigned; no need to sign it. Wills would know who sent it.

When Wills went to lunch with a business associate, Stannard followed and took a table facing him, smiling.

When Wills stopped for a drink on the way home, Stannard just happened to drop in to the same bar. On one occasion he even sat at the bar next to his prey and pressed the barrel of the gun against his quarry's side, whispering, "Not here Wills, later." Day after day the routine continued. He watched as the quiet confrontations with Wills took their toll on the younger man. He no longer had the arrogant look of a man in control of his own destiny.

Stannard worried that his boss would find out. He managed to investigate the cases assigned to him during the hours he was not engaged in pressuring Wills. By the end of the fourth day, he could tell that Wills's nerves were beginning to frazzle. Wills had always been the predator; he didn't know how to react when he became the prey.

Stannard saw Wills had no friends, no one to turn to during a crisis. A person like him seldom does. Stannard watched; he didn't sleep at home, not that it mattered now. Wills Parlous knew fear and would not leave the safety of his condo for the danger that waited in rural Wyandotte County. He did not allow Wills to take the initiative. Wills became more agitated. It didn't matter what time of the day or night he left his condo. Stannard followed close behind him.

By the end of the week, Stannard was as exhausted as his target. Neither man would be able to withstand the pressure much longer. Wills rarely stayed alone in his condo. He clearly wanted the company of someone, his father, who would have been able to help, but that wasn't possible. The son wanted money not a father and now he was alone. The constant pressure had worked. Stannard could sense the man's fear. *He had to know I can come for him at any time.*

On Saturday night, Stannard remained on watch but at a different location. He saw Wills leave the condo building. He did not appear to see Stannard anywhere. *He feels secure for the first time in a week. He must be going to meet someone he trusts, but who?* Wills drove out of the parking garage and proceeded to

Interstate 35. Stannard followed in a different rental car. Staying a discreet distance, he followed until they passed the Interstate 635 turnoff. At the Shawnee Mission Parkway exit, he pulled beside Wills and leered at him, holding up his service revolver. Wills reacted immediately. He shot ahead. Stannard followed on his bumper.

Wills changed lanes, the Spyder more maneuverable than the rental car, trying to put traffic between them. Fear registered in his eyes. By the time they passed the 75th Street exit, he was three car lengths ahead of Stannard. As they approached the "Y" split for the Overland Parkway, Wills drove in the Interstate 35 lane, only to swerve at the last moment onto the parkway. Stannard cut in front of another car. The driver honked, holding his hand on the horn. Wills saw his tormentor was still there. At the Interstate 435 interchange, he raced off the parkway and onto the interstate highway. Stannard followed but was cut off by a uniform company panel truck.

Stannard did all he could to catch up to the fleeing killer, but traffic blocked the way. At last only the panel truck barred his path to Wills. Then it happened.

The truck changed lanes without warning just as Wills glanced in his rearview mirror to see if he had lost Stannard in the traffic. The combination of events came together with perfect harmony. Wills swerved to avoid the collision but overcorrected, and the Spyder smashed into the concrete pier of a street overpass. From two cars back, Stannard saw what was happening and sped by as the Spyder disintegrated upon impact—then he saw the fireball. No one could survive that crash. Bad people, evil people, eventually come to ruin, sometimes in this world, sometimes in the next. Justice is often nothing more than a matter of fate or God's justice.

He pulled onto the shoulder of the interstate highway, just past the Quivira Road exit, and stopped, watched, looking in the rearview mirror of his car. Within minutes he saw the flashing lights of police cars and heard the wail of sirens converging on the scene. He saw death in his rearview mirror. *It's over where it started; justice has been done, justice for Russell, for Lorelei, for me.*

Stannard Jackson did not tell anyone what had happened. As the emergency vehicles pulled up to the accident scene, he put his car in gear and carefully pulled out into traffic, confident that no one could identify him. For the first time in his life, he had come close to committing a serious crime. Maybe he actually had. He knew with absolute certainty he bore moral responsibility for the death of another human being. He tried not to think about it. The man deserved to die, though not the way it happened. Even so, it was better this way than how he planned it. He did not know if he would have been able to shoot Wills. He had not thought it through carefully enough. Fatigue and the anxiety of simply getting it over with had led him to the crazed chase. *Would I have killed him? Yeah I think I would.* God had saved him, and for that he would be forever thankful.

He wanted to call Caryl but knew he would have to wait until morning. He wanted her to come home. He wanted to get their life back on track. He feared she would reject him. At last he understood the toll the years had taken on her as well as him. It was another act of selfishness. He thought about himself, but what about her?

It took only one day for the news of the crash to reach the attention of Detective Lieutenant Michael Pezzati. He called his friend and asked him if he'd seen the news. When told that he had, Pezzati asked if there was anything St Jack wanted to tell him. When he said no, the two friends changed the subject and made plans to meet for breakfast at Santa Fe Café the next morning.

Epilogue

A year after Wills Parlous crashed his car at the Quivira Road exit ramp on Interstate 435,

Stannard Jackson received his bonus from the company. The company president had made a special trip to Kansas City for the presentation at a luncheon honoring the man who saved the company $7 million. When they unveiled the check—for that truly was the way to describe it, because the document was twenty inches high and forty inches across—everyone in the room could see the amount, $100 thousand. Stannard gasped.

The president smiled. "You know, it took the lawyers a year to get that bank on Grand Cayman to turn loose of the seven million dollars you saved us. All I can say is, what you did was a whole lot harder. You know you have our thanks, but more important, we owe you an apology for doubting you could solve this mystery if we gave you enough time. I want you to know you have that apology, and it is publicly stated. If there is ever another time, please, please remind us of this event." He shook Stannard's hand, pumping it.

"You can count on it, but we both know there was a lot of luck involved." He thought about the meeting he'd had with his old pal Mike Pezzati the day before. He'd told him the police departments of the metropolitan area were putting together a special case squad. "After the work you did on the Parlous case, the boys at KCK put you up for the job of heading it," he'd said to Stannard. "They said to tell you as far as they were concerned, St Jack was back and they would be proud to work with you." *When Pezzati had brought up my problems with depression, he said they brushed them aside.* "They said they knew all about it and they understood it all had to do with the death of your son. Now that that is solved, they believe your demons have been put to rest," Pezzati had related. "Call them and set up an interview," he had urged. *Maybe I'll just do that instead.*

An awkward silence had passed as Stannard thought about his options. He let go of the insurance man's hand. "If Lorelei Parlous hadn't given us a confession implicating her stepson and his mother, we never would have been able to recover the money."

The president nodded. "Yes, that may be true, but I believe there was more to it than luck. By what twist of fate did Willsson Parlous meet his end at the same place as his father, and under similar circumstances?" He looked intently into Stannard's eyes. They gave away nothing.

Stannard responded, "That's something no one will ever know." *I'm certainly not going to talk about it here. For my part, I doubt fate had anything to do with it.* "I don't believe God micromanages our lives, but in this instance maybe he decided Wills Parlous had done enough damage in this life and it was time for him to find out just how wrong he had been."

The crowd of well wishers drifted away one by one.

The president didn't know what to say. At last he changed the subject. "I understand you and your wife have adopted a boy. How is that going?"

"Great, he is fifteen and a super kid. We, all of us, are trying to make a new start. We took him in as a foster child shortly after the Parlous case wrapped up, but it was several months before we decided to adopt. I may be a little old for him, but I'm looking forward to picking up where I lost my fourteen-year-old. He is just a little older." He sensed the CEO wanted to say something but didn't know what.

For some reason he felt the need to explain. "His grandfather was a friend of mine in the old days. He was a cop too. The boy's father became a fire-fighter. He died in an industrial fire down toward Grandview."

"That's too bad," was all the executive said.

"It's worse than that. The boy's mother died of cancer a year earlier." He paused before finishing his thought. "His father didn't just die in an industrial fire. It was a staged arson, and his father died in an explosion." He could read shock and horror on the man's face. "He had no close relatives; just some cousins on the east side of town. They're good people, but they're not in a position to take him in." He thought for a minute whether to say more. "I guess I owed him and the boy. His mother and father asked me to be his godfather, but I failed at that after Russell died. I wanted to make up for it."

He stopped to consider how it had come about. Caryl had not come home immediately. She stayed in Iowa for a month after the death of Willsson Parlous. Worrying about their own relationship, they decided to throw themselves into helping another damaged person. It was a risky undertaking, but they both realized it was a risk worth taking if they were going to save their marriage. He decided not to mention that. "Caryl and I thought it was the least we could do. We thought a lot of his grandfather and father.

His grandfather had been an assistant chief when I came on the police force. He helped me get a start. His father was a friend, a good friend. After a while it just seemed right to talk to him about adoption."

"What is his name?" the company president wanted to know.

"Trevon."

Neither man knew what else to say. They stood there in the awkward silence as Caryl and the boy walked up to them. Stannard held out his hand again to say good-bye and thank you.

Later that night when the house had settled down, Caryl sat on the arm of the chair and snuggled against her husband. "You liked that woman Lorelei, didn't you?" she stated.

"I did. There was something tragic about her for all her overt sexuality. I don't think she wanted to be a bad person."

Caryl thought about what he had said for over a minute before commenting. She didn't buy into that answer at all. Instead of challenging her husband, she swallowed hard and answered, "Maybe we just get tangled up in the web when we start to plot and scheme." She stopped for another long pause, trying not to look at him, knowing he had been drawn to Lorelei Parlous. The fact frightened her. *We are passing middle age. Was he wandering?* She felt the heat of jealousy rising before concluding, "At least you now know the truth about so much of the past." She had to let it go at that.

"I'm not so sure. It seems to me there were a lot of unanswered questions that will remain unresolved, since everyone involved is dead except for that creep Roberto." And he just vanished.

"Forget him," Caryl answered. "It's time for bed." She felt the wound being opened. Her husband would never be able to let go of some things. Yet, he expected her to understand him.

They both rose from the chair and walked down the hall toward their bedroom. At the doorway, St Jack looked back down the darkened hall. A light began to shine dimly deep in his intuitive brain. He saw a rental storage unit with a wooden desk chair standing in the middle of the room. But what captured his attention was the pair of worn-out sneakers in the corner. It caused his fertile mind to spin. *Why would Dr. Loren Parlous be wearing a pair of worn-out sneakers? And why did he have on sweats? It's like that picture hanging in Dr. Parlous's house—the one with the cowl-clothed monk. It isn't what it appears to be.*

Stone-Cold Alive
The Parlous Trilogy #2

Don't miss the second part of The Parlous Trilogy. Read on for a sneak peak of Stone Cold Alive as St Jack begins to see through the maze of deceit surrounding the death of Dr. Loren Parlous.

Watch for the conclusion to the mystery in Will Evil Never Die.

Chapter One

He stood alone in the dark, the first glint of an
orange-pink morning sky off in the east, the direction
of the city. Sweat soaked his short-sleeved dress shirt,
the warm night promising a hot summer day. An eternity seemed to pass as he stood there, though he did
not know how long it had actually been—staring at
the closed door to the rental storage unit. One thing
he did know was that the metal door was all that separated him from insensate evil. His heart pounded, his
temples throbbsed, blood rushed to his head. Inside,
things too horrible to contemplate were about to happen unless he opened the door and stopped them.
He stood frozen, unable to move.

The last minutes of the time when wickedness
roams the earth in darkness grudgingly gave way to
dawn. But with the dawn, he knew it would be too

late. The man trembled with fear. He had to open the door for his own sake, if not for those inside. He reached for the knob, hand trembling, the sour taste of fear rising in his throat. He hoped the door would be locked, yet he felt compelled to try. The knob turned silently—he jerked his hand away as if it had been heated by the very fires of hell. A low sob, a groan of despair, escaped his lips. If he could not open the door, at least he could shout for them to stop. He tried. His voice barely emitted a squeak. He tried to back away, but his feet would not respond. He remained like a coward, too afraid to run or fight.

Minutes passed. He could hear the scuffling of feet inside the outdoor storage room. Surely the man inside would scream out for help. He hoped that would break the spell and allow him to act, spurring him to action or flight. He heard nothing, silence, then the scraping sound of a chair being dragged across the concrete floor. Hesitantly he reached again for the doorknob. He had to do something. He felt the presence of the woman beside him. He could smell the aroma of her perfume, an exotic aphrodisiac. He felt the warmth of her soft, firm body press against his bare arm, the white silk fabric cool even in the heat of the summer night. He had been led to this place by her, and she wanted him to know the truth, all of it, not just the part she had told him in the letter. He wanted to know. No, he needed to know the truth, for her sake as well as his. She had been brave—why couldn't he?

"Open the door," she urged. "You have to open the door if you want to know."

He turned to tell her he lacked the courage, but when he did she was gone. She's dead. I must have imagined her. Still, the voice had the desired effect. He once again reached for the knob, this time turning it and pulling the door open far enough to peek through the crack. His eyes slowly adjusted to the dim light, but the truth still eluded him. He opened the door farther, and in the center of the storage unit he could make out the figures of three men. His eyes settled on the man in the chair, held immobile by duct tape, his arms secured around the back of the chair, a strip of tape pasted over his mouth making it impossible for him to cry out. The man was nude—his sweatpants and shirt thrown against the far wall next to a pair of worn sneakers. The chair had been tilted back by a young man. I know him. It's Willsson Parlous. Then it hit him. The man in the chair had to be Dr. Loren Parlous, the younger man's father. He appeared to be either unconscious or sedated. But who was the third man, the one wearing the blue shirt and khaki slacks who stood with his back to the door? It can't be Riki Simmoni. Even on his best day, Riki Simmoni never looked that good.

It was then he saw the scalpel. The man bent forward, the sharp medical instrument poised, and with just a few quick strokes he emasculated the man in the chair. Both men laughed as only those who worship Satan can laugh—then the man in the blue shirt handed the scalpel to the younger man and said something. The young man reached down and carved the unicursal hexagram into the torso of the man in the chair. Having completed their grisly task, they removed the tape across the man's mouth and removed the duct tape bindings. After pulling on his sweatpants and shirt, they taped his arms and legs as before, but making certain he would be able to free himself. They then turned off the single bulb that hung directly over the man in the chair and retreated to the far corner of the room, where they stood in the shadows, their faces hidden from view, waiting. The time dragged on, possibly half an hour, the man at the door couldn't tell, and all the while the men in the corner continued to chant, "See the eyes. She wants you dead. They are the eyes of death—your death. See the eyes. She wants you dead. They are the eyes of death—your death. See the eyes. She wants you dead. See the eyes. They are the eyes of death—your death. See the eyes. She wants you dead!"

Over and over they chanted in a low monotone as the man in the chair slowly awakened.

Suddenly he jerked awake and felt the pain in his groin. He groaned. The droning in the corner stopped. Only the sound of breathing could now be heard. The man freed his arms with what strength he had left, and with the dim light coming through the open door illuminating the room, he hobbled to the door.

Outside now, he saw the yellow Corvette with the personalized license tag HEADDOC. It was his only hope—but only if the men who took him there had left the keys in the ignition. He saw the keys and sobbed again! Hope! Dr. Loren Parlous was literally running for his life. Barely able to drive, gravel flew behind the car as he sped out of the storage yard heading for the interstate highway and sanctuary. Frightened, desperate to escape, he drove the car up the entrance ramp just as the oncoming car reached the point of collision.

"Watch out!" Stannard Jackson bolted upright in his bed.

His wife, Caryl, reached out to touch him, hoping he had awakened. "It is the dream again, isn't it?"

"Yes, it's always the same. I can't shake it, and I can't figure out what it means. It's driving me crazy." For the past two years he had suffered from the dream. At first it came only infrequently, but now it haunted him twice a week. "They're all there—Dr. Parlous, his son, Wills, and the other man whom I can never see. I always thought it had to be Riki Simmoni, but…but it can't be." Stannard Jackson, the man once again known as St Jack, rose from the bed and walked down the hall to the kitchen. He poured a glass of water from the pitcher in the refrigerator, took a long drink, and waited for the shaking to stop.

His wife of thirty years followed. "They're all dead, you know. Everyone involved in the case is dead."

"I'm not so certain. My involvement stopped with the recovery of the insurance money.

After Wills Parlous died, the police were satisfied with the letter Lorelei Parlous wrote and never pursued the case beyond that."

Caryl bridled at the reference to Lorelei Parlous. She knew her husband had been attracted to the woman—a woman who, like a black widow spider, devoured her husband. What was it about women like that that attracted men? "You liked her, didn't you?"

He felt the iciness of her voice. He wanted to say no, but it would be a lie. "I did. There was something tragic about her. She made a mistake when she married Loren Parlous. All she wanted was out…" He stopped, knowing that to be a lie too. She had participated in the murder of her husband, and in the end she too had been murdered. "You never had to worry about her, Caryl. I love you, always have—always will." His mind raced back to the death of their only son. Russell had died at the hand of Parlous and his son, Willsson, of that he felt certain. After all, he'd seen the proof in the photograph Lorelei Parlous had found in her dead husband Dr. Loren Parlous's personal papers, the photograph he received after Willsson killed her too. He felt the grief for his dead son rise in his throat along with the love for his wife. If it hadn't been for her, Stannard Jackson would have been lost, committed to an asylum for the insane or the victim of a suicide.

Caryl let the wave of emotion waft over her. It wasn't like her husband to be so demonstrative. "Don't let the dream upset you, dear. They are all dead—it's just a dream."

He nodded. *All dead, maybe. But why do I have the feeling there was always more to the*

Parlous case than we discovered? No one ever accounted for that creep Roberto Bertonelli, who operated the shop in Westport, Roberto's 17th Century Bazaar Bizarre. Could he be the man in the dream—the one whose face I never see?